STEALING SUNSHINE

By the Author

Venus in Love

In Every Cloud

Stealing Sunshine

STEALING SUNSHINE

by

Tina Michele

2016

STEALING SUNSHINE
© 2016 By Tina Michele. All Rights Reserved.

ISBN 13: 978-1-62639-445-2

This Trade Paperback Original Is Published By
Bold Strokes Books, Inc.
P.O. Box 249
Valley Falls, NY 12185

First Edition: January 2016

Credits
Editor: Cindy Cresap
Production Design: Susan Ramundo
Cover Design By Sheri (graphicartist2020@hotmail.com)

Acknowledgments

Huge thanks go to my girl, Holli! Without our late night porch chats with bottles of red wine, this story wouldn't be what it is today. To my family, you buncha clumsy nuts on the same tree—I get it honestly.

As always, a sloppy smooch for each of my beta readers this time around. To Cindy, I promise this is the last time you need to repeat yourself. Big thanks to Det. Campbell for helping me put the fact in my fiction.

CHAPTER ONE

Belle Winters stood patiently in the foyer as she waited for her date. Although it wasn't the sort of date she hoped for, she was still looking forward to a lovely night out. "We're going to be late." Belle hollered up the stairs in her most threatening voice, which wasn't saying much. When there was no answer, she called out again, "Kyle King, you better not be changing."

"I'm ready!" Kyle said as he appeared at the top of the steps in a perfectly tailored tuxedo. "Holy crap, honey! You look amazing!" He trotted down the steps with his mouth wide open.

"Don't look so surprised." Belle flashed a shy smile.

He grabbed her hands and held them out. "I am not surprised by your beauty. I am overwhelmed by it, sweetheart."

This time, Belle's face burned. "Thank you. And of course, you look dashing as always."

"Oh, this old thing?" He wasn't fooling anyone. Belle knew firsthand that Kyle had that suit special ordered and tailored for the event. It was his husband Andrew's opening night as a principal dancer with the Florida Ballet Company, as well as their ten-year anniversary.

Belle had met Kyle her first day of work, and they'd been inseparable ever since. A fact confirmed because she also rented the apartment over their garage.

She'd known him before he had even met Andrew, but she couldn't remember what life had been like before they were a couple. They were her family and she was blessed to be able to share such an occasion with them.

"Ready, gorgeous?" he asked her as he scooped his wallet and keys off the hall table, slipped them into his pocket, and then held out his arm for her.

"Why, yes, I am," Belle said as she slipped her arm into the crook of his elbow. Kyle held the door for her as Belle gathered her long dress into the car. "Are you nervous?" she asked as he released a long, calming sigh as he jabbed a key into the ignition.

"Is it that obvious?"

"Um, yes. That's the house key you're trying to start the car with." They both laughed at his distracted blunder before he selected the correct key and started the engine.

"Okay. I'm a wreck," he admitted.

"Do you want me to drive?" She knew he would say no; he preferred to be in control, especially when he was anxious. He looked over at her and she knew his answer. "Just thought I'd offer."

"By the time it takes us to switch places we'll be there."

He was right about that. Within minutes, they were pulling up to the front of the newly renovated Orlando Metropolitan Performing Arts Center. It was a beautiful state-of-the-art venue with a facade of glass and steel that glowed with warm and inviting light. It had taken three years and just under one billion dollars to reconstruct a monumental addition to the downtown Orlando Arts District.

Belle was beyond impressed with the stunning design and contemporary architecture. She could only imagine how excited Andrew was to participate in its inaugural event—in addition to his own personal milestone achievement. The valet opened her door and helped Belle out into the crowd of pristinely dressed attendees. Diamond-clad women milled about as they greeted each other with kisses and compliments before they headed inside to continue their required acknowledgements.

Belle fidgeted with her dress and hair as she tapped her bare neck which was void of an obligatory million-dollar bauble. Kyle's voice in her ear startled her. "You are more beautiful than any of these pretentious women. Own it, sweetheart." Belle smiled at him.

He was her very best friend, and he always knew how to make her feel special even when she felt her most inadequate.

She took a deep breath and allowed Kyle to lead her into the foyer with all the confidence she didn't feel. But the night wasn't about her, and she was blessed to be a part of it. They stopped often as the other guests recognized Kyle and gave him their congratulations for both him and Andrew. It made Belle happy to see so many people who adored them as much as she did—although she was certain that no one was more proud. Any insecurities that she had faded each time Kyle introduced Belle as his dearest friend.

When they slipped off to the side of the room during a welcome lag in attentions, Kyle plucked two glasses of champagne off a passing tray and handed one to Belle. "Oh, thank you. To you and Andrew, the most amazing people in the world and my very best friends." Belle held up her glass for Kyle's when, across the room, a figure caught her eye. Time seemed to slow to a near halt when her eyes met the ones that stared back at her.

A dark-haired woman, dressed in a crisp black suit gazed at her through the crowd. The hundreds of people disappeared and their accompanying chatter faded into silence. Belle was frozen in time by the woman's unabashed gaze, and she was helpless to pull herself from it. Her heart pounded in her chest as the woman mouthed her name. *What? How does she know my name?* As the woman's lips moved again, Belle heard her name, as if through a fog, but it wasn't a woman's voice.

"Belle!" Kyle said as he lifted his glass into her line of sight, but Belle was unfazed. Only when the woman smiled and Belle blinked was the connection lost.

The bustle of the people and noise sparked to life, and Belle felt an undeniable jolt of loss run through her. The sensation reminded her of the many dreams she'd been ripped out of when she woke, yet there was no blanket to cover herself with this time.

"Belle. Are you okay?" This time she heard Kyle loud and clear.

"What? Uh, yeah. I'm fine." She looked at him, and his face was awash with concern.

"What are you looking at?" He looked behind him for an explanation. It took him a second to see what had her hypnotized. "Wow. No wonder. That smile almost put *me* in a coma just now."

Belle shot him a look of disbelief. "Shut up. I was not in a coma. I was, well, I got distracted. There are a lot of people here. I thought I recognized someone. That's all."

"Recognized someone? Who? Because I know all of your friends, and that handsome woman in black is not one of them. But maybe—"

"What? No. Not her, someone else." Belle looked around the room and then down into her champagne glass.

"You could go—"

Belle knew Kyle was about to suggest that she leave her comfort zone and approach a complete stranger, but a chime rang overhead. "It's time! Let's go find our seats." Belle grabbed his unfinished glass and set them both on a nearby table before she gripped his elbow and led him into the hall. Before they left the lobby, Belle couldn't help but sneak one final peek of the woman. It was then that she saw the beautiful blonde who whispered into the woman's ear. Belle was struck with an overwhelming and unexpected sense of disappointment. "Of course," she murmured to herself.

❖

In a dim and cool room, Pete and Jesse sat on either side of a long oak table. They sat in silence looking as unkempt as they did suspicious. Roz entered the room without a word and unrolled a large blueprint onto the table. He lobbed a small bronze statue at Pete who did not expect the weight of the item. Although he caught it, he looked at Roz with contempt. "This thing weighs a fucking ton. It could've broken my damn hand, asshole."

"Shut the hell up, Pete, and pin that end down." Roz hovered over the table and did very little to try to hide his utter lack of concern.

Pete stood and slammed the bronze down on the table. "Oh, it's like that is it? I'd like to see you find someone else put up with this bullshit."

Roz straightened and took three quick steps toward him. Before Pete knew what had happened, Roz punched him in the face and knocked him back into the chair.

Pete screamed in pain and grabbed his nose as blood gushed through his fingers. "What the fuck, man?"

Roz grabbed him by the collar and pulled him close. "Listen to me very carefully. There are a hundred more brainless morons where you came from, and they are willing to do whatever I tell them without talking back." He twisted the fabric of Pete's shirt. Roz tightened his fist until Pete's bleeding face tinged a deep purple. "But if I were you, I would pray that I don't pick one of them." Pete's mouth moved, but no words came out. Roz held his grip and flipped back his sport coat to expose the dull black .38 in his waistband. "You are expendable. Do you understand me?" Pete slowly nodded his head in comprehension, and Roz released his grip.

Pete sputtered and gasped for air. He ripped his collar open around his neck and exposed the blood red marks where the fabric had burned into his flesh. "Yes, sir, I understand." He struggled to speak as the blood ran from his upper lip and down onto his shirt.

"Now that we've gotten that dirty bit out of the way, can we please get back to this?" He calmly asked in spite of the thrill he had from almost strangling another man to death. Both men nodded in agreement, but neither dared to speak. They watched with determined focus as Roz drew his finger, still covered in blood, across the paper in a path he had been over a hundred times before. It was something that he could have done with his eyes closed, but he needed to be sure that they could do it as well and in real time.

Roz looked over at Pete, who held his bloody face in his shirt, and rolled his eyes. "Jesus, Pete, get a napkin before you get blood all over my Persian Tabriz carpet, and then I *will* have to kill you." Roz chuckled, but he was the only one. He looked over at Jesse. "You. Walk me through it while dipshit gets a tissue." It was only then that Jesse chuckled and Pete flashed him a dirty look.

Jesse ran his finger over the map as he listed the targets. "Les Barques de Peche, Auvers Sur Oise, La Musicienne…"

CHAPTER TWO

Tara Hicks sat in her car and prepared herself for the spectacle that was about to begin. She'd done it a thousand times before, yet each and every time it played out the same. She would enter the room and be swarmed by both familiar and unfamiliar faces. Tara would smile and kiss cheeks as she thanked each one for coming and for their generous donations. She knocked her head back onto the headrest and sighed.

"It could be worse."

Tara glanced over to the passenger's seat at her best friend, Cate Summers. "Really? How?" Tara hated the obligations that came with being a member of the Hicks family. To say that her parents, Linda and Oliver Hicks, were two of Orlando's most affluent socialites was an understatement. They were all but considered the king and queen of the arts and social scene in Central Florida. Not to mention they were the heads of the architectural firm responsible for the multi-million dollar design and renovation of the Orlando Performing Arts Center, as well as the single most generous benefactor and fundraiser of the Florida Ballet Company. All that made it bearable was the presence of Cate, who had just as much experience with such events as Tara did. "It's just another ass-kissing event to get more money out of my parents. I don't even know why I'm here."

"You're here because your parents told you to be here. You are Tara Hicks, darling, the future face of Hicks Architecture Group." Cate reached over and squeezed Tara's hand.

"Cate, you and I both know that I have no desire whatsoever to be an architect or run the company."

"I know. But they won't stop trying until you pick something." Cate knew that the more they pushed her to choose a path the more Tara rebelled against it.

"I have a path, several, in fact." Tara smiled.

"You do realize that part-time photographer-bartender-cab driver is not so much a 'path.'"

"It is for someone like me. Can you imagine *me* in one job for the rest of my life? And I haven't been a cab driver, yet." The valet opened her door, and Tara took a deep breath. "Here we go."

Cate waited for Tara to round the front of the vehicle. "I can't even imagine you with one woman for the rest of your life, but that doesn't mean it wouldn't make you happy." Cate took the arm that Tara offered.

"Ha! I am the happiest person you could ever know." They both knew it was a lie.

Even for all of her disinterest in being an architect, she had to admit that she was both impressed and proud of her parents' accomplishments. Their talent was evident in the beautiful structure around them. "Wow!"

"Yeah, no shit." Cate was impressed as well.

Just as she expected, it hadn't taken more than thirty seconds for the greetings to begin. "Hi. It's good to see you. Yes, it's stunning. Thank you. I'll be sure to tell them." It was nothing more than a looping audio track. The redundancy and passionlessness of it all made her want to crawl out of her skin.

When the crowds dissipated, Tara sipped her drink as she waited for Cate to return from the restroom. A flash of red caught her attention on the other side of the room. Tara was captivated by the woman with long, flowing black hair that fell in waves down the back of a stunning crimson dress. She watched with intrigue and an unwavering gaze as the mysterious woman greeted so many familiar faces. How was it that this woman moved in the same circles and yet she'd never seen her before that night? When the woman stepped off to the side of the room, an attractive man approached and handed her a glass of champagne that he'd picked off a passing tray. He too looked familiar, but she couldn't place his face or think of his name. Their closeness was undeniable. Tara felt an unexpected tinge of disappointment at the unmistakable intimacy of their interaction, but she was too mesmerized to look away.

She watched the emotion in the woman's eyes as she held up her glass and spoke to her companion. Tara wished for the room to go silent so she could hear the sweetness of her voice. When their eyes met, Tara's breath caught and she heard the solid thrumming of her heart. She dared not move for fear that the connection would be broken. Without knowing what she would say, Tara opened her mouth to speak, but her voice failed her.

When the man raised his glass between them, the spell was broken and the woman looked away. Tara felt a cool rush of loss flood her body, and she stepped forward in a desperate attempt to regain the connection. But her movement was stopped by a melodic chime overhead and a firm grip on her arm.

"Are you ready?"

Tara blinked and glanced over at Cate. "What?" She was caught off guard both by Cate's sudden return and the swirl of unfamiliar emotions within her.

"The show. We should get to our seats." When Tara didn't move, she leaned in close. "Tara, is everything all right?"

"Huh? Yeah. I'm fine. Is it time? We should go in," Tara said before she looked back across the room where the woman in the red dress no longer stood.

CHAPTER THREE

B elle selected a track on her cell phone's music player and pressed play. She slipped the phone into her back pocket and pushed an earbud into each ear. Belle hooked several wire leads to the back of her work belt and headed up the ladder toward the ceiling mounted hanging rail. Belle was an exhibition and art technician for the Emily J. Grayson Museum of Art. While it wasn't one of the museum's most glamorous positions, it was one that Belle loved and enjoyed immensely. She spent most of her time moving, hanging, or storing some of the world's most valuable and priceless artworks. She reveled in the opportunity to be as close to a painting as the artist himself—close enough to see the painter's delicate brushstrokes or even a stray paintbrush bristle that the artist left behind two hundred years earlier.

Belle had begun her journey in the art world when she was seventeen. The Grayson Museum was her escape, her haven from a mad and harsh world. When she looked back on her life, it was void of any true connection except for those moments when she surrounded herself with the beauty and majesty of the greatest art of masters. Belle found a home at the Grayson, something she never had anywhere else.

She slipped two wire leads into the rail, and they swung loosely against the wall. They would soon hold the weight of both the art and its history. Belle climbed down the ladder and eyed the empty space that would soon be filled with a gilt framed Degas. She could see the detail of the painting as if it already hung before her. She sang along to the song that played in her headphones as she shifted the ladder to her next position.

Most modern art galleries and museums preferred the isolated display methods for their art. This allowed the viewers to absorb the art's beauty and delicacies without the intrusion of the other pieces in the room. Belle preferred a more robust method of display known as a salon style. She wanted to be overwhelmed and bombarded with the beauty of the pieces all at once in a grand display of passion and brilliance. It reminded her of Hubert Robert's painting of the *Design for the Grande Galerie in the Louvre*. Although she understood how, in a world overwhelmed with technology and instant access, the more personalized approach would be favored. Maybe it was because she often got as much one-on-one time with a piece as she wanted.

Belle climbed down and once again stepped back to inspect her spacing when she bumped into something. Ever cautious of her surroundings, she spun around to make sure it wasn't a rack of priceless art. She screamed in shock when she came face-to-face with Kyle. She ripped her earplugs out and shoved him. "What the hell!"

Kyle laughed at her startled reaction. "Hi. Whatcha doin'?" he asked in his most innocent voice.

"I hate when you do that. And I'm working. What the hell does it look like I'm doing?" Belle despised being scared or startled, especially when she was in full concentration.

"Sorry. So, are you at a stopping point for lunch? I just finished proofing the last marketing pamphlets, and I am starving."

Kyle was the director of development for the museum. Whenever there was a free moment in their day, they would walk downtown for lunch or sit in the park and people watch. "Sure. Do you want to get a sandwich from Eli's Deli and go to the park?"

"You read my mind, as always."

Belle and Kyle picked up their lunch from the restaurant and headed to their favorite spot under one of the large oak trees that lined the park green. Some families gathered on blankets and watched their children play tag, while others tossed Frisbees and tennis balls for their dogs. Belle and Kyle sat on a bench with their meals and enjoyed the sunshine and smiles in the park.

Kyle was the first to break their companionable silence. "Andrew and I are meeting some of his company friends at The Lamb later tonight. I think you should come."

Belle looked over at him with trepidation. "Oh, I don't know."

"Come on, Belle. It will be fun. We'll get out, get some drinks, have some laughs."

Belle knew she wouldn't win any argument she put up against Kyle. He never took no for an answer, most often when it involved getting her out of the museum or the house. "You know I get so weird around Andrew's dance friends, with their perfect hair and even more perfect bodies. They aren't human I tell you."

"Give me a break. They aren't any more beautiful or perfect than you are. They're just people. And they like you." Kyle never passed up an opportunity to make Belle feel good about herself. He looked at her with a stern yet endearing face.

Belle laughed at her defeat. "Fine, I'll go."

"That's my girl." Kyle flung an arm around Belle's shoulders and pulled her in for a tight squeeze.

"One of these days I will tell you no and mean it." Belle said it, but not even she believed it. The truth was that she liked going out with her boys, and for the most part, their friends were hers, too.

Two men pushed a stroller past them, and they both cooed in unison. "I want that," Kyle said.

Belle felt a small knot twist in her gut, but she took a deep breath and pushed it away. "I think you would make wonderful parents." She meant it. They knew no bounds on loving or being loved, and Belle couldn't have imagined two people more deserving or more capable of parenthood. "You should do it."

"What?" Kyle looked at Belle with surprise.

"You should. I think it would be fantastic. I've always wanted to be an auntie." Belle had no siblings. Aside from Kyle and Andrew, she had no one, so they were her family. "Aunt Belle."

"I don't know if Andrew is ready for that. I mean, he just made principal. He's at the top of his career. I don't think he'd want to give that up to change diapers and get spit up on."

"Well, it's something you two would need to discuss, but I wouldn't count him out. You don't have to give up on your dreams just to have a family. "

Kyle and Belle looked back toward the men. They sat on a large blanket under a bright rainbow umbrella while they laughed and played with their daughter. Kyle's sigh was filled with hope. "Maybe."

❖

Tara and Cate reclined in their lawn chairs and watched the children that splashed and squealed in the pool. "Aunt Tara, come in the pool!" Two identical bright-eyed girls peeked up from the side of the pool with ear-to-ear grins.

"Eden, Olivia, go play. Your aunt doesn't want to get in the pool right now," Lucy Atwater told her daughters. The girls groaned in disappointment at her dismissal. She handed Tara and Cate their drinks and sat on the end of Tara's chair.

Lucy was Tara's sister, more specifically, her twin sister. Although Tara most often referred to Lucy as her older sister since she'd been born first. Tara looked around her and comforted the twins. "Maybe later, girls." The response elicited a renewed set of squeals before they swam off to race each other across the length. Tara smiled. "I just love them."

"Enough to spend the day with them on Friday while Charlie and I go meet with a client in Tampa?" Lucy raised her eyebrows in hopes that Tara would say yes.

Of course Tara was going to say yes, but the way Lucy asked made her feel a little peeved. "Why do you say it like that? You know I would spend all the time in the world with them if you needed me to."

"I didn't mean anything, T. I just didn't know if you would be…available."

Tara knew that was Lucy's segue into bringing up Tara's career choices, or lack of them. "Yes, I'm available. I work tonight and Saturday so I can take them all day." She still had to sit through dinner with the family so she wasn't in the mood to discuss the inevitable topic of her life twice in one day.

The housekeeper appeared with towels for the girls and announced that dinner was almost ready. Lucy patted Tara on the leg. "Thank you. The girls will be very excited to spend the day with you." Lucy helped the twins out of the pool and rushed them inside to change for dinner.

"I'm sure she didn't mean anything by it," Cate said as she slipped her shirt on over her head.

"I know she didn't. But you know they will." By that, she meant her parents, as it had in effect become a family dinner tradition.

As expected, dinner went just as it always had and ended when Tara announced she had to leave for work. She didn't stick around to hear any further comments regarding how she was wasting her talents and time on odd jobs and women. She'd heard it all before, and she finished the lecture in her mind as she drove to the club.

Of all the jobs Tara had ever had, the one she held on to was her bartender position at The Lamb. It was the one that her parents hated the most. They had often told her that being employed as a bartender at a nightclub was not something they believed to be a reputable position for someone of her status. They would have much preferred that she live solely off her trust fund than serve mixed drinks and beer to rowdy bar patrons. But Tara needed more than that, and being behind the bar gave her a small sense of freedom and individuality that she lacked in the other areas of her life. It wasn't a job she saw herself in forever. Mostly because she didn't see herself finding any one thing that could hold her attention for that long. The idea of choosing one path, one job, or even one woman filled her with a sense of permanence that she knew would suffocate her.

Tara slipped past the bouncer at the door and patted him on the shoulder in greeting. The smell of stale beer and wet mops hit her like a brick, and she smiled. "You have problems, Tara," she said to no one in particular. It was going to be a good night; she already felt it. And if she was lucky she would end her night with a gorgeous and willing woman on her arm. *Fingers crossed.*

As soon as the doors opened, she had no shortage of eligible and interested ladies lined up at her end of the bar, and it would stay that way all night. Tara could work any crowd she was in, whether it was at a ballet fundraising gala or a two-for-one ladies' night. The one difference between the two was the location. She knew everyone and everyone knew her, or at least they knew as much as she wanted them to. That was the freedom she got from being the mysterious bartender with no commitments and pretty good drinks.

CHAPTER FOUR

Belle waited in the short line to get into the club. Standing alone in a line of people who all knew each other was awkward. It was something Belle hated, but it was the price she always paid when she insisted on driving herself. On the other hand, having the ability to leave whenever she wanted gave her a sense of contentment in an otherwise nerve-wracking environment. She got her wristband from the doorman and slipped inside.

It wasn't hard to spot the tables that Kyle, Andrew, and all his friends hovered around. When Andrew saw her he smiled and waved. He met her halfway. "Isn't this place great?" He wrapped her in a hug and kissed her cheek.

Belle looked around the bar. "It's something." The music was loud and the bass thumped in her chest. It was an awkward, yet invigorating feeling, and she welcomed it. The room was filled with hundreds of people split into their own island groups throughout the club. Some stood, some danced, and some sat, but not often did two of the cliques intersect. There might have been a stray that could flit between two or more groups, but for the most part the islands floated alone. Belle had to wonder how anyone ever met anyone, especially a potential partner, in such an environment. The odds weren't much better than expecting a Papa John's driver to deliver true love with a large pepperoni pizza.

Andrew led Belle over to the rest of the group and introduced her to the one person she didn't recognize. Hazel, a tall, slender woman with fire-red hair, shook Belle's hand that she held out in greeting. "Nice to meet you."

"You too," Hazel said with a slight accent that she couldn't quite place. Belle didn't have a chance to ask before Hazel's attention was drawn to an attractive group of women that passed by.

Belle was a little rebuffed by Hazel's action, but she wasn't surprised. She was there for reasons beyond socializing with Belle. Belle couldn't help but wonder how long it would take for the gorgeous woman to find what she sought. When a handsome woman approached and offered her a martini, Belle had her answer. She couldn't remember the last time she'd ever been hit on, probably because there wasn't a single time in her recollection that she had been. Belle wouldn't have even known what to do if she had been approached by a random woman and offered a drink. She was a mix of both thankful and disappointed at the lack of such an experience.

She was intrigued by Hazel's confident interaction with the potential suitor. When Hazel thanked the woman for the drink and dismissed her, Belle couldn't help but ask, "Not your type?"

Hazel giggled. "Let's just say that if I were interested, I'd have let her know long before she ever realized she wanted it."

Belle was floored. "Wow. Well, I imagine no one's ever accused you of not knowing what you want."

"No. They haven't." Hazel winked and sipped on her free drink.

Belle wouldn't have been surprised if someone had told her that her mouth was agape. It wasn't, but she was most shocked by the woman's arrogance and a tiny bit impressed by her brash confidence. Belle looked over at Kyle and Andrew with a silent plea to be rescued. They both laughed at Belle's distress before Kyle made his way over.

"How's it going, ladies?" Kyle asked.

"Good. Hazel and I were just discussing the finer points of the dating game." Belle's voice oozed sarcasm, but Hazel was too busy prowling for her next drink to notice.

"She is very—" Kyle began to say before Belle interrupted him.

"Voracious? Arrogant?" Belle offered.

"I was going to say abrupt."

"Of course you were." Belle and Kyle laughed. "I need a drink."

"I was just headed over to the bar." Kyle motioned behind him, and that's when Belle saw her. It was the woman from the ballet, the one that took her almost three entire days to get out of her mind. And even then, parts of her lingered in Belle's memory.

"Oh, shit. What is she doing here?" Belle grabbed Kyle's shoulders and lined him up between her and the bar.

"What is who doing here?" Kyle attempted to turn around to see what had Belle on edge, but she jerked at him.

"No. Don't turn around."

"What the hell?" He shrugged her off and looked behind him. "Is that…?"

"Yes. It's the girl from the ballet. Stop staring." Belle turned around so that her back faced the bar and the woman who stood behind it. She wore a tight black tank tucked into a pair of low-slung jeans. Her hair was smoothed back and tucked casually behind her ears where its medium length brushed against her long neck.

"Why are you hiding from her? There are a hundred people in here. You'd have to be standing right in front of her for her to see you. And that's not a bad thing, sweetie. She is hot!"

Belle knew exactly how gorgeous the woman was. She didn't need Kyle to point that out to her. "She is. I'm n—"

Kyle stopped her in mid-sentence. "Don't even say it. That's bullshit and you know it."

"Kyle, she would never—" Belle started to say before he cut her off again.

"I'm going to the bar to get drinks. Come with me." He grabbed her arm, but she pulled it back.

"No way. I'm quite content waiting right here with Hazel." Belle stepped back over to where Hazel had just reeled in another woman.

"Really?" But Kyle knew there was no way Belle would go with him. "Okay. Maybe I'll bring her back with me."

Fear flashed through Belle. "Don't you dare." She was serious, but she also knew that Kyle was joking, sort of. "Please don't," she begged.

"Oh, sweetie. I'm kidding. I would never do that to you. What would you like to drink?" He rubbed her arm in comfort.

"A sunrise and a shot of Patron." She needed more than that to slow her racing heart, but it was a start.

Belle watched Kyle cross the room. He waited at the bar for the woman to take his order. She greeted him with the most dashing smile Belle had ever seen and her stomach fluttered. A voice in her ear startled her, and she jumped.

❖

Tara leaned over the bar and kissed one of her regulars on the cheek, when over his shoulder, she recognized a familiar face. It wasn't just any usual face she would have expected to see that night. It was the woman in red she'd seen at the Arts Center. Once again, out of the hundreds of people in the room, Tara was instinctively drawn to her. She wore a low-cut blue blouse and jeans with her long, dark hair pulled back into a loose ponytail. Tara would have kept staring if not for the customer who appeared between them. Tara blinked the woman into focus. "What can I get you?" Tara said.

"Vodka tonic," the woman replied with a sly grin, but Tara didn't notice.

"Sure." Tara mixed the drink, slid it across the counter, and took the cash that the woman held out. "Change?"

The woman's face expressed a disappointment at the impersonal service she was not used to. "No. But—"

"Thanks." Tara turned toward the register. When she turned back, neither the bar customer nor the woman across the room were still there. Before Tara could scan the room for her, another customer was in front of her.

This time she recognized him as the man she'd seen with the mystery woman nights earlier. "Hey, there."

"Hey. How's it going?" he asked.

"Not too bad. You look familiar, but I don't think I've seen you in here before," Tara said in hopes of gaining more information about the woman he was with.

"You do, too. I'm Kyle, and nope, it's our first time. I'm here with my husband and his friends from work." Kyle shot a glance toward the table where his friends gathered.

"Nice. From work, huh?" Tara looked at the group of exquisitely built men and women he gestured to.

"Florida Ballet Company. My husband, Andrew, is a dancer."

Tara realized why he looked familiar both this evening and the night before. "Andrew Pearce? The newest principal?" Tara asked.

"Yes. How did you know?" Kyle was surprised and he puffed with pride.

"Oh, I've seen a few shows." Tara was beyond vague.

"My best friend and I were there the other night for his debut performance. Her name's Belle, she's..." Kyle turned around to point her out without pointing.

"The beautiful one in blue looking over here? Yes, I recognized her earlier." Tara stared past him. She recognized the awkward softness of her voice and failed to hide her smile when Kyle turned back toward her.

"Yes. That's the one, and I should get those drinks."

"Of course, on me." Without taking her eyes off of Belle, Tara poured the drinks and slid them across the bar to Kyle. "Thanks," she said before he walked away.

"For what?"

"Telling me her name."

❖

"Mmm. Who's that delicious nibble Kyle is talking to? She just might be the one I'm looking for tonight."

The butterflies turned to lead in Belle's gut. Hazel could have any woman she wanted in the bar that night, but she had to set her sights on that one. "Oh, I don't know. Just the bartender, I guess." Belle tried to be nonchalant. When Kyle turned his head in their direction, she looked too, and both Belle and Hazel gasped.

"Oh. My. God," Hazel said. Her tone was deep and voracious when the woman smiled at them.

Belle's face burned, but she didn't speak. She couldn't have even if she'd wanted to. She felt paralyzed with fear and desire.

Even as Kyle headed back toward them, Belle was caught in the woman's gaze. It was only when she heard Hazel growl in her ear that the connection was broken.

"I'm going to go let her know what I want." Hazel smoothed her short skirt, flipped her hair, and strode confidently toward her prey. Belle watched in disbelief as Hazel swooped down onto the bar like an osprey.

Andrew met Kyle at the table just as he returned and handed Belle her drinks. "Uh oh, seems like Hazel found herself a little mouse to play with tonight," Andrew said as the three of them watched her move in.

Belle threw back the shot of tequila and without a chaser. "Yep. Seems so."

❖

Kyle smiled slyly and headed back across the room toward his party. Tara never would have broken the eye contact if it hadn't been for the tall redheaded woman who whispered something into Belle's ear that caused her to look away. Tara wanted more than just a distant look. She wanted to be closer—to look into her eyes and to hear her voice—but it was more than a usual want, it was an unfamiliar need.

Tara knew what want felt like. She also knew what it looked like, and she saw the intensity in the eyes of the fire-haired woman that stalked toward her. In that moment, Tara couldn't remember if there was a difference between the two. The desire in the woman's eyes was obvious. There was no doubt in Tara's mind what she was about. A fire built inside her as she imagined just what she would do to her. She might coax her into a bathroom stall and take her fast and hard against the wall. She could have almost guaranteed that *Red* liked the excitement of hot and dirty public sex. It wouldn't have been Tara's first shot at having a random woman's legs wrapped around her in the club's bathroom. But as the woman slid to a stop in front of her, Tara realized one thing—it wasn't what she wanted.

Tara scanned the room in hopes of catching Belle's gaze again, but all she found was disappointment as she watched Belle slip out of the club, alone.

CHAPTER FIVE

R oz sat in his office and stared at a photograph of himself thirty years younger. Beside him in the picture was another man who was long since dead and someone Roz once considered his only friend. The image was taken just days before he was betrayed by this man he'd once trusted with his entire future. The man he'd once admired in life and now despised in death: Giles R. Grayson.

Roz threw the framed photograph across the room, and it shattered into several pieces. "Son of a bitch!"

Jesse appeared in the doorway. "What's going on, boss?"

Roz pushed himself away from his desk. He stood and gestured to the mess on the floor. "Get a broom and clean this shit up. Then meet me in the back room." Roz needed to test his men again. He needed to make sure his plan was executed without the slightest error. He knew that the success of his scheme relied too much on the complete understanding of the goal and its intricate details. But he would succeed even if it cost his men their lives. They were no more than pawns in his game, and he would win this one, no matter what.

Roz turned off the lights as he entered the room. He and his men were blanketed in silence and darkness for a brief moment before the large screen at the end of the room illuminated. Once his eyes adjusted to the light, Roz asked, "Title, artist, location? You." He pointed at Pete who fidgeted with the bandages on his battered face.

Pete squinted at the screen and confidently answered, "*Charring Cross Bridge*, Monet, French Masters Exhibit, east wing, north wall, third from the right."

"Good," Roz said before he clicked the remote and changed the image on the screen. "Next." He motioned this time toward Jesse who sat in silence on the other side of the table.

The look on his face was blank as he stared at the projection. Roz slammed his fist on the table and Pete and Jesse jumped. "Um…, it's…uh…" His voice shook as he struggled to recollect the information.

"You have three seconds or I will be glad to jog your memory," Roz said.

"I got it! *Pastoral*, Matisse, Grayson Collection, east wing, west wall, second from the left." Jesse sighed in relief, but Roz didn't praise him.

Roz moved to Jesse's side and leaned over his shoulder. "It's all the Grayson Collection, you idiot. It's the name of the Goddamn museum, for Christ's sake. Try. Again."

"Yes, sir, sorry. It's in…the um, oh! It's the Impressionist Landscapes Gallery."

"Better." Roz patted him on the shoulder. Jesse's tightly wound nerves caused his body to jerk from the unexpected touch.

Pete chuckled and muttered under his breath, "Pussy."

Roz glared across the table at him. "What was that?"

"I called him a pussy. You do realize that if we fail it's going to be his fault? With his twitchy ass nerves and shit. I bet his little baby hands are all sweaty sitting over there with you breathing down on him." Pete pushed himself away from the table in frustration.

Roz didn't give a rat's ass how much Jesse's hands twitched or perspired. All that mattered to him was getting what he deserved, and getting two moron petty thieves to do the hard work for him. Roz pulled the gun from his side. With his weapon in one hand, he pressed both hands onto the table and leaned forward toward Pete. "Listen to me very, very carefully. You will not fail. Because if you do, I will kill both of you. Without a single thought about whose 'fault' it was. Do you understand me?"

Both men responded, "Yes, sir."

"Good." Roz stood up straight, holstered his gun back onto his side, and straightened his sport coat. "Now, where were we? Ah, my favorite," he said as he clicked to the next image. "It's your turn, Pete. Dazzle me with your knowledge."

❖

Tara pulled her Jeep up to the gate, and it opened. As soon as she stopped in front of the house, both of her nieces burst out the front door and jumped up and down with excitement. Tara's heart filled with joy at the sight of her precious girls. Before she could get her seat belt off, Eden and Olivia had her driver's door open to help her out of the truck. Tara smiled at their bright faces and scooped them both up into a bear hug. The girls squealed as Tara slung them around under her arms and carted them like potato sacks into the house.

Lucy stood in the foyer with a smile almost identical to Tara's in every way. "What are you doing to my children?"

"Children? These aren't children. These are sacks of potatoes I found in the driveway." Tara set the girls down.

"We aren't potatoes, Aunt Tara."

"Oh goodness!" Tara exaggerated a playful surprise. "I could've sworn I'd just carried in potatoes. Let me see here." Tara reached out and tickled the twins, which renewed their laughter. "Huh…are you sure?"

Both girls responded. "Yes!"

"Well, since you aren't potatoes, I guess I should put you back outside." Tara reached down to scoop them back up, but they ran down the hallway out of her reach.

"They've been driving me nuts every day since I told them about spending the day with you," Lucy said as she hugged her hello.

"Excellent! I'll be sure to fill them up with sugar all day today so we don't lose that momentum."

"Don't you dare." Lucy and Tara heard the whispers of the girls hiding in the other room. "You girls need to get dressed if you want to spend the day with your aunt."

"Okay, Mommy!" the girls said as they zipped past and up the stairs to their room.

"Too bad they don't listen that well when you aren't here." Lucy grinned.

"What can I say? I'm the awesome Aunt Tara."

"Yeah, yeah. Come in the kitchen. Silva just made coffee."

Tara followed her down the hall toward the kitchen and the smell of fresh brewed coffee. She sat at the table where Silva, the housekeeper, set out two cups along with sugar and cream in a pristine and polished silver coffee service. "Thank you, Silva. Can you run upstairs and make sure the girls are putting the clothes on their bodies and not all over the floor?"

"Yes, ma'am," Silva said before she grinned at Tara and left the room.

"What was that?" Lucy asked when she noticed the look Silva gave Tara.

"What?" Tara asked not so innocently.

"Don't what me. And please tell me that you didn't sleep with my housekeeper!"

"No, Lucy. I didn't have sex with Silva. I mean, I could, but no. I didn't," Tara said.

"Good. Please don't. I like this one."

"No worries, sis. I'll leave the help alone. Plus, if I needed that, I could easily find it elsewhere. Not that I've been in the mood of late." The last part came out more as a grumble than anything else.

"You? Not in the mood? Are you ill?" Lucy set her cup down and reached out for Tara's forehead but was swatted away.

"No. I'm not ill. I'm just not looking for that right now."

Lucy sat at the table across from Tara, the look of concern on her face was clear. "Um, okay."

"It's nothing. Well, I'm sure it's nothing." Tara began to say before Lucy interrupted her.

"Oh no."

"Lucy. I'm not sick. It's nothing like that, but there's this girl, a woman. I don't know anything except her name. Other than that all I know is that I can't seem to get her out of my head."

"Oh! Thank God." Lucy sighed in relief. "So who is she?"

"That's the thing. I have no idea. I've seen her twice, and both times there's been this connection that I can't explain. It's intense. But each time she's just disappeared before I could get a chance to talk to her." Tara sipped her coffee while Lucy absorbed the information.

"Wow. Okay. So, what now? I mean you don't have any idea who she is?" Lucy asked.

"Nothing. All I know is that her name is Belle and that isn't much to go on."

"Well, how do you know her name?"

"Her friend Kyle at the bar told me. She was there with him and his husband, Andrew Pearce."

"From the Florida Ballet? Is she a dancer?"

"Yes and no. I don't think so. She isn't anything like those women at the company. She's different. Her beauty is so natural and much more mysterious. Not like them in any way." Tara let her mind recall Belle's long black hair and deep, intoxicating stare.

"You could call the company. See if anyone by that name works there?" Lucy suggested.

"I can't do that. That's one step below stalking." Plus, Tara had already thought of that and decided against it.

"What about social media? You could find Andrew online and maybe search his friends list?"

"Wow, Luce! I think that's what they consider stalking." Tara laughed but couldn't help thinking that it wasn't a bad idea.

"I'm just trying to help." Lucy smiled mischievously.

"Thanks but—" Their conversation was interrupted by the girls who came barreling into the kitchen.

"Aunt Tara, we're ready!" Eden and Olivia announced simultaneously.

Tara laughed at the sight of the two girls dressed in the wildest outfits they could imagine. "What in the world are you two wearing?" Lucy asked them.

A proud Eden twirled in front of them in her hot pink leopard skirt and not-so-matching blue sequined scarf. Olivia offered a deep curtsy to show off her lime green and purple ensemble which she finished off with a long teal beaded necklace. Tara covered her mouth to hide her smile.

"You are going out with your aunt dressed like that?"

"Yes!" they replied.

"Okay then." Tara loved that Lucy never wanted to stifle their creativity or confidence so she always let them wear what they wanted, within reason of course.

"Well, I love it!" Tara proclaimed.

Lucy's husband, Charles, came into the kitchen at that moment. "What in the world is going on in here? And who are these beautiful young ladies dancing in my kitchen?"

"We are going out with Aunt Tara, so we wanted to look special," Eden declared as she wrapped her arms around her father's leg.

"Well, you both look very special and beautiful, too. Where are you going dressed so lovely?" Charles squeezed Tara's shoulder. "Good morning, sis."

"I was thinking we could go to—" Tara began to offer a suggestion but was interrupted by Olivia.

"The art museum!"

"Yeah!" Eden seconded the idea.

"We are going to the art museum," Tara confirmed.

"Yay!" The girls cheered at their victory. "Aunt Tara, there is this one painting by Vergo called *Poppy Flowers* that I think you will like a lot."

Lucy smiled but corrected her. "It's Van Gogh, sweetheart. But very good try!"

"Right. Van Gogh. Mommy says it's worth a lot of money so we aren't allowed to touch it. But you can get super close, like this." Olivia smooshed her hand against her face to demonstrate, and Eden giggled at her.

"Wow. I can't wait. You girls will have to teach me because I don't know anything about art."

"We can. We've been lots of times," Eden said.

"Great." Tara was very much looking forward to the day. Tara stood up from the table. "Are we ready then?"

"Yes!" Eden answered while Olivia nodded. They hugged their parents and ran out the front door.

"Okay." Tara laughed. "Drive safe, and we'll see you tonight."

"Have fun," Lucy replied as Tara followed the girls out the front door.

The twins were already loaded and strapped into the backseat when Tara got out to the Jeep. "Can you take the top off?" Eden asked as Olivia nodded her head in agreement.

Tara looked at the sky for any sign of impending rain and nodded. The girls cheered as Tara unsnapped the cover and folded it up neatly in the back. She loaded herself into the driver's seat and smiled into the rearview mirror as she watched Olivia help Eden tie her scarf around her head like a mini Audrey Hepburn.

Chapter Six

Belle loaded a gilt framed painting onto the customized transport cart. She adjusted the art until she was confident that it was secure before she strapped the piece into place. The most crucial need for protection of any piece was during transport, even if it was a short distance. Every curator or handler of art was well aware that damage to a priceless work of art occurred most often when it was being relocated. Belle was always hyperaware of technique and procedure when she moved any art. She couldn't imagine being responsible for any damage that occurred while under her care.

Her love and appreciation for art was impressed upon her long before she began her career as an art technician. It was a love that grew out of her search for safety and a place to call her own. She had spent many days sitting alone in the Grayson Museum as she stared at the beauty that hung from its walls. She found solace and peace in the company of passionate artists and their masterpieces. She had always wished for a place where she belonged, and the Grayson Museum was that place. It had been since the day she first came as a wounded sixteen-year-old. Every moment she had outside of school she spent wandering the exhibits and galleries. If she could have slept there instead of going home to her fourth loveless foster family, she would have.

She still remembered the first day she met Giles, who was more of a fixture in the museum than she was, if that were even possible.

She sat on a gallery bench in the Impressionist Landscapes Gallery and chose the painting she would get lost in that day. She often had a journal or notebook with her where she would write down random observations or sketches of the work. She would sometimes note color and technique or jot down questions about the artist or artwork that she could research later. An elderly man that she recognized but never before met sat beside her. They sat in companionable silence for several minutes before he spoke to her. "Monet. Impression Sunrise or Soleil levant. *It was painted in 1872 at the port of Le Havre in Southern France. They say it was this painting that began the Impressionist movement in the nineteenth century."*

Belle had written every word down in the notebook on her lap. Instead of writing down her question as she usually would, she asked him instead. She stared at the words she'd written. "Why is it called Impressionist?"

He acknowledged her shy inquiry and answered her question in great detail. She feverishly wrote his every word into her journal.

Belle smiled at the memory from so long ago. It wasn't the first time she had recalled the very moment she had fallen in love with art. It was a common occurrence, since she worked every day in the very place that it'd happened. She missed him, but she knew he would always be with her. She felt him in the art that they both loved a fraction less than they loved each other. She saw him in the framed portrait that smiled back at her as she came and went.

Belle positioned the last painting on the cart and strapped it in place. She circled the cart and checked each hook to make sure that there was no way they could come loose. She unlocked the wheels and pushed the cart to the freight elevator where her assistant, Katrina, held the doors open. Belle pushed the cart in and rode up to the gallery level. She was anxious to get the pieces hung as the exhibition was scheduled to open in a week. When she and Katrina arrived in the empty gallery room, her excitement increased exponentially. They locked the cart in the middle of the room, and Belle pulled her portable speaker from her bag and set it on a small table in the corner of the room. A song by P!nk blared from the tiny speaker, and Belle laughed when Katrina just about jumped out of her skin. She turned it down to a reasonable decibel and slipped her white glove back on.

"You and your music." Katrina laughed off her shaken nerves and began to release the hooks on the cart.

Belle unrolled the design schematics prepared by the exhibition coordinator and double-checked her placements. She pointed to the far side of the east wall. "We can start with *la Musicienne*." The exhibition was one that Belle had been looking forward to for some time. The Tamara de Lempicka exhibit would prove to be a popular one. To Belle, de Lempicka's work was evocative and sensual even with its crisp lines and bold colors. Belle had done extensive research on the reclusive Art Deco artist, and she was fascinated by her cool and detached approach of capturing her favored genre, portraiture. Belle also couldn't dismiss the underlying sexual energies of her female subjects which were fueled by her open bisexuality.

Belle sang along to the music as she and Katrina painstakingly hung each painting in its place. After each one, Belle measured the hanging distance for the standard 105cm and checked the positioning with her handy pocket level. If she was anything, when it came to work, she was precise. There was no doubt that Belle loved her job, and it showed in every possible way. She smiled with pride after the last piece was placed and she stepped to the middle of the room to admire the completed exhibit.

"Katrina, come here and look. It's perfect." Twenty-two paintings in all and they spanned a lifetime of struggle and success. She took Katrina by the shoulders and spun her in a circle that followed the chronological and technical evolution of de Lempicka's finest works. Belle couldn't help but be moved by it. They stared for a few moments more until Katrina pushed the cart away, and Belle's attention was interrupted by Disney's *Sleeping Beauty* show tune, "Once Upon A Dream." "Oh! I love this song. Dance with me." Belle reached for Katrina but she was too quick.

"Whoa! No way. Did you not learn your lesson from the last time?"

TINA MICHELE

"But it's a tradition," Belle said as she swayed to the music. "Fine. I'll dance by myself." Belle held her arms around her invisible partner as she whirled around the large room and sung along to the words.

Katrina always laughed at Belle, not just for her dancing but for having a Disney musical station programmed on her streaming radio. Belle didn't care either way.

❖

From the moment Tara and the girls had arrived at the art museum, it was nonstop smiles and mini-lectures. Tara didn't think there was a single painting or sculpture in the building that the girls didn't know at least the title or artist of. Although they could have told her anything and she probably would have believed them since she hadn't the faintest idea about any of it. All she knew was that she enjoyed every moment of it.

They entered another gallery where both girls decided it was time to sit, and Tara's legs were thankful. "Aunt Tara, come sit down." They scooted apart from each other so she could sit between them.

"Does this mean you're tired and ready to go?"

Both girls looked at her in surprise and opposition. "No!"

Tara raised her hands in surrender. "Sorry. I just thought—"

"This is what you do. You sit and look at the art and then think about it," Eden explained before she leaned forward, propped her elbow onto her knee, and then rested her chin in her hand.

"Like that one. It's my favorite." Olivia pointed at the painting in front of them.

"Wow. That's beautiful." Tara walked over to read the placard. *Taming the Flamingo*, Louis Comfort Tiffany, 1888. The watercolor depicted a beautiful woman draped in a dress of shimmering fabric as she held out a graceful hand for two pink birds. Tara was enamored by the subtle rendering of the woman's smooth skin and the reflections of light captured in the water-filled orb that hung almost divinely in the air. She turned back to the girls with a questioning look. "Tiffany? Like the lamps?"

The girls looked at each other and giggled. "Yes," Eden proclaimed.

Olivia's response was more animated. She jumped up from the bench. "They have a whole room just for those!" She grabbed Tara by the hand. "Let's go see it."

Eden hopped up and grabbed her other hand before they both pulled her out of the room. Tara found herself humored by her complete faith in the knowledge of two seven-year-old girls and equally curious to learn more.

On their way they passed a set of closed double doors with a sign that read "Closed for renovations. Art Deco Portraiture: Works of Tamara de Lempicka." Tara was intrigued and made a mental note to return after the exhibit opened. She was amused at how influenced she was by the passion of two little girls. In the doorway of the Tiffany Room, Tara pulled Eden and Olivia to a halt. They looked up at her with confused faces before she knelt and pulled them into a bear hug. The girls squeaked as she smooshed them together and gave them a little shake for emphasis. When she let them go and stood up, neither of them moved. They glanced from her to each other and back in stunned silence. Tara laughed and said, "What?" as if she had no idea what had just happened. She smiled and left them standing halfway into the hallway.

"Hey! Wait for us," they sang out as they ran one to each side and took a hand.

They wandered quietly as the three of them studied the large colored stained glass artworks mounted in the walls. Each piece was lit from behind to show the painstaking detail in the glass. Tara had a newfound appreciation for the artist as more than a mere name behind a brand of lamps.

As she moved through the room, the faint sound of music caught her attention. Blocking the archway to another room was a thick purple curtain behind a folding room divider. Just like on the closed doors in the hallway, there was another sign that announced the upcoming exhibit. Tara's curiosity was piqued, and she leaned in closer to a small opening in the curtain. On the opposite side of the room she could see two women. They each held one side of a large gold framed painting while they secured it to the indistinguishable wires that hung from the ceiling. The women stepped back and assessed the placement of the boldly colored reclining nude.

Tara couldn't take her eyes off of it. The crisp detail of the curved figure was visible even from where she stood. One of the women unlocked the large cart and wheeled it toward the door as the other stepped into its place and spun in a circle in the center of the room. Tara's heart leapt in her chest. It was Belle.

Tara pushed in closer to the divider. She watched as Belle and the other woman laughed before Belle began to waltz around the room by herself. Tara smiled at the innocence and carefree dance to what she thought sounded like a song from a Disney movie. She couldn't hear the words, yet the whole world around her faded into a cheerful swirl of color and light. She watched Belle swing and sway to the music, and Tara felt an overwhelming sense of joy. She wanted to be the invisible partner Belle shared that moment with.

"Oooh, Aunt Tara! You're not supposed to do that."

Tara jerked back at the sound of Eden's voice next to her. "Shit! I mean—shoot. Shoot. Not shi—right. Do what? I'm not doing anything. Just closing the curtain so it doesn't ruin the surprise." Tara pulled the curtain closed and resisted the urge to look again.

"Can we look, too?" Olivia asked.

"Um, no. We should go." Tara pointed toward the doorway on the other side that led to another gallery.

"Aww, we won't tell," Eden stated.

"Promise," Olivia said.

Tara knew she should have stuck with her first answer, but she wanted to see Belle again as much as the girls wanted to break the rules. "Okay, but just real quick. Come here." Tara pushed the girls together and opened the curtain enough for the three of them to see into the other room. The girls oohed and aahed at the sight of a now darkened room lit by the overhead spotlights on the artwork. It was a dramatic scene, but coolness rushed through Tara when she realized Belle was gone. "Why does she keep doing that?" Tara whispered to herself as she closed the curtain, which prompted a series of disappointed moans and groans from the twins.

Tara felt a tug on her arm and looked down at Eden who stared up at her shyly. "What's wrong, sweetie?" Tara asked.

"I gotta go to the potty."

"Oh! Of course you do." Tara was jolted out of her haze and into a sprint for the nearest bathroom.

As Tara waited in the hall for the girls, her stomach growled and she looked at her watch. She was shocked at the time and scolded herself for her absentmindedness. "They're probably starving to death. Lucy's going to kick my ass." For all the fun she was having with her nieces, she forgot that they were children, and she was the adult. When the girls came out of the bathroom, she advised them that they were going to get lunch.

"See. I told you that she didn't forget," Olivia said to her sister.

"Why didn't you tell me you were hungry?" Tara asked as she mentally slapped herself on the forehead. The girls shrugged. "Okay. Let's go." It was as they were leaving that Tara noticed the advertisement for a part-time security position posted on the reception desk. Without thinking, she stopped the girls and asked the docent behind the desk for an application. She rolled the papers and slipped them into her back pocket. Tara held out her hands for Eden and Olivia. Each gripped a finger and they headed out of the museum for lunch.

CHAPTER SEVEN

Belle screamed like she'd just been electrocuted and ripped the earbuds out of her ears when something tapped her shoulder. She spun around and her face burned. "What the hell, Kyle!" The blood pounded in her ears as her heart raced in her chest. He knew full well that she despised being scared, and she hated that Kyle was always so damn amused by it, every single time. "Why?"

He tried but failed to hide his amusement. "I'm sorry. But your face went from ash white to crimson red in a split second."

"Then why do you insist on doing that? You know I fucking hate it." Belle was beyond angry. She didn't understand why in the ten years she'd known him he still did it or why she wasn't used to it. As her heart rate decreased, the heat in her face subsided and so did her annoyance.

"Don't be mad. I don't do it on purpose." She glared at him with the last of her anger. "Most of the time. It's those damn headphones. I never know when you have them in."

"Call my name, dumbass. If I don't answer then I can't hear you." Belle took a deep breath. "Sorry. You're not a dumbass."

"I know. It's okay." Kyle pulled out the chair at Belle's desk and sat down.

"Not busy today?" Belle asked as she turned back to the crate she had been unloading before Kyle interrupted her.

"Eh. Not really. I was bored so I came down here to bother you for a while." Kyle twisted like a child back and forth in his chair.

Belle lifted a framed etching from the box and slid it into its designated storage slip against the wall. Hundreds of similar slots stretched the length and height of the environmentally monitored vault. Air pressure, temperature, and humidity levels in the room were controlled for the protection and conservation of the materials and artifacts stored inside. It was common for workers who were not used to the environment to become lightheaded. "Are you feeling okay?" Belle chuckled as she watched Kyle spin in two full circles in her chair.

"I'm fine," he said when he stopped himself before he could make a third rotation. "A little dizzy now."

"I think we should go outside and get some air." Belle grabbed his elbow and helped him out of the seat.

"Yeah, I think you're right."

"This is what you get for coming down here and scaring the crap out of me." Belle laughed at his lightheaded expense. "Deep breaths," she advised him.

They took the elevator to the gallery floor level as Belle preferred not to have Kyle black out and tumble down the steps. By the time they made it upstairs, Kyle was back to normal. "I always forget about the air down there."

"Maybe that's why you always forget how much I hate when you sneak up on me."

"Yeah, that's it." Kyle grinned and exited the elevator.

Belle followed him out before she stopped and remembered something. "Meet me in the lobby. I forgot my purse downstairs." Kyle nodded and Belle stepped back into the elevator as the doors closed.

Belle grabbed her purse from her desk drawer and took the stairs back up to the lobby. She pushed open the door, and it stopped short as someone grunted in pain on the other side. "Oh! I'm so sorry." Belle froze in place and her voice caught in her throat. "I, um…" It was her—the woman from the ballet and from the bar.

"Hi," the woman said in a soft, smooth voice.

"Hi." Belle responded so quietly that she wasn't even sure she'd said the word out loud.

"Hey there!" Kyle said interrupting the awkward silence Belle found herself in as she stared into the ice blue eyes of the woman in front of her. "That was a good knock with the door. Are you all right?"

She looked to Kyle. "Hey, Kyle, right? Yeah, I'm great," she answered and then returned her glance to Belle and smiled.

Belle's stomach fluttered like a swarm of butterflies. *How does she know his name?* Her heart pounded in her chest, and she felt the heat sear through her body.

"I'm Tara," she said as she held out her hand.

Belle glanced down at the hand being offered. She was afraid to touch it for fear that the woman would somehow feel the energy that surged through her.

"This is Belle, Belle Winters," Kyle said.

"It's a pleasure to meet you, Belle."

Her smile was kind and bright, and Belle's stomach twisted at the sound of her name in Tara's voice.

"Me, too. I, yes…it's nice to meet you." Belle wanted to crawl under the security desk and hide.

Tara smiled brighter at Belle's inability to communicate. "I don't want to keep you. I'm sure you were on your way to somewhere more important."

"I…we, no. I mean yes. We were going—"

Kyle interrupted her. "We were going to take a walk. Get a little fresh air. I think we both could use it."

"Excellent. That sounds like a wonderful idea. I'm sure I'll see you around, Ms. Winters."

"I'm sure you will," Kyle said before he reached for Belle's hand and pulled her from the spot she was frozen to.

"Thank you," was all Belle had managed to say, and it made no sense. She wanted to run out the front door, and had Kyle not had such a firm grip of her hand she would have. When they got outside, Belle panicked. "What the hell was that? I sounded like a moron!"

"Aw, sweetie. I thought you were adorable." Kyle grinned from ear to ear.

"Adorable? Did I even make one complete sentence? What was she even doing there?"

"Um, it looks like she was working."

"Wait. What? What do you mean 'working'? She doesn't work there." Belle stopped walking and waited for Kyle to answer.

"Belle, she was wearing a guard uniform. I'm pretty sure that's not a new trend. Eh, at least I hope it isn't." He made a humorous sick face, but it was lost on Belle in her flustered state.

"A uniform? What? Since when? How did I not see that she was wearing a uniform?" Belle battered him with questions.

"I'd say because you never took your eyes off of hers. Which is understandable. Have you ever seen eyes so blue before?" Kyle said with a grin.

"I've never. They were incredible." For a split second, Belle wished she was still looking at them. Then reality hit her. "She works here? I haven't been able to get this woman out of my head for weeks and now she works with us? And I just made a complete jackass of myself in front of her." Belle sat on a park bench and buried her face in her hands. "This can't be happening. Third time's a charm, I guess."

"Third time for what?" Kyle asked as he sat next to her.

She peeked out from between her fingers. "For me to completely embarrass myself in front of her."

"I don't think she even noticed your, let's call it a sudden inability to communicate."

"Oh, she noticed. Why wouldn't she have noticed? A woman like her?" Belle dropped her hands and looked at him.

"For the same reason you never noticed what she was wearing."

"I don't even know what that means," Belle stated.

"I know." Kyle stood and held out his hand to pull Belle up off the bench. "But I'm sure you'll figure it out soon enough."

Belle took his hand and stood. "Not before she *figures* out every other woman on the property," Belle murmured to herself. All Belle needed to figure out was how to avoid any more awkward encounters with the striking new guard, Tara.

❖

Tara spent an entire forty-hour week in the most intensive training program she had ever experienced at all of her jobs combined. There had been several occasions during her training that she asked herself what the hell she was doing. But each day, she learned something new, and each day after that, she returned with a curiosity of what she would learn. It wasn't her first experience working in a security position. However, the museum environment proved to be a far more complex and regulated set of tasks and procedures than when she had patrolled concert venues. The reason she took that job was as a means to enjoy a variety of free shows. Tara hadn't yet figured out why she had taken or kept this job, beyond the obvious, which was, of course, Belle. Yet, after a week of being sequestered in a room for no less than eight hours a day, she had yet to even catch a single glimpse of her so-called motivation. Tara assumed that to be the reason for her anticipation as she arrived to work that morning for her first real day on the job.

She assembled with the rest of the security staff for the thirty-minute morning roll call training—a required start to every guard's day. It was where command staff disseminated various information relating to the day's onsite art students, special groups, and exhibit closures or changes. It was also a time used for training on other areas of museum workings. Staff and curators from the different departments would conduct short lessons in a wide range of museum disciplines. She overheard another guard groan when the daily topic was announced—art handling. Tara learned the very basics of the topic during her training. To her surprise she found herself interested in learning more. She took out her pen and small spiral notepad in case she learned any information that would be useful to her. She scribbled the subject header on the page just as a woman's soft and familiar voice spoke.

"Hi, everyone."

Tara's eyes flashed toward the front of the room where Belle stood and addressed the group. Her hair was braided and fell forward over her shoulder. In spite of her desire to be closer, Tara stayed toward the back of the room. She had an unobstructed view that allowed her to stare without disturbing Belle's concentration.

Before Tara knew it, Belle thanked everyone for their time and excused herself from the room. Tara hadn't heard a single word that had come from the lips she couldn't look away from.

"Hicks?" A tall, gray-haired man repeated her name until she responded.

Tara snapped out of her trance and every eye in the room was on her. "Yes, sir. Sorry." She offered no explanation for her absent-mindedness.

"Okay. Your partner is out sick so I'm going to have you tag along with me for now." There was a mixture of low gasps and quiet snickers at his announcement.

Tara accepted the assignment. Although she was curious about the varied responses in the room, she thought it was a great opportunity to train with the head of museum security. She didn't see the downside. Joseph Jones was a dedicated, no-nonsense man with a wealth of knowledge that she was eager to tap into. There was no doubt that Tara would learn a great deal during her time at the Grayson Museum, no matter how long or short that time would be.

She and Joe started their rounds after the meeting was dismissed. Like a perfectly oiled machine, each guard reported to their station and began the day. As the two of them made their way through the building, Joe stopped here and there to give Tara an important lesson in the "art" of protecting art.

"It is imperative that we never let our guard down. Serenity and silence is our enemy. It is easy to become complacent in a comfortable environment with high security and low risk. But there is always the foreseeability of crime against the collection," Joe explained as they passed through an empty gallery.

Tara remembered reading that in her handbook, but it was the way Joe had said it that drove it home.

She said, "I understand," and meant it.

He twisted the knob of a locked door and, content with its security, he moved on. "Our biggest and most important responsibility is to the protection of the objects and persons within this building. Sharp implements and dirty hands both pose significant risk of damage to any artwork," he said as he straightened a steel post that held up a barrier rope. "The 'do not touch' rule goes for everyone, including us."

"Yes, sir," Tara said just to be sure he knew she was indeed listening.

"Everyone keeps a notepad with them to record various situations or suspicions. But never, under any circumstance use any undesignated surface for writing." He stopped next to a large wooden table in the center of the room and pointed to a small corner section. "See there?"

Tara leaned in for a closer look. "Those markings? Yes, what are they?"

"Those are the worthless indentations of a ballpoint pen on a priceless piece of history. Needless to say, he no longer works at the Grayson."

"Damn." Tara remembered all too well the time she used her Spirograph on her mother's antique Rococo side table. She would've preferred to have been fired than to have endured her mother's wrath. But she now understood.

She followed Joe downstairs. She didn't think the building could be any cooler than the constant seventy-two degrees, until they reached the vault. A thick glass wall framed with steel every ten or twelve feet ran the entire length of the building beneath the museum. A solid steel door at one end looked impenetrable, and Tara had very little doubt that it was. Inside the first room was a small area with desks and vertical storage slots and cabinets covering every inch of available wall space. The next was far more expansive with enormous floor-to-ceiling sliding panels on each side of the room. Each one held any number of precious paintings not on display in the gallery upstairs. Tara shivered both from the cold and the impressive sight.

Joe and Tara greeted the vault guard who wore a large coat as she made her rounds through the area. "It's always a refreshing sixty-nine or so degrees down here. I would suggest a jacket on those days. And be glad you aren't in there," he said as he pointed into the vault. "It's a controlled atmosphere. It never gets over sixty-four degrees, humidity is a steady fifty percent, and the oxygen level is less than seventeen percent. It takes a special person to work in there, and you don't have the degree. Speaking of the devil, there she is."

"Who? Oh." Tara's pulse increased when she saw Belle, who was no devil.

"Belle, our lead art technician and all-around wonderful girl." Joe waved at Belle to try to get her attention, but she didn't see him. He chuckled. "That wall could be solid concrete because she doesn't notice a thing on the outside when she's working. All right, let's head back upstairs."

Joe pressed the button on the freight elevator, but Tara didn't dare move a muscle. When the doors opened, Joe called her name, and against every want she had, Tara followed him into the elevator.

CHAPTER EIGHT

Once Tara completed her training and orientation, she was reassigned to the second shift and began her official part-time position. She was surprised by how much knowledge she had gained about the inner workings of museum security, but also by how much it interested her. Joe never did partner her with anyone else after her first day with him. He took her under his wing, and she let him. She didn't see the harm in learning something new. After all, she had started more than a handful of college majors that she found interesting until she didn't anymore. This one wasn't any different.

After closing, the guard staff reduced from over thirty employees down to just two. Per protocol, one person was assigned to monitor the control room while the other made their rounds through the building. As required, in order to eliminate complacency or boredom, Tara and the other guard, Scott, took turns in each position throughout the shift. It might have been her trainee attitude or her previous job experience, but she didn't put much confidence in Scott's abilities as a guard. She couldn't help but think that Joe had scheduled them together in order for Tara to keep an eye on him. It was a responsibility that she hadn't expected, but she was honored by his faith in her.

With her portable radio in hand, Tara took her turn at walk, testing the alarm systems. She patrolled each room, testing door security and purposely tripping the motion and vibration alarms. She couldn't resist the urge to make a game out of it by attempting to sneak through the room without activating the sensors. Each time she failed, Scott laughed and buzzed over the radio like a game of Operation.

"You think you can do better do you?" Tara asked him.

"Hell yeah! I am the reigning champion," he declared. "I could do it with my eyes closed."

Tara had no doubt that he was pretty good at it since he'd managed to find all of the same blind spots and inconsistencies that she had. She made a quick note in her notebook to mention the finding to Joe. Tara wondered why Scott hadn't done the same or if he had, why the deficiencies weren't corrected. As she continued, she noticed that the doors to one of the galleries had been slid shut. Light shone out from under the door, and she radioed back to Scott. "Hey, man. I've got a closed door in the east wing."

Scott responded, "I see you. That's the Giles Grayson Gallery. No worries though. Ms. Winters is in there."

"She is? It's almost ten o'clock. Why is she still here? I didn't know she was here."

"Yeah. She always spends the last few minutes of her day in there. It is pretty late for her though. She looks fine. I wouldn't bother her, especially if she has her headphones on. I made that mistake once." Scott laughed.

Tara was curious, but she listened to Scott and fought the urge to disturb Belle. She hesitated for a moment before moving on past the closed room. "What happened?" she asked as she continued down the corridor. If Tara couldn't see Belle then maybe she could try to garner some information from Scott.

Her radio crackled. "Where?"

"When you made the one mistake?"

"Oh. Well, I scared the shit out of her. By accident, of course. She wears her earplugs all the time when she works and can't hear a damn thing with them in. I came up behind her, and she punched me right in the eye. My own fault."

Tara laughed at the vision of Belle coldcocking Scott. He was by no means a small man, so the idea of Belle laying him out gave Tara another reason to admire her. "I'd like to have seen that."

"I learned my lesson, that's for sure."

Tara moved on with her testing, but she still wanted to know more. "So, what else can you tell me about Ms. Belle Winters? East wing, secure." Tara liked the way her name sounded when she said it out loud.

"Copy that. Like what do you want to know?"

"Anything, everything," Tara stated.

Scott laughed in her radio. "Oooh. Okay. Well, she spends all of her time here. The art is her life."

"So, no boyfriend or husband?" If Scott had come back and said that she was straight, she'd have been surprised.

"Ha! No. But she could have a girlfriend. Belle is a lesbian. Although, I've never seen her with anyone, male or female, except Mr. King. She's nice, but like I said, she's all about the art. She keeps to herself unless you ask her about a painting or whatever. Hey, go check out the staff corridor door. I've got a weird flicker on camera two."

"On my way." Tara knew nothing about art except the few things she'd learned during her training, morning roll call lectures, and of course, her nieces. Like anyone, she appreciated a beautiful painting or sculpture when she saw one, as her parents were avid patrons and collectors of the arts. But that was it. It wasn't something she ever found herself interested in, until now. Tara entered the corridor and looked for the camera Scott needed her to investigate. "I don't see anything. Which one was it?" she asked as she looked up into one of the cameras.

"That one. It's not there anymore. The screen sort of flashed. Just once. It may have just been a moth. Or maybe a ghost." He chuckled and moaned in her ear.

"I don't see anything. But mark down the timestamp so they can check it tomorrow." Tara wrote the same information in her notebook.

"Ten-four. East entrance, secure."

Tara hoped to see Belle on her way back to the control center to relieve Scott, but when she passed by the Grayson Gallery, the door was open and the room was empty. Tara was disappointed that she missed yet another chance to not only see Belle but talk to her. "Stupid ass moths," she grumbled to herself.

Scott stood and stretched his back when Tara returned to the desk. "Watch and learn."

"From the master, right?" Tara laughed and sat in the disturbingly warm seat. She stood back up.

"Yes, ma'am. West wing challenge is a go." He spun around like a James Bond wannabe, and they both laughed as he disappeared around the corner.

Tara sat back down on the seat after it had cooled a bit. She made a mental note to get two chairs behind the desk. She watched Scott avoid every sensor with skill. Tara was both impressed and a little concerned. It shouldn't be that easy for anyone, even someone as practiced as Scott was. After Scott went back and performed the tests, she secured the room. As she watched Scott on one screen, movement on another grabbed her attention. It was Belle, and she was leaving. "Of course she is. That's what she does." Several lights flashed on the console in front of her. She looked down and reset the sensors that Scott's flailing arms and Belle's badge had activated. When she looked back up at the staff corridor monitor, Belle was gone.

❖

Before Belle left work for the night there were a few things she needed to get finished. Things that she could have gotten done before nine o'clock had she not spent the last half of her day thinking about running into Tara and the rest of the time trying to avoid it. She wasn't even sure why she was trying so hard. Belle knew that she could be friends with Tara. The problem was the more-than-friends feeling that she got every time she saw Tara. Women like Tara— gorgeous, confident, sexy, and unattached women—didn't settle down with the shy, creative, awkward, and guarded ones like Belle. Her head knew this, yet, for some reason Belle couldn't convince the rest of her body of it.

Belle pushed the last open panel back into place and slipped out of her sweater. If she didn't take it off before she left the vault she would wear it home and freeze her ass off the next day. She jotted down a few notes and reminders onto the pad on her desk before she turned off the lights and set the overnight alarm. The heavy steel door slammed behind her, and she trotted up the stairs to the main floor. Every night, regardless of the time, she spent a few minutes alone in the Grayson Gallery. While most of his collection was scattered throughout the entire museum, it was in that room that she felt his presence the strongest. She didn't believe in ghosts or angels, but he had, and if he was one, she imagined that's where she would find him.

She slipped into the room and slid the hidden pocket doors closed behind her. Belle sat on a bench and started her music as she pulled her legs up and crossed them beneath her. She let out a relaxing breath and surveyed the room as she did every night. She wanted to let him know in her own way that she and his art were safe, just as she promised him so many years earlier. Belle sat in silence, like she had so many times with Giles. They would sit for hours and not speak or even look at each other, but she was comforted by his presence. As she sat on their bench without him, she pretended he was there with her. When she was finished, she turned down the lights and pushed the doors back into their place.

The staff entrance and exit was located on the far end of the west wing of the building beyond the modernist and sculpture galleries. It was a narrow corridor flanked on either side by two steel doors, each with a badge reader and keypad. A long two-way mirror ran for several feet along one wall. During the day, guards sat on the other side and watched the comings and goings of the museum employees. No one ever stayed as late as Belle did, and for some reason no one was ever concerned about her walking out with a painting stuffed down her pant leg. She cringed at the thought of the damage that a priceless piece of artwork would sustain from such an action. Belle swiped her badge and entered her key code to exit the building.

It was a typical Florida night, hot and muggy even at ten p.m., but the sky was clear and bright. All employees of the museum parked on the bottom level of the parking garage across the street.

On most nights, she didn't mind the short walk as it allowed her to defrost from her day in the vault. It was those unexpected Sunshine State thunderstorms that could turn a short, dry walk into a long, wet run. Thankfully, this was not one of those nights. She walked along the side of the museum building toward the garage. When she heard footsteps behind her, she turned around. She expected to see a woman walking her dog or lovers on their evening walk downtown, but it was neither. Two men dressed in hooded sweatshirts followed along behind her.

On such a warm night, Belle couldn't imagine why anyone would want to wear a sweatshirt. Their steps synced with hers, and the hairs on her arms stood straight up. When Belle increased her pace so did the men. She looked around her for any sign of other people, but there were none. She sped up to a brisk walk, but she still heard them close behind. Belle's heart pounded in her chest and a voice in her head told her to run, so she did. She took off as fast as she could. The sound of their pounding feet behind her drew closer as she rounded the corner of the building. One of the men reached out for her arm, but she jerked it away. She almost lost her footing when her ankle twisted in the mulch along the sidewalk. Belle screamed in pain but didn't stop. She saw the front door to the museum and nothing else. She didn't know what else to do, so she ran toward it.

Belle screamed for help and hoped someone would hear her. She cut across the grass toward the door and prayed someone would be there. As she reached the glass doors, she held out her arms for the handles, knowing they would be locked. When the door opened, she leapt forward. Solid arms wrapped around her and pulled her into the building. Belle buried her head into the tight embrace of her savior and panted.

CHAPTER NINE

Tara had watched the entire ordeal unfold before her eyes. Two men dressed in dark clothes trailed along behind Belle, and Tara's heart raced. She stared at the monitor and called out for Belle to run. She radioed for Scott. "Get up here, now!"

Scott responded without hesitation. "On my way! What's going on?"

"It's Belle, hurry!" She watched the monitor as Belle turned the corner and disappeared. Tara's eyes flashed over to another screen that showed Belle headed for the front doors. "Shit!"

Scott came running from around the corner and slid to a stop as Tara bolted past him toward the main entrance. "Where are you going?" he asked as she hit the emergency release on the steel gate. "What the—open the door. Now!" he hollered after her.

Tara flung open the doors just as Belle leapt for them. Tara pulled Belle into the building and watched the two men skid to a halt at the sidewalk. They paced and waved their arms before they ran back toward the garage.

Tara wrapped Belle in her arms and whispered. "It's okay. Shh. You're safe. It's okay." Belle sobbed into her shirt, and Tara could feel warm tears on her skin. "Shh. You're okay." Tara comforted her as Belle's entire body shook with fear. Tara refused to loosen her arms as she led Belle inside toward the guard station where Scott stood wide-eyed. "Close the gate," she said as she motioned to the overhead security grille.

He swiped his badge and entered his key code near the front door and a heavy steel grille dropped. "Who the hell were they?" he asked as he followed along behind them to the control desk.

Tara had no idea, and from the way Belle ran from them, she couldn't imagine that she had either. Tara eased Belle down into the chair, but Belle's grip around her shoulders remained tight. "Hey. Look at me. Belle?" Tara cooed.

Belle eased her arms down from around Tara and looked into her eyes. Tara's heart squeezed in her chest to see the fear in Belle's eyes. Tears and mascara stained her beautiful face. "Are you okay?" It took several seconds for Belle to focus on Tara's face, but when she did the tears began again. "No. No. Don't cry." Tara reached up to wipe away the tears.

Belle shivered. Tara assumed it was a reaction from the touch as she felt it as well. But when Belle wrapped her arms around herself, Tara realized there was a more rational explanation; she was cold. She leaned forward, and Belle closed her eyes. As she reached around Belle for the jacket that hung from the back of the chair, she heard a sigh. It was the first sound Belle had made since she heard her screaming outside the door—a sound that made Tara's stomach turn. She wrapped the jacket over Belle's shoulders and pulled the front closed around her.

"Thank you," Belle said before she gave Tara a gentle smile.

More beautiful words Tara had never heard. "You're welcome" didn't seem like an adequate response. Yet, before Tara could say a thing, an alarm sounded on the security console. Scott, Tara, and Belle all jumped at the alert and scanned the monitors. Two police officers stood at the front door, and the flashing lights of their vehicle strobed behind them.

The intercom system buzzed. The officers identified themselves and requested entry. When Tara had pressed the emergency release button during the ordeal, an automatic call was sent out to both Joe as head of security and local law enforcement. Scott looked over at Tara for direction. He was as white as a ghost, and it was clear to her that he had never experienced such an event. The intercom buzzed again, and Tara reached over and pressed the button on the console to respond. "Stay here with her," she told Scott then Tara looked at Belle. "I'll be right back." Belle nodded.

Tara raised the security door. Per protocol, Tara relayed the officer's badge numbers to Scott who verified the information with dispatch. She swiped her badge and key code to open the doors for them. Tara described the incident as she led them back toward the desk and Belle.

Scott was on the phone relaying the same information. "Yes, sir. The front door, sir."

Tara cringed, knowing that she breached regulations in order to open the doors for Belle. But she would do it again in an instant. The officers asked Belle a series of questions, many of which she couldn't answer. As Tara suspected, Belle neither knew nor recognized the men who had tried to attack her, nor did she know why she had been their intended target. The officers questioned both Scott and Tara, who couldn't offer much more than what Belle had already told them.

As the officers finished gathering their statements, Joe arrived. He looked furious until he spotted Belle, and his expression morphed into concern. "Belle, sweetheart, are you okay?"

"I'm okay, Joe. My ankle is on fire, but I think it's just sprained."

Tara had no idea that Belle was injured. "Do you need something? Ice?" Tara didn't want to leave Belle's side, so she asked Scott to get the icepack from her lunch cooler.

The officers completed their notes, and Joe walked them out. Scott handed Tara the icepack, which was almost melted. "It's not very cold anymore, but it should help a little." She slid her hand down Belle's calf and lifted her swollen ankle. "Damn," she said as she placed the pack onto Belle's lower leg. Belle stared at Tara but said nothing as she cared for her injury.

Joe returned from the front and stood over Tara and Belle. "Hicks. You violated the single most important regulation of your post. You compromised the security of the entire building and—"

Belle pulled her leg from Tara's hands and stood. She flinched from the pain, and Tara jumped up to catch her. "Joe. She saved my life. I don't know what would have happened to me if she hadn't opened those doors when she did." Tears filled Belle's eyes as she spoke. "You can't fire her."

Joe looked at Belle with kind eyes. "Belle, I'm not going to fire her. She did the right thing. It was against every tenet of established protocol for this museum, but you're right. She very well might have saved your life."

"Thank you, Joe." Belle smiled and sat back down.

"I still have to write you up for the breach. We can't go breaking all the rules in one night." Joe winked at Tara.

"I can live with that," Tara said.

Joe held out his hand for Belle. "I'll walk you to your car unless you want me to call Kyle to come get you."

"I can drive but I…" Belle looked at Tara. "I think I'll sit here a little while longer."

Joe glanced between Belle and Tara. "Oh. Well, okay then. I'll see you tomorrow. And I'll need your reports on my desk in the morning," he said to Scott and Tara.

"Yes, sir," Scott said, but Tara was distracted by the deep gray eyes that stared into hers.

Joe laughed and walked away.

❖

Belle sat in the chair behind the desk while Scott and Tara completed their incident reports. She took the opportunity to watch Tara unabashedly. She allowed her eyes to rake over Tara's strong and confident features. Belle was surprised by how well the figureless black uniform hugged Tara's body. She closed her eyes and recalled the protective embrace of that body as it had pressed against hers. She'd never felt so safe in anyone's arms, especially not a stranger's. When she opened her eyes, she was startled to see Tara looking back at her. Belle felt her face flush, and she chuckled.

"All done here," Tara declared with a grin.

Belle was thankful that Tara couldn't read her thoughts, at least she hoped that she couldn't. "Great. Well, I should go." Belle moved to stand, but Tara leapt forward.

"No. What? You can't go back out there alone. I thought maybe you could stay? I have another hour or so. You could come with me on my rounds and keep me company."

Belle wanted to scream yes, but she didn't. "Oh. I can't." Tara pouted and Belle laughed. "What I mean is, I don't think I can walk that far on my ankle." She gestured to her swollen foot.

"Oh! Not a problem. One sec." Tara disappeared, and Belle looked over the top of the desk to see where she had gone. She laughed when Tara reappeared pushing a wheelchair.

"Oh my gosh. No. No way." Belle covered her grin with her hand. "You are not pushing me through the building in that thing."

"Oh, come on. It'll be fun." Tara laughed as she swerved the chair playfully around in front of her.

"Seriously?" Belle blushed.

"Yes." Tara locked the wheels and held out her hand for Belle.

She contemplated for a moment before she took it and allowed Tara to help her into the chair. "I cannot believe I'm doing this."

Tara grabbed her logbook and handed it to Belle. "This ain't a free ride. You've gotta work for this. Plus, I need free hands to steer." Tara logged the start of her patrol into the computer and then announced, "Here we go!" She pushed off, but the chair didn't move. "Ugh!"

Belle shrieked with laughter as she jerked forward in the seat. "The brakes!"

"Um, I knew that." Tara released the wheel locks. "Let's try that again." She pushed the chair forward smoothly. "Much better."

"Yes." Belle giggled again. Stop giggling, you idiot, she told herself. "Where to first?" Belle asked as she scanned the checklist in her lap.

"Start at the top." Tara reached over Belle's shoulder and pointed to the first line. Belle inhaled the faint scent of cologne that she hadn't noticed during the incident. It was intoxicating and fit Tara well.

"Right. I knew that." Belle read the first few lines out loud. "East corridor, gallery one—Impressionist Landscapes and east wing lavatories." Each line had a place for a time, initials, and notes.

"Yes, ma'am. This train stops at all stations on the east line."

"Wow." Belle was excited to see everything from a new vantage point.

Tara swung the wheelchair back and forth across the hallway as she tested the sensors. "If you get seasick let me know."

Belle anticipated that an entire hour of swerving through the building would make her nauseous, but she would worry about that if and when it happened. "I'm good."

"Excellent." Tara radioed back to Scott that the east corridor was secure before she leaned over Belle once more. "Check that first box and initial."

Belle hoped that Tara would continue to point out each line over her shoulder so she could catch another hint of her cologne. "Impressionist!" Belle pointed to her right when she thought Tara was about to pass the gallery. Tara turned the chair, and Belle squealed in surprise. "Ahh! You drive like a maniac."

"If it keeps making you laugh like that then I will keep doing it." Tara pulled the chair into the center of the room and stopped.

"What's wrong?" Belle looked around for Tara.

"Nothing. I have to check the motion and vibration sensors, and unless you want me to ram you into all of these displays, I think this is easier."

Tara smiled at her own joke, and Belle's stomach fluttered to life. "Yeah, I think that's a good idea."

Belle watched as Tara circled the room activating the silent alarms. When Tara stood in front of Monet's *Sunrise*, her heart skipped. "I love that painting."

Tara stopped and looked at the piece. "It's nice."

Belle's mouth dropped open. "Wha...Nice?"

Tara looked at Belle with wide eyes in complete surprise. "It's beautiful?"

Belle wheeled herself over and stopped just short of Tara's shins. "Nice? Beautiful, that's it? Those two words are all that come to your mind when you look at this painting? Seriously?" Belle's question was forceful and her voice was stern. "Look at it again."

Tara did as she was told and turned back toward the painting. "Try again. Say the first word that comes to your mind."

"Calm."

Belle sat up straighter in her chair. "Better. Why?"

Tara looked at Belle and was flustered by her intensity. "Well," Her eyes went back to the artwork. "I guess because it's how cool and calm the colors are. The way the sun reflects off the water. It's like you can feel the silence and haze of the morning as they float along here." Tara pointed out the small boats in the lower half of the painting.

"Very nice." Belle relaxed into the back of the wheelchair. "This painting is *the* painting to which all other impressionist artists are compared. It's Monet's ability to capture nature in short, bold strokes of color to give us an *impression* of what he saw or what we might see. He painted to give us an emotion, a feeling, not just a scene. This painting began one of the most important eras in the history of art." Belle watched as Tara continued to stare at the piece in front of her. "I'm sorry."

Tara turned her head toward Belle. "What? For what? I've never heard or felt so much passion for anything in my entire life. I don't know what to say. But please, don't be sorry for that. Ever."

"I just wanted to—" Belle began to say but was interrupted by Scott over the radio.

"Hey! Are you two all right? Cause either my screen is frozen or you guys are practicing for a new sculpture exhibit."

They both laughed at the break in the tension. Tara looked at Belle kindly and smiled. "We are perfect. Impressionist Landscapes, secure."

Belle wanted to smack herself for her outburst. There was no reason for her to be so abrupt and forceful with Tara. She often forgot that not everyone cared about things or art as much as she did. She was brought out of her sinking mood when Tara grabbed the handles of the chair and whistled like a train. "Next stop, east wing potties!" Belle closed her eyes and screamed as Tara sped her out into the hallway.

Chapter Ten

Tara enjoyed pushing Belle through the halls as she performed her duties. She couldn't remember the last time that she had such innocent and childish fun. After the heaviness of her impromptu art lesson with Belle, Tara began to view every painting and sculpture with a newfound appreciation. She felt that Belle was embarrassed by her outburst, although she didn't come out and say it. But Tara felt quite the opposite. It opened up a new way of thinking for her, and each piece became more than an inanimate object she was hired to protect.

They spent more time in each room than Tara did on her rounds, but it didn't feel any longer. As they weaved in and out of the rooms and around displays and walls, Tara listened to every small fact and piece of trivia that Belle tossed out. There were no more tense moments of passionate intimidation, just interesting tidbits of data that Tara stored in her mind. Belle maintained the checklist as they secured each room on their route, occasionally flipping up the page to write on the notepad beneath it. Tara couldn't make out anything that Belle scribbled on the page, and that made her all the more curious. Whenever she asked what Belle had written, she was given the same response: "Nothing much." She didn't believe her for a second, but Tara figured that if it was something Belle wanted her to see then she would show her.

So far in their patrol, Tara's favorite room had been the de Lempicka exhibit—in the same place where Tara had seen Belle for the first time at the Grayson. From the first moment she'd seen the works of de Lempicka, she was intrigued by them. Each time she went through the gallery on her rounds she had spent a little extra time in there out of pure fascination with the art. This time the effect of the work on her cut deeper into her soul. Tara assumed it was because she was seeing everything with a new appreciation, but part of her felt that it was Belle's mere presence that had heightened her sudden ardor.

They secured several more rooms after that one before they headed back toward the main lobby. One room remained to be tested before their time together would be over. Tara's mood turned sullen at the thought of the evening's end. When they entered the Giles Grayson Gallery, Tara parked Belle's chair near the entrance. As she made her way around the room, she noticed that Belle had moved in toward a bench in the center of the room. When Belle locked the wheels and pushed herself out of the seat, Tara ran over to her. "What are you doing?"

"I just want to sit here for a minute." Belle hopped over and sat on the bench that faced a large painting of yellow flowers. "Van Gogh," Belle stated.

"Didn't he paint sunflowers?" Tara asked.

Belle laughed. "He did. But he also painted poppies."

"Oh. Right, I knew that," Tara joked. Tara knew that Belle knew better than to believe her and they both laughed.

"Sit," Belle said as she patted the bench beside her.

"Yes, ma'am!" Tara did as she was told, not that Belle would have needed to ask her twice.

"*Poppy Flowers* or *Vase with Viscaria*. That's what this piece is called. It was painted by Van Gogh in 1887. It belonged to Mr. Giles Grayson until he died and left his entire collection to the museum."

Tara recalled the title as the one Eden and Olivia had told her about. She also contemplated the name Grayson for a second. "Giles? But then who is Emily?"

"Emily Jean Grayson was Giles Grayson's sister. She and her daughter died during childbirth when he was eighteen. They were very close, and I don't think he ever got over it." Belle stared at the painting.

"Oh, man." Tara could feel the emotion in Belle's voice as she spoke of him.

"His sister was an artist and she adored Van Gogh. This was the first painting he ever acquired, not long after she died. He always said that she was as beautiful as the yellow in those flowers and brighter than the sun. It was because of her that he called it his sunshine collection."

Tara hung on every word Belle spoke. "Then she must've been truly beautiful."

"He's the reason I'm here," Belle said.

Tara didn't quite understand what she meant. "Was he your grandfather?"

"No. He was my savior. And before he died I promised him that I would care for this painting, and all the others, the same way he did."

Tara thought she now understood the reason behind her fierce passion for art, and Belle continued.

"I was sixteen when I met Giles. Here, in this room. It was different then. The Monet painting from the other room hung where this one is now. I was searching for my place in the world, and this was where I felt safe. For five years, he taught me everything he knew about art, life, and family. Things that, at sixteen, I didn't know the first thing about. When he died he left me the money to go to college with the promise that I would continue my education in art and return here to look after his collection."

Belle's story hung heavy on Tara's heart. There were gaps that Belle left out, but Tara could only imagine the pain that filled in those spaces in her life. "I am so sorry."

Belle looked at Tara and tears hung in her eyes. She struggled to absorb the information that Belle had just shared with her. As much as she fought against the consuming love and influence of her family, Tara couldn't fathom her life without them.

Belle wiped her eyes and cleared her throat to compose herself. She smiled and shrugged. "I have no idea why I told you all of that. I guess I just wanted you to understand why…who I am. Not that you wanted to know." Belle was unnerved by her unsolicited honesty.

"I'm glad you told me. It's what makes you, well, you. And I want to know." Tara reached out and covered Belle's hand with her own. Now Tara truly understood, and she yearned to know so much more. "We should go. Scott will be—" As if on cue, Tara's radio crackled to life and Scott announced the shift change. They laughed at the coincidence as Tara helped Belle back into the wheelchair and pushed her back to the front of the museum. Tara and Scott debriefed the third shift guards and logged out.

Tara gathered her things as Belle waited in her chair. With Belle in a wheelchair, Tara challenged Scott to a race to the staff corridor and he accepted. After a countdown, the three of them sped down the hallway as Belle screamed. Tara pulled back at the last minute to keep from crashing into the door, and Scott finished first. Belle teased Tara for letting him win, and the three of them cackled with joy.

They left the chair in the hallway. Scott and Tara each took one of Belle's arms over their shoulder and carried her out of the building. They all looked around for anything or anyone suspicious. Content with their observations, they headed to the garage. Tara insisted on being used as a supporting structure even after Belle refused to be carried any farther. Tara enjoyed the closeness that Belle's unfortunate injury allowed. They said good-bye to Scott and left him at his truck before they continued on to Belle's car.

When they reached the vehicle, Tara was reluctant to release her, but had to in order for Belle to retrieve her keys. Tara opened the door, helped Belle into the vehicle, and closed the door between them. Tara tapped on the roof and stepped away for Belle to pull out.

Belle rolled down the window and called Tara over. "Hey. I just wanted to thank you again, for everything."

Tara leaned onto the door. "You're welcome. We should do it again."

"Uh."

"Without the hooded creepers, of course."

"Right. I'll see you tomorrow." Belle began to roll the window up, but stopped when Tara put her hand on it. "What's wrong?"

"Nothing at all." Tara didn't know what had come over her, but she couldn't let Belle leave yet. She leaned into the car and placed her hand on Belle's cheek. "I'm glad you're okay." Before Belle could speak, Tara pulled her in and kissed her on the lips. It was a simple kiss, but Tara's heart raced, and she knew that she shouldn't have done it. She pulled back out of the window and stepped away from the car. "Have a good night, Belle."

Belle touched her lips. "Yeah, you too," she said before she pulled out of the spot and drove away.

Tara made sure Belle was gone before she cursed at herself for kissing her. "What the hell, Tara?" She slapped her hands onto her head and walked to her Jeep.

❖

Roz stood in a room filled with hundreds of people as they milled about around him making idle small talk and dishing out backhanded compliments. Everybody who was anybody in the up-and-coming modern art world was at Art Basel, and then there was him. He was invisible in the world that he wanted so desperately to be a part of. Roz meandered in and out of the exhibits like a fly on the wall and watched with jealousy as men and women made million-dollar deals on a chance that their investment would produce substantial returns.

As a fine art graduate, Roz had the eye for the job. He also had a salesman's attitude and tenacity. What he didn't have was a way into the world he knew he belonged in. He perused the displays with purpose and a confident appearance when he felt someone watching him. Roz looked around the room when he spotted a tall middle-aged man staring at him. The man was attractive and suave, and Roz couldn't resist returning a smile from across the room.

He turned his attention away and back to the art that hung before him. He stared at it blindly as his mind flashed back to the man whose eyes he could still feel upon him. He read the placard over and over, never retaining the artist's name or title of the piece.

A soft, low voice spoke behind him and his heart raced. "I'm not much into modern art myself. Can I ask what has you so captivated with this one?"

Roz replied without looking at him. "I'm not sure. To be honest, I don't understand what people see in most of this stuff either. I prefer the classics and masters." Roz dared to look at the man who spoke with rumbling smoothness. His eyes were the color of steel but far from cold.

"I'm Giles Grayson," he said as he held out his hand to Roz.

His name flowed from his lips and lingered in his ears. Roz could hear him say it a thousand times and never grow tired of such a perfect name. "I'm—"

"Roz?"

Roz heard his name, but it wasn't his voice. As he drifted from his dream, he heard Pete call him again. His blood boiled, but he wasn't sure if it was the dream or being woken. "What?" he asked as he flung himself forward in his chair. He looked around the men for someone who wasn't there. "Where is she?"

"Well, you see…"

Roz stood up behind his desk and leaned forward over it. He moved with calculated leisure as his temper flared inside his gut. "No. I don't see. Because if I did see, I would see that stupid little bitch bound and gagged behind you. Do you see?"

"We…she…" Jesse stammered.

Roz raised his arms and then slammed his hands down onto his desk. "She what?" His temper boiled up from deep in his chest to the top of his head.

"She got away," Jesse answered while Pete stood silent and reserved.

Roz took a deep breath and held it for several long seconds before he exhaled loudly. "Okay. No problem. There's always next time." He moved around from behind his desk and smiled as he slithered up to a nervous Jesse.

"Really?"

Roz's hand shot out and clutched at Jesse's neck. "No, not really, you fucking moron."

Jesse pulled at Roz's hand as his face turned red and he tried to speak. When Roz let him go, Jesse sputtered and gasped for breath as he turned toward Pete.

"What did I tell you about letting me down? Did we forget how worthless your lives are to me already?"

"No, sir."

"Well, I suggest you both take this as your final warning and figure out what you're going to do to fix this little problem you made for us. But for now, it's best that you get the hell out of my office."

Neither of them hesitated when Roz dismissed them. Pete turned to leave as Jesse held his neck and scrambled out behind him.

CHAPTER ELEVEN

Tara scooped three wine glasses into her hand and slipped a bottle of Syrah from the wine rack while Lucy made herself comfortable on the front porch. Cate had yet to arrive for their monthly girls' gab and gossip fest, but it wasn't out of the ordinary. Unlike Tara, both Lucy and Cate had successful long-term careers. Lucy and her husband were freelance corporate attorneys for a staggering number of businesses and organizations throughout Florida, including Cate's independent organic market and food delivery.

Cate had started her company out of her passion for food and her frustration with the lack of quality natural products in the area. When she first opened Nature's Bounty, Tara spent almost as much time getting things off the ground as Cate had. She honed her arsenal of skills as stock girl, cashier, and delivery driver, and developed her own taste for natural fruits and veggies. She set the glasses onto the table next to Lucy and sat down. Tara wedged the wine bottle between her legs and jabbed the one-legged pirate corkscrew into the top. As she poured out the dark liquid in the waiting glasses, Cate sauntered up the sidewalk carrying a large brown box.

"Fresh organic delivery for Ms. Hicks," Cate announced as she came up the steps and set the box onto the stoop. "I threw in some wine because, well, because who doesn't always need more wine."

"Oh! Dibs!" Lucy called out before Tara had a chance to say anything.

"Hey, get your own, lush." Tara reached her arm out to stop her sister from stealing her gift.

Cate laughed. "Don't worry, Luce. I have yours in the car."

Tara frowned. "And here I thought I was your best friend."

"You're twins. Haven't you learned how to share yet?"

Lucy responded curtly, "Nope."

"Okay, then." Cate looked down at the table. "Is that mine?" she asked as she reached for the beverage.

"No." Tara grabbed the glass and held it and hers close to her chest. "You don't get any until you say that you like me better."

"Oh, for goodness sakes." Lucy groaned. "Are you serious?"

Tara looked at her incredulously. "Yes, I'm serious." She looked back at Cate and waited for her to say it.

Cate rolled her eyes and reached out for the glass. "Fine."

"That doesn't count. Say. It." Tara raised her chin with pride.

"It."

Lucy laughed and sipped her wine. "Good thing I didn't have the same requirement. I'd be so thirsty. Mmmm." She took another long sip.

"I can take that away from you," Tara said as she motioned to Lucy's glass.

Lucy pulled her arm back. "And I'll bite your damn hand off if you come any closer."

Cate laughed. "Fine, dammit. You're my favorite. Now give me my booze and nobody gets hurt."

Tara handed Cate her glass. "Was that so painful?"

"Excruciating." Cate took her wine and sat in the rocker next to Tara.

"I now call this meeting to order." Tara held out her glass in a toast as Lucy and Cate clinked theirs with hers.

The Friday Fest girls' night had become a tradition for them when Tara first bought her home in Thornton Park. The east side of Lake Eola was a bustling neighborhood mixed with historic homes, bars, restaurants, and art galleries. The first Friday of each month drew crowds of people into the community for sidewalk wine tastings and impromptu art exhibitions on the quaint tree-lined streets. They sometimes took their meeting out with the crowds, but for the most part they were content to squat on the porch with their bottles of wine to chat and people watch.

"How's everything at the store, Cate?" Lucy asked.

"Super busy. You know what I think about Monsanto, but it's doing wonders for sales."

"Have you thought any more about opening that second location?"

"I have. I just don't know if I'm ready for that again. I'm seeing profit, I have exceptional staff and supply, and I'm now getting to enjoy some free time again. I'm not sure I want to give that up yet."

Tara nodded in agreement. She knew how much time Cate put into her business, and she was glad to be spending time with her again. "That's understandable."

"Speaking of free time, how's your new job going, Tara?" Cate asked.

"It's good. I like it. A lot.. It's pretty laid back most of the time, with the exception of last night, of course. There's quite a bit to learn as far as the art goes, but everyone there is helpful and knowledgeable."

"A lot?" Lucy asked.

"Wow." Cate said.

"Yeah. I mean, I never gave much thought to art in general, but there's something to be said about the meaning and passion that goes into a work of art. Don't you think?" Tara's mind drifted back to the passion she felt in Belle's voice as they stood in front of Monet's *Sunrise* the night before. The silence brought her out of her short daydream, and she looked at they eyed her with surprise. "What?"

Lucy and Cate looked back and forth at each other a couple times before Lucy spoke. "I don't even know where to start."

"Then don't *start*."

"I wasn't starting anything."

Before Tara could get defensive, Cate spoke up. "What happened last night? You said something about it being laid back 'for the most part.' Except for?"

"Oh, that." She knew they were more interested in her sudden and unexplainable interest in art, but she was far more comfortable with a different topic. Tara leaned back in her chair as she recalled the incident from the night before. Lucy and Cate leaned forward in their own chairs and hung on every word that Tara said. It was a good story, full of action and suspense, complete with a damsel in distress. Although Belle wasn't the typical fairytale damsel, Tara couldn't help but smile at the thought of herself as her knight in shining armor.

"Damn, Tara. That's crazy. To think of what could've happened had you not opened that door in time," Lucy said.

"What if they were armed?" Cate added.

Tara hadn't even thought about that until Cate had said it. She had no second thoughts then or now. She still would have done it all the same. "You know, I don't know. I'm glad it didn't come to that, and I'm sure they were just a couple of punk kids anyway. Although, I can't say that the whole thing didn't have a particularly pleasant outcome, considering." Tara smiled at the memory of Belle's squeals and laughter as they barreled through the halls with the wheelchair.

Cate looked at Lucy and raised an eyebrow. "Clearly, she is leaving something out. Wouldn't you say?" They looked back at Tara and waited for her to continue.

"That's it." That wasn't *it*, but Tara didn't see the point in trying to explain the connection they made or the kiss they'd shared. She hardly understood it enough herself. Tara shouldn't have been surprised when neither of them took that as an acceptable conclusion to the story.

"I call bullshit!" Lucy said.

"I second that. You think we're just going to believe that you pulled her inside, called the police, and both of you went on your separate merry ways—the end? I don't think so. What aren't you telling us?" Cate asked.

"Nothing. It's Lucy's turn. How's work, sis?" Tara sipped her wine, and begged in silence for them to accept the subject change.

"Fat chance, missy. You're keeping something from us. And it's something juicy enough to give you that goofy smile on your face. Spill it."

The timer for the porch lights clicked on, and Tara was thrust onto a bright and empty stage. "There's nothing to spill. She didn't want to go home, so she stayed and helped me with my rounds. We talked and laughed, and I may or may not have kissed her when I walked her out to her car." It's not like Tara had never kissed a stranger before. Hell, she'd done much more than that with plenty of women she'd just met. There was no sense in putting unnecessary meaning into it beyond what it was—just a kiss. She and Belle had both been overwhelmed with adrenaline and excitement earlier that evening so she chalked it up to nothing more than that.

"You kissed her?" Cate laughed. "Of course you did. That was a stupid question. Only you could have just survived a life or death situation and still tried to get in her pants."

Tara was a bit rebuffed by Cate's accusation. She hadn't forced herself onto Belle, and it's not like she'd planned it. Something had just come over her, and Tara took a chance. "I didn't try to. That's not why I did it. It just felt, never mind. I shouldn't have kissed her, I know that." Up until that moment Tara had only remembered the uncontrollable attraction for Belle. But now she'd begun to feel like maybe she had taken advantage of her in a stressful situation. "It might not have been my best decision. I see that now."

"I don't think Cate meant that, Tara."

"I didn't. Not at all. I was just giving you shit."

"No. You're right. She was vulnerable and scared, and I just did what I always do. Belle doesn't deserve that."

"Well, as an outsider, maybe your timing was a little out of place, but that doesn't mean it was wrong. Would you still have kissed her if the situation had been different?" Lucy asked.

Would I have? Tara thought back to the very moment she'd first laid eyes on her at the ballet. Without a doubt, she responded, "Yes." But her admission didn't change the fact that she had made a mistake the night before in more ways than the one.

"So you like her?" Cate asked as she leaned forward in her seat and grinned.

"Like her? Yeah, I like her. I mean she's nice. Everybody likes her."

"You know damn well that's not what I mean. Do you think you'll *date* this one, you know, more than once?"

Tara's heart began to race. *Date?* They just met. She'd spent a mere total of two hours with her since then. Yeah, she was attracted to Belle and they'd kissed, but nobody said anything about dating her. Tara didn't do that. "Why?"

Lucy and Cate both huffed and slumped back into their chairs. "Another one bites the dust," Lucy said.

"Nobody's bitten the dust. I'm just not the dating type. At least not in the way you see it, and you both know that. Dating is messy, and it makes me feel claustrophobic. Why does everything have to boil down to that? With all its labels and restrictions?" This was the reason Tara wanted to avoid telling them in the first place. They both wanted her to find "the one," someone to settle down with. But Tara was comfortable with the freedom she had established in her life, and settling down wasn't something she was interested in. "What's wrong with just enjoying the things that come and go?" Tara winked at her double entendre.

"Wow!" Cate said.

"There's our Tara. You had us worried that you might have found a reason to rethink your outlook on life," Lucy added.

"No worries there. Believe me." She'd said it, but for the first time she felt just the tiniest sliver of doubt in her statement. "More wine?" They nodded as the awkward conversation came to a close.

❖

Kyle helped Belle out of the car. He had insisted on driving her to both the doctor and to work that day, and refused to leave until she was ready to go. "It's just a sprain. I don't need you to carry me," Belle said as he slipped his arm around her waist.

He let go and stepped back. "Fine, but hurry up. I need to go tell Andrew about your wheelchair rodeo and smoochies with the hot security guard."

"You're enjoying all of this far too much. Do you know that?"

"Hell yes, I am. Well, except for the scary part before the handsome rescuer swooped in and saved you."

Belle never asked for help. She had learned at a young age never to need or rely on anyone else. But she was secretly glad for Kyle and his nurturing ways. He pulled her up the driveway. Soon after they moved in, Kyle and Andrew converted the bottom level of the large detached garage building into a private ballet studio. The spacious one-bedroom apartment on top was where Belle called home. She eyed the outside steps and dreaded the climb on her sore and swollen ankle.

Noticing her trepidation he said, "Don't worry. I'll have Andrew carry you up later."

"Neither of you will do any such thing."

"Whatever, Miss Independent. Come on!" He opened the door and stood out of the way so Belle could maneuver her crutches through the doorway.

"Oh my goodness, girl! Look at you!" Andrew gasped and held out his arms toward her.

"I'm fine. I just need to sit." Belle backed up against a large black armchair and plopped down into it.

Andrew stood with his hands on his hips as she got comfortable. Belle propped her leg onto the table and he gasped. "Oh damn, is it broken?" he asked as he covered his grimaced mouth.

Belle looked up and laughed out loud. She'd known him for years, but the sight of him in his skintight unitard always made her chuckle. "Do those things have to be so revealing?"

Andrew opened his arms and thrust out his groin. "What? You no like?"

"I like," Kyle said before he kissed him hello. "Babe, guess what little miss over here did last night?"

"Besides almost scare us half to death?"

"Yes. But I'm not talking about that. I'm talking about afterward, the small juicy little detail that she failed to tell us." Kyle slipped away from Andrew. He sat on the arm of Belle's chair and wrapped his arm around her shoulders.

"Ooh?" Andrew sat on the edge of the table and leaned forward in anticipation. "Do tell."

"It's nothing, you two." Belle knew how they loved to over-dramatize just about everything, in particular the things that happened to her.

"Now, now. If you don't spill, then I will." Kyle raised an eyebrow.

"You are making much more out of a silly kiss than there is." It was just a kiss. Belle didn't see the point in blowing it out of proportion or reading into it.

"A kiss? You kissed her?"

Kyle clapped his hands together and grinned from ear to ear. "She did!" He said louder than he'd expected and covered his mouth.

Belle looked up at him and rolled her eyes. "You're such a drama queen." She looked over at Andrew. "And no. I did not kiss her. *She* kissed *me*."

"Eh. A technicality. So? How was it?"

Belle had thought of nothing but that kiss since the moment it had happened the night before. She replayed the scene at least a hundred times over. She could recall every detail, from the dark desire in Tara's eyes to the smooth softness of her lips. "It was fine." She lied.

Kyle laughed at Andrew's disappointed snarl. "Ha! Like you expected anything other than that? Shame on you!"

"For once, can't you indulge me?"

"Fine. It was amazing. When I close my eyes, I can still see her face. I can feel her hand on my cheek as she looked into my eyes, and my heart still races when I think about those few silent seconds before her lips touched mine. I don't know if I'll ever feel her kiss again, but at least I have that perfect moment to remember." Belle touched her fingers to her lips.

Kyle and Andrew sat in stunned silence at Belle's unexpected and honest confession. Andrew pushed himself off of the table and cleared his throat. He looked at Kyle, pressed his hand to his chest, and tapped his fingers. "Oh. Well, okay then."

Belle was surprised by the relief she felt to say those things out loud to someone, even if the situation made her uncertain. "Was that what you were fishing for?" Belle smiled at the looks of shock and awe still plastered on their faces.

"Um. Sure. That's good enough for now," Kyle said.

Belle laughed and pushed herself up from the chair. "I need to get some ice on this thing. So I'll leave you two here to process." She propped herself onto her crutches and swung herself to the door. Andrew attempted to reach out and help her, but she shooed him away. "I got it. Just hold the door." He held the door for her as she shuffled outside and made her way up the steps to her apartment.

When she got upstairs, she flopped herself onto the couch in exhaustion. She could have had Kyle or Andrew help her, but she was a stubborn control freak who would rather struggle than rely on someone else. Yet, for the first time since she could remember, she'd let herself trust someone—someone she didn't even know. The thought that Tara was that someone who'd been able to weaken her defenses made Belle feel uneasy and vulnerable. Before she realized it, she'd let Tara in, and it had happened long before the kiss.

CHAPTER TWELVE

Tara volunteered her entire Monday to assist and participate in the annual Grayson Museum Family Day. The annual event took advantage of the closed museum to host a private viewing for staff, family, and friends. Staff volunteers manned information tables, displays, and hands-on activities, while others conducted special tours and behind-the-scenes peeks. Tara hadn't thought twice when the volunteer signup sheet had made its way around to her. While her art knowledge and skills still left much to be desired, she gladly accepted the position of runner, which according to Joe was no more than hired muscle. She didn't mind in the least. She'd done far worse for much less in the past. And since it gave her an unlimited number of opportunities to run into Belle over the course of an entire day, the experience was priceless.

Tara picked up a large banquet table and flung it onto the cart. It made a loud bang, and Tara heard a sharp yelp from a nearby room. As she hollered an apology, a startled woman shot out into the hall from a nearby gallery.

"What the hell?" Belle said as she clutched at her chest.

"Belle! I'm so sorry! I didn't realize." Tara stared at Belle as her face flushed from stark white to bright crimson.

"Oh. Well, it's okay. No problem." Belle fidgeted. "I should go," she said as she motioned back toward the room she had come from.

Tara didn't want her to go. "Wait!" she said a little louder than was necessary. "I mean, do you need anything? A table or chairs?" Tara inched closer toward Belle.

Belle stepped back and bumped into the wall behind her. "No. No. I'm good. I have my cart. I should get back to it." She sidestepped quickly. "I'll see you later." Belle smiled and pushed a stray strand of hair behind her ear before she disappeared back into the room.

"Okay, then." Tara had never before been so intrigued by someone like Belle. To Tara, she was as difficult to interpret as abstract art and no less complex, but there was something even less explicable that drew her to Belle. And she didn't intend on stopping until she had figured out what it was.

She pushed the cart of tables past the gallery Belle had retreated to. Tara sauntered by in order to catch another glimpse of Belle who gingerly examined a small vase as she hummed along to the song in her headphones. Tara slowed to a near stop in an attempt to freeze the moment into her mind. As if sensing her presence, Belle tilted her head up and looked at her. Tara flashed her a wide smile. When Belle grinned shyly in return, Tara's heart fluttered. She felt her face redden as the heat rose through her. Belle chuckled and returned her gaze to the object before her, and Tara was released from her spell. As she pushed the cart forward, it took her more than a few seconds to remember where she'd been headed in the first place.

Tara's mind was filled with the vision of Belle's sweet smile. The idea that someone she didn't know had her so captivated was disconcerting. She seldom, if ever, spent so much time thinking about just one woman. And certainly not about a woman that she'd not even slept with, let alone spoken to. A handful of brief but memorable moments were burned into her mind, and Tara had yet to convince herself of their true danger. Like a child testing her limits, Tara risked letting Belle linger a little while longer. She wasn't a child, after all. She helped set up the last of the tables and headed off to find her next assignment as the families were soon to arrive, hers included.

She could still hear the squeals she'd gotten from her nieces when she gave them the invitation to Family Day. She'd given them the invitation the week earlier so that they could harass their mother about it constantly. It was one of her many joys, irritating her sister. As she imagined Lucy's "I'm going to get you for this" face, her phone rang. *Speaking of the devil.*

Before she could even say hello, two screeching voices blasted her ear. She made out a couple words like "fun," "most awesomest," and "Aunt Tara," so she was good with that.

Lucy got on the phone, and Tara chuckled at her winded breathing. "Do you have any idea what it's like to herd these girls into a car to come see you?"

"It can't be that bad. They would've loaded themselves up last week and waited had you let them."

"Yes. Thanks. It's been a wonderful week of that!"

"You're welcome." Tara laughed at her exhaustion. It was one of the best parts of being a beloved aunt.

"So, we got them loaded and should be there in about five minutes."

Tara looked around the lobby as the families had begun to arrive, and she smiled. It was going to be a great day. "Excellent! I can't wait. The girls are going to love this." She hung up and slid her phone into her pocket. Out of the corner of her eye she spotted a figure peering out from a doorway. It was Belle. She stood quiet and invisible tucked just inside the gallery entrance. Belle fingered her necklace as she absently stared into the crowd of cheerful families.

The look in her eyes was one of sadness and longing. That much could be seen even from where Tara stood. The brightness that her eyes had held earlier that day was nowhere to be seen. Tara remembered the night they spent in that very gallery where Belle now stood. She hadn't asked at the time, and she kicked herself for being so blind, but it all began to come together as she looked into the emptiness in Belle's eyes. The only family she'd ever known was gone. Tara couldn't begin to imagine the hurt Belle was feeling in that moment. She wanted to go to her and console her as best she could, but Belle had spotted Tara and her concerned gaze. The look of sadness was replaced with surprise before she disappeared into the room behind her.

Before Tara had a chance to follow, she heard her name echo through the lobby. Olivia and Eden rushed toward her with open arms and wide smiles. Her heart swelled as it always did around her precious girls. She maneuvered them back to her sister as they waited for the festivities to begin. She glanced back toward the Grayson Gallery hoping to see Belle once more, but she was gone.

❖

Belle picked and plucked at the items on her cart. One of her favorite days was Family Fun Day. It excited her to see all of the bright, smiling faces—children and adults alike—as they absorbed and participated in the activities of the day. It reminded her of when Giles had opened her eyes to the same beautiful world. But it was days like this that she missed him the most.

Like every year before, Belle stood off to the side and watched as the staff greeted their families as they arrived. They mingled and chattered in the lobby while the children bounced around like loaded springs itching to be sprung. She watched the most curious of them peek around at what adventures awaited them. Those were her favorites. She imagined that had her childhood been different, she would have been that kind of child.

Before Belle could let her mind drift away to what might have been, she spotted Tara who stared at her from across the room. The look on her face was questioning and concerned, and Belle felt exposed. She wasn't sure how long Tara had been staring at her, but it was too long. Belle slipped backward into the room and pushed her cart toward her activity station to wait for the families.

It wasn't long before the group shuffled into the Tiffany Studios gallery where Belle had her workspace set up. She gathered the group around her area as she prepared to demonstrate one of her many responsibilities. The result of her demo was twofold. She got to do her job while teaching others about it.

Everyone circled around as the children pushed in close. "Careful. This is very fragile. So we want to make sure that we don't push each other." The last thing she needed was to have a hundred-year-old Tiffany vase crash to the floor and shatter into a million tiny shards. Most of the children took a few steps back, while several parents gripped their child's shoulders and pulled them in close. Content with everyone's distance Belle began her lecture. As she started to describe the collection of Tiffany lamps behind her, she saw two tiny faces darting back and forth at the back of the crowd.

Belle set the vase down and asked, "What do we have back there?" She stood on her toes to get a better look over the crowd.

Two bright-eyed girls gasped and turned to stone as they stared back at her. "We…" one began to say before the other finished.

"We couldn't see."

They might have been the most precious pair of twin girls Belle had ever seen. They were identical, but most distinguished by their bright and original choice of clothing and accessories. Not a single thing matched on either of them, and there was no shortage of animal prints and glitter. Belle was smitten. "Come on up here."

They looked up at the man beside them with wide eyes. After a brief moment, he smiled and nodded in approval. Smiles spread wide across their faces as they made their way to the front through the parted crowd. They aligned themselves with the other children and clasped their hands in front of them. Simultaneously, they echoed, "Thank you."

"Oh my goodness. Aren't you two the best in the world? What are your names?"

They answered for each other as they pointed. "That's Eden."

"And she's Olivia."

Belle looked up at their father and smiled. He gave a knowing grin and just shrugged. "Okay, let's get started. Can anyone tell me what this is?" Belle asked as she pointed to a table lamp behind her. She got the answers she had expected, except for two.

"Art new bow," said Eden.

"Tiffany," added Olivia.

"What?" Belle looked down at the girls in surprise.

"Art new bow?" Eden asked that time.

"So close! It's Art Nouveau. And you're right! How about you, Olivia? Can you repeat your answer?"

"Tiffany," she responded quietly.

"Yes! Very good! This is a Tiffany table lamp in the Art Nouveau style. Excellent!"

The girls beamed with pride as they looked back toward their grinning father. Eden waved her little fingers and he blew her a kiss. Belle's heart twisted in her chest. He was the luckiest man on the planet, and she was jealous.

Belle cleared her throat and continued her demonstration. After slipping on a pair of latex gloves, she gently lifted the lamp and set it onto her cart. She prepared a number of supplies and laid them out so everyone could see. She also passed around a few spare items that she had for examples—large swabs, cleaning cloths, and polishing wipes. While several of the children had become bored and had begun sword fighting with the oversized Q-Tips, Eden and Olivia stood steadfast and enthralled with her lesson.

She leaned down toward the girls. "Would you like to help me?"

Their mouths gaped open and their heads spun around toward their dad. He smiled and nodded his approval once again. They answered, "Yes!"

Belle walked them around to her side and handed them each a clean swab. She demonstrated the technique before she let them take a few gentle passes across the stained glass as Belle held the base of the lamp in place. As they grinned and swiped, movement in the hall caught her attention, but it wasn't the activity coordinator and Kyle as she expected. Two beautiful women stood in the doorway, but she recognized just one. Tara did not move or speak; she stood in silence and stared at Belle. And Belle was paralyzed by her intense, unwavering gaze.

When Eden spoke, Belle was startled from her thoughts and her arm swung up sharply. The girls screamed as the lamp tipped forward and everyone in the room took a collective gasp. Belle lunged for the lamp and caught the base before it toppled over onto the floor. She set the lamp upright and breathed a sigh of relief along with everyone else. She chuckled to ease the anxiety in her chest and the tension in the room. Eden and Olivia stood off to the side in shock still clutching their swabs. "It's okay! That was my fault. Just shows us how careful we have to be, right?" Belle smiled.

The girls smiled back. "Right!"

"Can we keep these?" Olivia asked as they both held out their tools.

"Absolutely. And thank you for all your help." Belle crouched to shake their hands.

Instead, the girls wrapped Belle in a hug, and her heart swelled. They gripped their prizes, trotted off to their father, and followed the rest of the group from the room. Belle cleaned her station and put the lamp back where it belonged. Leave it to her and not the twins to almost smash a priceless Tiffany lamp. She blamed Tara. Tara had a hold on the very core of Belle, and she couldn't break free no matter how much her mind wanted her to.

She pushed her cart into the hall toward the vault to prepare for her next demonstration when she stopped in her tracks. Tara hugged the beautiful woman in her arms before she smiled sweetly and kissed her on the cheek. Belle's stomach lurched and a knot rose in her throat. Since the night by her car, she had dreamt of the moment when Tara would hold her the way she now embraced this other woman. Belle watched as Tara released the woman and waited for her to walk away before she turned around. Belle tried to disappear before Tara spotted her, but she wasn't quick enough. Belle pushed her cart into the open elevator and pressed the button again and again. She begged for the doors to close before Tara got to her. When the doors closed, Belle breathed a sigh of equal relief and disappointment. She should have listened to her head all along. Now she knew.

CHAPTER THIRTEEN

In the vault, Belle pushed her cart into the corner of the room and plopped down into her chair. She was overwhelmed with so many emotions she wasn't sure if she cried which one it would be for. While they were her favorite, Family Days were never easy for her. She always missed Giles, but these days were the ones she found difficult and the ones where she felt most alone. Even the beautiful twins she was enamored with left a sad mark on her heart. And then there was Tara. The one she couldn't get out of her mind and who could change Belle's entire mood with one look. She wanted to cry; she could feel it welling up inside her.

She couldn't let herself cry for Tara. There was no reason to let a stranger have that much control over her feelings. But she would agree that the disappointment of seeing her arms around another woman added to the swirl of thoughts in her head.

She liked Tara. She could admit that much, to herself at least. But why? She told herself that they had nothing in common. The problem with that reasoning was that Belle didn't know enough about her to be certain of that. She realized that the few times they'd spoken Belle had done all of the talking and even that had been minimal. And it's not as if Belle had any right to be upset or jealous of whoever Tara chose to embrace, but a part of her was. The part that yearned to be held, touched, and kissed. It was a need that went beyond the physical. It was a void in her very soul that ached to be filled. For a short time, the unexpected love of a kind and generous man eased the deep ache within her. Giles had given her hope, but he was gone.

It was his love that gave her the courage to let in Kyle and Andrew. They were all she had, and while she cared as much for them as they did for her, she still felt incomplete. From the first moment she saw Tara at the theater, something sparked inside her. It was unfamiliar, a persistent tug that she couldn't ignore even though she wanted to. Belle shivered from the cool air and pulled her sweater over her shoulders. She took a few deep breaths and let her arms hang lifelessly at her sides before she leaned over, closed her eyes, and dropped her forehead her desk. She rocked her head side to side as she twisted in her swivel chair. It gave her a calming sort of feeling.

"She has a girlfriend," she said to herself, and then responded to her own declaration. "Of course she has a girlfriend. As if someone like her wouldn't have one. Hell, she probably has a handful of them." She sighed, and without moving anything else, she turned her head to the side. Her forehead peeled off the surface of the desk and the spot burned with warmth. She opened her eyes and tried in vain to look at her forehead. The closest she got was a cross-eyed view of her nose. When she heard a loud bang, she flung herself up and looked toward the sound.

Kyle grinned at her and waved as no less than twenty others stood along the length of the glass wall and watched her. Some laughed and smiled outright, while others attempted and failed to hide their amusement. She couldn't hear them through the vault walls, but Belle didn't need to in order to get the full dose of embarrassment. She raised her head and forced a smile. She looked at Kyle, who pointed to his own forehead and laughed almost loud enough for her to hear him through the glass. Belle rubbed her hand over the spot and smiled shyly. When she didn't think it could've gotten worse, she saw Kyle motion behind him with a covert finger, and she spotted Tara. She slapped her hand over the spot and spun around.

"You've got to be shitting me!" No one could hear her, but it would've been her luck that Tara could read lips. She took several deep breaths and turned back around. All of the eyes were still on her, all of them. She stepped over to the intercom system and flipped it on.

"Hey, everyone!" She waved at the crowd.

"Sorry we caught you off guard, Ms. Winters," Kyle said with barely restrained enjoyment.

"You did. I was having a moment. It's easy to forget that the three-inch-thick walls are glass. But I'm better now that you're all here." Belle's eyes met Tara's as they always seemed to do. When Tara smiled, Belle's stomach fluttered. Thankfully, Eden and Olivia caught her attention. Belle waved. "Hey there, girls." They giggled at each other and hopped up and down with excitement. They still clung fast to the used swabs they had been given as souvenirs and waved them at Belle.

When Kyle spoke, everyone's attention shifted to him and off of Belle—everyone except Tara who continued to stare at her. As Kyle described the features and function of Belle's storage vault, the group listened intently. Belle was hypnotized by Tara's gaze until the beautiful woman appeared and slipped in close to whisper into Tara's ear. Belle's stomach dropped, and she turned away just as Kyle wrapped up.

"Thank you, Mr. King." Belle addressed the crowd outside. "So can anyone tell me what these racks behind me are for?" She gestured toward the floor-to-ceiling slides that lined the length of the room. Several people gave answers like "art" or "paintings." Belle smiled. "Correct, but not just any art or paintings." She reached over and pulled one large panel far out into the middle of the room.

"We have masterpieces." Belle pointed to the framed pieces and rattled off a list of names. It wasn't until she said Picasso and Dali that she got the raised eyebrows and interested looks she searched for. They weren't her favorites, but everyone knew their names. She found that familiarity was often a gateway, and she loved opening it up for them. She answered a few last questions and thanked them for coming before Kyle herded them toward the elevator to their next stop. Which she believed was food, so it explained the few glassy-eyed stares she got toward the end of her talk.

She watched as everyone loaded onto the large freight elevator. It was built for the weight, but Belle was glad she didn't have to squish herself in with all those people. Eden and Olivia peeked out from the group and waved good-bye and Belle smiled. "Too bad kidnapping is illegal," she joked to herself before she turned away and headed back to her desk.

She reached down to pick up her sweater from the floor where it had fallen when she jumped up earlier.

"Kidnapping is very much illegal."

Belle screamed at the sound of the voice and flung the sweater into the air, knocking over a cup of pens and pencils that sat on her desk. "What?" She looked around and realized the voice had come from outside the vault. Tara stood near the door and leaned up against the glass casually. Belle glanced over at the intercom panel and realized that she hadn't turned it off. "I didn't mean that. I wouldn't. I'm not a kidnapper. I swear."

"I don't know. It sure sounds like something a kidnapper would say." Tara smiled.

Belle laughed. "Yes. True. But oh my gosh, they might have been the cutest little girls I've ever seen in my life. Did you see how engaged they were? I could just squeeze them and—" Belle stopped herself so she didn't sound any more like a child abductor.

"They were most beautiful and smart."

"Well, I think I've embarrassed myself plenty for a single day. I think I'm going to lock myself in the back for the rest of my life." Belle fidgeted with the stray strands of hair that fell in her face.

"The back? There's more back there than this?"

Belle smiled. "Yes. It takes up pretty much the entire lower level. Sculptures, photography, textiles. They all have different humidity, oxygen, and light requirements, so they're in their own areas and vitrines back there." Belle motioned behind her.

"Oh, wow! I bet that's an interesting sight."

Was she asking to see it? It wasn't a question, but it sounded like interest. Should she ask her if she wants to come back? Belle didn't have anything else to do. Maybe for a minute? When Tara laughed, Belle blinked. "Huh?"

"I just said it must be interesting and then you went somewhere. The lights were on, but…"

Belle blushed. "I was thinking. Would you…do you want to come in and see?"

"Yes, I'd love to."

Belle was surprised by Tara's quick and excited response. "Okay." Belle grinned as she pressed the exit button and opened the door for Tara.

❖

Tara stepped into the vault and shivered. "Holy cow! How is it not snowing in here?"

Belle chuckled. "It's only sixty-seven degrees. You get used to it. I have an extra sweater." Belle pulled a frilly pink sweater off the back of her chair and held it out to Tara. Belle looked from Tara to the sweater and back again. "I'll trade you," she said as she shrugged an arm out of the one she was wearing.

"No, it's okay. It's not that bad." Tara was more concerned with looking cool than feeling cool. Although she despised being cold, she decided that she could tough it out.

"If you get too cold let me know."

Tara's mind listed off the various ways she would choose for Belle to warm her back up if she did get too cold. "I'll do that," she said thickly. Had she known her voice would've sounded so deep she wouldn't have opened her mouth at all. And to her dismay, the tone wasn't lost on Belle either. For once, it was Tara's turn to burn with embarrassment. They stared at each other in silence for a few brief seconds before they both eased the awkward tension with laughter. "I have no idea where that came from!"

"Oh my gosh. I didn't mean to laugh at you. I was just caught off guard." Belle covered her mouth and spoke through her fingers. "I'm sorry."

"It's all right. It's just puberty. I'm expecting my first chest hair any day now."

Belle gave a chuckle and a snort and then buried her face in her hands. "I did not just do that."

"Yep, you totally snorted." Belle turned and started to walk away, but Tara grabbed her by the wrist. "Wait. Come back."

Belle turned back to Tara but hung her head. "I am such a mess. Every time I'm around you I make an ass of myself somehow."

Tara drew Belle in toward her. "Hey. Look at me." She slipped her hand under Belle's chin and lifted it up. "I remember every time I've ever seen you, and you've never done any such thing."

Belle was smart, passionate, and beautiful. Sure, she was a little clumsy and awkward as well, but it was charming, and Tara couldn't get enough of everything that was Belle. Belle's eyes sparkled as they stared deep into Tara's. The intimate connection both fueled her desire and alarmed her senses. She fought between pulling away and pulling Belle in close. Tara drew her fingers softly from Belle's chin down her smooth neck. She could feel the quick pulsing of Belle's heartbeat under her touch. She gripped her shoulder as Belle tilted her head back. Tara watched Belle's soft lips part, and instinct drew hers down to them. Suddenly, Belle turned away and gasped. She stepped out of Tara's arms and crossed her own in front of her.

"What?" Tara asked as she followed Belle's line of sight toward a woman who stood on the other side of the glass. "Oh. Now I see why it was so easy for us to sneak up on you earlier." Lucy raised an eyebrow and waved at them through the glass.

"Umm, you should probably go," Belle said as she walked toward the vault door.

"Why?" Tara would just need a minute to say good-bye to her sister. "Come on. This will be painless." Tara motioned for Belle to follow her.

❖

Belle stood still and looked at Tara. "What?" She had no desire whatsoever to meet Tara's girlfriend, and less so after she'd just caught them in such a compromising and heated moment together. And it was hot. "It's a little awkward."

"Why? It's fine. She doesn't care. You shouldn't."

"I don't think it's a great idea." Belle assumed Tara had multiple relationships, but to be so open about them didn't sit well with her.

"Sure it is. Come on." Tara took Belle's hand and led her out into the hallway toward the beautiful woman. They came to a stop in front of her, and Belle smiled nervously.

Tara slipped her arm around the woman and pulled her into her side. In much the same way as she had when Belle saw them in the hallway earlier. Belle's stomach twisted into a knot.

Tara smiled and introduced her. "Lucy, this is Belle. Belle, this is Lucy, my sister."

Belle's stomach untied so fast she felt a little nauseous. "Your sister?"

"Yes." Tara and Lucy smiled, and Belle saw the resemblance.

"I had no—" She was interrupted by the clacking sound of tiny shoes trampling toward them. She peeked around Tara and Lucy and saw Eden and Olivia sprinting toward them followed by their tall father. "Girls! What are you doing down here?" Belle asked.

"Ms. Winters!" they said.

They skidded to a stop between them and looked up at her. "Hi!" Then they turned to Tara and Lucy. "Hi, Mommy! Hi, Aunt Tara!"

Belle felt like she'd just been hit with a brick. "Aunt? They're your..." She pointed between the girls and Tara, unable to get out a complete sentence.

Tara laughed. "Yes. The girls you wanted to abduct belong to me. Sort of."

Belle looked at Lucy in shock. "I didn't. That was a joke. I would never."

Lucy and Tara laughed. "They haven't stopped talking about you all day. I'm going to have to pry those Q-Tips from their sleeping hands." Belle's heart soared.

The girls squealed, "Nooo!" And everyone laughed.

"Ms. Winters?" Eden asked.

"Do you want to come to our house for dinner?" Olivia finished.

"Oh! Um."

"Girls, you just ate," Lucy said.

"Aww, tomorrow?" Eden asked.

"Well, I don't—"

Before she could finish, Olivia asked, "Ms. Winters, do you have a boyfriend?"

"Olivia!" Lucy said with surprise.

Belle laughed. *Kids really can say anything.* "No, Olivia. I don't have a boyfriend."

Eden spoke up. "A girlfriend? Aunt Tara doesn't have a boyfriend either. She has girlfriends."

"Eden!" It was Tara's turn to be shocked.

Belle slapped her hand over her mouth. "Ha!" Belle watched Tara's face turn from pink to red.

"What?" Eden asked.

Tara looked at Belle. "I don't have *girlfriends*."

Lucy interrupted the awkward tension in the air. "Kids! Whatcha gonna do? Okay, girls. I think we've made things uncomfortable for your aunt, so we should go. It was nice to meet you, Belle."

Belle was even more caught off guard when Lucy hugged her good-bye. She watched as Tara embraced her sister and the girls before they left. It was the first time she'd ever seen any family act with such affection toward each other. She stared with curiosity.

The twins waved one last time as they stepped into the elevator before Tara turned to a shocked and astounded Belle. "Wow. Aunt Tara, huh?"

Tara grinned. "That's me."

"I don't know why, but I'm sort of surprised by that. Not at your sister's ability to have kids, but to see you so, I don't know, involved?"

"Oh. Why's that?" Tara crossed her arms and tilted her head to the side.

"No. I didn't mean it like that. It's just that you're so…ugh." Belle sighed. "I'm sorry."

Tara smiled and stepped toward Belle. "Don't be sorry. Let's just say, I don't let very many people see that side of me. Or anyone. So whatever ideas you have about me are the ones I want you, and everyone else, to have."

"Oh. I see." Belle didn't believe her in the slightest. She couldn't imagine that someone with so much affection toward her family could be as disconnected and distant as she wanted others to see.

"It's just who I am."

Belle and Tara stood in silence for several long seconds. Belle knew very little about Tara. All she had to go on was what she saw and what Tara offered. Maybe she was telling the truth. Belle stood quietly and began to sway in place—torn between staying and leaving.

"I'm sure Eden won't mind, well, she might, but I can keep a secret if you can. So would you like to have dinner with me on Friday?"

Belle's stomach fluttered to life. Tara reached out and took Belle's hands in her own. Tara's hands were soft and strong, and their heat sparked a fire inside Belle.

Belle held her breath as she stared into Tara's eyes and felt her hands slide up her arms. She gripped Belle's shoulders and pulled their bodies close. Her pulse quickened and she fought to keep her legs beneath her. "Friday?" Belle asked almost breathlessly.

Tara's face drew close to hers. She looked deep into Belle's eyes. "Friday," she said before her soft, warm lips pressed against Belle's.

She wanted more, but Tara pulled away and brushed her fingers across Belle's cheek. "You're freezing. You should get another sweater."

Belle could've been hypothermic, but with the fire Tara had built inside her she wouldn't have known. "Okay." Tara turned away. Belle stood glued to the floor, pressed her fingers to her lips, and watched as Tara bounded up the stairs and disappeared.

CHAPTER FOURTEEN

Belle stood in front of her full-length mirror and fidgeted with the sixth outfit she'd tried on in twenty minutes. She tugged and turned, sucked and tucked before throwing herself onto her bed like a defeated twelve-year-old. She lay on her back and stared at the ceiling. "What am I doing?" Belle was ignoring all the warning bells that clanged in her head. They were so loud she could've been a human carillon tower. In spite of Tara's admitted commitment issues, Belle couldn't help but remember the way she was with her family. She hoped that there was more to her than what Tara wanted people to believe.

A knock at the front door made Belle's heart jump. "Shit!" She froze in panic. "She cannot be here yet!" she said as she grabbed her phone to check the time. As she brought it over her face, it slipped from her fingers and hit her square on the bridge of her nose. "Ow!" She squeezed her nose with her fingers and sat up. Her eyes watered as she squinted to see the time. It was way too early to be Tara, thankfully. She walked to the door with her nostrils still pressed together and let Kyle and Andrew in.

"Please tell me you didn't drop your phone on your face again."

"No! It's fine, I won't tell you."

"Good grief, girl!" Andrew said.

"Stop mushing it. You're going to make it worse." He pulled her hand off of her face. "But more importantly, why aren't you dressed yet?"

"I can't find anything. I've tried on six different outfits already."

"And this is the best you came up with? Oh, hell no! Come on." Kyle grabbed her by the arm and pulled her down the hall toward her bedroom and Andrew followed behind.

When Kyle went into her closet she said, "You won't find anything in there. Most of it's right here." Belle sat next to the large pile of mangled clothes she'd tossed onto her bed.

"Not true!" He came out of her closet with three dresses.

"Seriously? Those are so fancy. And I wore that red one already."

"Oh, right," Kyle said as he tossed it over her footboard. "So you have two."

Belle had never worn either of the dresses that Kyle held up for her to choose. She'd bought them, and the red one, at the same time the year before. She had tried on all three of them and couldn't decide. And since at the time she didn't have any evening or cocktail dresses, she bought them all. Her eye was drawn to the one with black cap sleeves and lace trim. She remembered that it scooped low in the front and offered an ample view of her breasts. "You don't think that's too much?"

Kyle held it up to her. "I think it's just enough."

Andrew offered an "mhmm" in agreement.

She had no idea where Tara planned to take her. She didn't want to be either over or under dressed. "I'll try it. But if it's too much I'm going back to this." Belle motioned to the unremarkable blouse and slacks that she wore. When she compared her existing outfit to the elegant black dress, she was very much aware of its inadequacy. She took the dress from Kyle and went to the bathroom to change.

As soon as Belle had the dress on she knew that it was what she was going to wear. She felt comfortable and sexy without pulling or tugging on herself or the fabric. When she stepped out of the bathroom, both Kyle and Andrew confirmed her choice.

"Whoa! Now that's what I'm talking about!"

"Gorgeous!"

Belle blushed at their praises. "Thank you. I just need to figure out what to do with all this." Belle gathered her long hair into her hands and flopped it onto the top of her head.

"Well, you've got the right idea but terrible technique. Come in here." Andrew pushed her back into the bathroom to help her with her hair. She was so glad to have the two of them in her life. They were the best friends she could've asked for. Belle began to tear up and Kyle caught her.

"No. No crying tonight. Well, not unless she takes you to McDonald's."

"Thank you." Belle smiled and then closed her eyes while Andrew worked his magic.

Her boys sat in the living room while Belle finished her makeup. She could hear them rattle the mini-blinds to look out the window every time they heard a car pass by. When Tara did arrive, she thought they were going to spin themselves into the floor with excitement. And that did nothing to ease her vibrating nerves. "Breathe," she told herself. She stepped into the living room and took several deep, calming breaths. When Kyle and Andrew saw her, they both gasped.

"Holy shit, sweetheart. I have no words, darling," Andrew stammered.

As Kyle was about to speak, the doorbell rang and all three of them shrieked. "She's here. Shit! She's here." Belle said as she paced.

"Shhh! Everybody shush! Relax." Kyle let out a long sigh and lowered his arms to his sides. "I'll get the door." He sauntered to the door and took one last breath before he opened it. Belle hadn't expected them to be as nervous as she was, but they were, and she loved them all the more for it. "Oh, hello there, Tara. My husband and I were just leaving. Andrew."

Kyle jerked his head toward the door. "Oh, right. Yes. You have a wonderful night, dear," he said before he kissed Belle on her cheek and followed Kyle out the door. "Good night," he said to Tara with a wide grin.

Tara watched them head down the stairs before she turned to Belle. "I wasn't expecting th—oh, wow." Tara froze in mid-sentence on the threshold.

"Yeah, sorry about that. They insisted on staying just to make me uncomfortable."

"I don't even remember who you're talking about, because I can't think of anything except you and that dress." Tara stepped into the foyer and closed the door behind her.

Belle had never seen the look that Tara had in her eye. It was raw, almost ravenous. "Uhm, I wasn't sure if this would be too much."

"Oh, sweetheart. No. It's just perfect. You look amazing."

Tara stepped toward her so quickly she stepped back and bumped into the wall behind her. "Ooh."

Tara reached out her hand for Belle. "Careful. Are you okay?"

Belle slid her hand into Tara's. The contact sent a searing heat over every inch of her body. Her pulse quickened and she swallowed hard. She opened her mouth to answer, but she had no words. She nodded.

"Good. Shall we?"

The best she could manage was "mhmm." She followed Tara out the door and down the steps.

With Tara ahead of her, Belle could take a few moments to admire Tara's frame and figure without fear of being caught. She wore a fitted navy blue button-down tucked into a pair of black slacks that hugged her solid and muscular thighs. She was so fixated on watching Tara's body she almost missed the last step. Tara turned around just as she caught herself on the railing.

"Everything okay?"

"Absolutely." If Belle wanted to make it through the evening without a stumbling face plant she was going to have to stay focused and avoid getting distracted by pretty much everything there was about Tara. It was going to be a long night, which wasn't necessarily a bad thing.

❖

Tara couldn't think. Belle was stunning in every sense of the word. Her dress highlighted every soft curve of Belle's body. Tara hadn't thought it possible to be more enamored with the girl in the fluffy gray sweater with a burning red splotch on her forehead, but she was wrong. This was a whole different side to Belle she couldn't get out of her mind. This moment wasn't going to make that any easier.

Tara opened the door for Belle and helped her into the Jeep. Her fingers burned where they touched Belle's smooth skin. She stared at her for longer than necessary as she tried to remember what she was supposed to do next. "Ah!" She checked that Belle was in and closed the door.

As she moved around to the driver's side, a wave of anxiety washed over her. This wasn't like her at all. She was acting flummoxed and awkward around some girl. She'd had her fair share of *some girls* and they had never affected her this way. She never would've allowed it. So when the hell did this one become the exception? However it had happened, the idea that this one had made her very claustrophobic. She took several deep breaths and reached for the handle. When she looked up and saw Belle's beautiful sparkling eyes staring at her, the strangling fear eased.

"So I thought we would head over to the Vine Cellar and have a drink before dinner, if you'd like."

"That sounds nice."

"Great. Although I suppose I should've asked you if you even like wine."

Belle looked over and grinned. "Well, lucky for you I do."

"It does seem that I'm on quite a winning streak so far." Tara was talking about more than just her guess that Belle liked wine. It had taken some extreme measures and quite a bit of time to get the stunning and intriguing Belle beside her. She couldn't give all the credit to chance. "You can't win the game if you don't play it. No matter how lucky you are." As soon as she heard herself say it, she cringed.

"Wow," Belle said.

"Belle, I am so sorry. That came out far more arrogant and chauvinistic than it was meant." Tara pulled into the spot near the bar and turned to face her. Belle stared out her window in silence. "Belle."

"Don't worry about it. We all say things we regret, whether it's true or not. Although everything we say is grounded in some manner of truth."

Tara reached out for Belle's hand and held it in hers. "Belle, please. All I meant by that was—"

"I'm a game."

A knot in Tara's throat choked her. "No. You—"

"I don't know what that means. It's okay. You said it before, it's who you are."

She had said that. And anyone in the world would draw the exact same conclusion as Belle had. "Look at me. You're not a game. I just meant that anything worth having isn't handed to you. You have to work for it, earn it, and prove that you are worthy of having it. And I am failing miserably at it this very moment." Tara hung her head. They were enveloped in silence for several long and painful seconds.

"Yeah. I think they call it a strike." Belle chuckled.

Tara looked up at Belle in confusion. "What?"

"Tara, everything in me told me not to say yes when you asked me out. There might have even been flashing lights and sirens. Even now I have no idea why I'm here with you. But I am."

"You are." Tara leaned in closer to Belle.

Belle leaned back. "Although I'm not sure why that is after you compared me to a sporting event."

"I didn't mean—"

"It's fine, Tara. It doesn't matter. I see the person you want me to and it's just the kind of thing I imagine she'd say. Your reputation remains intact."

Tara wasn't looking to keep her reputation. She was trying to explain to Belle that this time she felt something was different. But it was clear that Belle already had her mind made up. Tara could keep pushing it or she could try to push past it. "So, did I strike out or do I still have a couple of swings left?"

"Um, I don't know. I'm not so great at sports metaphors. How many strikes are there in football?" Belle smiled.

Tara laughed. She didn't know if Belle was serious, but it just didn't matter. "I'll take as many as you'll give me."

"Then just keep dribbling; you might still win all the points."

Tara laughed harder. "Oh, I can't. Please tell me you're kidding." There was no way Belle was serious.

Belle burst out laughing with Tara. "Ha! Yes, Tara, I'm just messing with you."

As they laughed together, Tara added funny to the list of all the things she already adored about Belle.

CHAPTER FIFTEEN

B elle sat and waited for Tara to open her door. She would've done it for herself except that Tara told her to wait. Clearly, Belle's independent nature was not lost on Tara. However, Belle indulged herself and allowed Tara to demonstrate her skills.

Although they had laughed it off for the most part, Belle couldn't get the word out of her head. *Game.* Belle knew Tara's game. She'd seen her in action on at least three occasions. The third turned out to be her sister, so it didn't count. But she'd seen enough to know who Tara was. Now, Belle was one of those women. Tara opened the door and helped her out onto the sidewalk. Her simple touch sent a searing heat through Belle's body.

She was drawn into her, from the first moment she laid eyes on her. Before she'd even known her name or heard the sound of her voice, Belle was spellbound by Tara. She could've been nothing more than a picture and Belle would have still felt an undeniable pull toward her. Each time she appeared in her life, she became more difficult to cast aside as just another random face. Tara had somehow become another studied masterpiece in her mind—an artwork she could recall from memory as vividly as the strokes of grass on Cezanne's *View of Auvers sur Oise.*

As they walked toward the bar, Tara took her hand and entwined their fingers. Belle looked down and couldn't imagine anyone else's feeling as perfect. She looked up when Tara pulled her to a stop. A large crowd of people poured out onto the sidewalk. They mingled and chatted as they used their cigarettes and glasses of wine for conversational emphasis. Belle's anxiety reared its ugly head. She held her breath in an attempt to keep from hyperventilating. She didn't realize that she was squeezing Tara's hand with a death-like grip until she said something.

"Whoa. That's quite a grip you have. Are you okay?"

"Shit. I'm sorry." She tried to let go of Tara's hand, but it tightened around Belle's.

"Hey." Tara brought Belle's hand up and kissed it. "It's not as bad inside. The ruffians spill out here so they can smoke. It's a little more reserved in there."

Belle looked around. There wasn't a single *ruffian* anywhere in sight. If there were she would've felt a little less panicked. It was the Louboutin pumps and Gucci bags that made her nervous. She thought about Kyle and Andrew and how this would be someplace they would love, and love to drag her into. Belle looked at Tara and forced a smile. "Great."

Tara wasn't convinced. She took Belle's hands in hers and pulled her close. "We can go in for a few minutes. If you still feel like this, we will leave. Or we can just go now," Tara said.

"No. We can go in. I'm okay." Belle took a deep breath and smiled.

"Good, let's go." Tara turned and led Belle through the crowd. She nodded to several people who called her name and showed Belle to an empty table near the back.

Belle slid awkwardly onto the chair and held her clutch on the table in front of her. She looked around at the room lined with endless shelves of wine bottles and automated stainless steel machines. Tara was right; it was a more subdued crowd inside, and as Belle looked around she began to notice a more varied collection of clientele. Her anxiety began to ease.

She looked at Tara who smiled at her. "Better?" she asked as she held two wine glasses up and clinked them together.

Belle laughed. "So far. Do I get one of those?"

"Of course." Tara handed Belle one of the glasses and helped her slide off her seat. "After you."

Before they could make their way to the nearest machine, someone called Tara's name. She and Belle looked in the direction of a beautiful blonde who made her way over. "Of course," Belle mumbled under her breath.

"Cate! Um, what are you doing here?" Tara said quietly, but still loud enough for Belle to hear.

"What?" the woman asked.

"I didn't know you were going to be here."

"We're all here, Tara. What's the big d—" She looked around Tara and spotted Belle who fidgeted next to the table and pretended not to be listening. "Is that *her*?" she whispered.

"Shit." Tara sighed. "Yes." Tara turned toward Belle and brought the woman over.

Seriously? Belle recognized her as Tara's striking date from the ballet opening. Belle offered an awkward smile as the woman beamed from ear to ear.

"Hi, I'm Cate!" she said with an overdose of excitement.

"Uh, hi. Belle."

Tara moved in between them. "Belle, this is Cate Summers, my best friend. We grew up together—me, her, and my sister, Lucy."

"Good Lord, you're beautiful." Belle couldn't believe she'd just said that out loud. She wanted to crawl under the table and die from embarrassment. "I don't know why I just said that. I'm not even drinking, I swear." Belle held up her empty wine glass as proof.

Cate laughed. "Thank you. And I will say the exact same thing about you. That dress is stunning."

Belle blushed. "Thank you." To be polite, Belle was about to ask Cate if she wanted to join them when they were bombarded by a mass of people. Belle looked at Cate in surprise. "What?" Belle's earlier sense of panic returned. Tara greeted the new arrivals, and Belle looked for an escape route. The last thing she wanted was to be inundated with crowds of Tara's *closest* friends.

Cate spoke over the noise that came with the crowd. "I'm so sorry."

"It's okay." Belle grinned weakly. "I'm just gonna go." Belle tried to squeeze herself through the horde.

As if Cate could sense Belle's distress, she reached over and touched her arm. "Hold on a sec," she said before she turned and grabbed Tara by the shirtsleeve.

Belle couldn't hear what she said, but Tara looked at her with apologetic eyes as Cate whispered into her ear. Belle felt invisible as people bumped and swerved into her. It was almost like drowning in a sea of people. Belle saw Tara hug Cate and give a few people a gentle tap or two on their backs.

Cate pushed her way back to Belle and rubbed her arm. "I talked some sense into her."

"What?" Belle had no idea what that meant.

"She just needs a good flick in the forehead sometimes. Lucky for her, this time it was just figuratively." Cate smiled as Tara came and stood next to Belle.

"I don't understand." Belle looked from Cate to Tara and back.

"I have a much better idea," Tara said as she held up a bottle of wine. "Do you want to go somewhere a little less *here*?"

Belle looked at Cate who nodded at her. Belle smiled. "That sounds like a great idea."

Tara raised an eyebrow at her. "Eh, how can I trust you? That's the same thing you said about this place."

"Hey, not fair!"

Cate and Tara laughed. "I give you permission to flick her in the forehead," Cate said.

"I might need it."

"Trust me, you will. Okay. Now go." Cate surprised Belle with a tight embrace and then smacked Tara on her arm as they left.

Belle had no idea what else the night had in store, but she found that she was curiously excited about it.

❖

So far the night was going worse than Tara could have expected. There was a reason she never got so involved with the nuances of a date, because she didn't have to impress anyone. Even if the night went poorly the only thing she was out was sex, and even the worst dates never ended without it anyway.

With Belle, it had been different from the start. She couldn't say that she hadn't thought about the way her skin would feel pressed up against her own, or the taste of her body on her tongue. But since the moment she'd seen Belle dancing alone in the empty gallery, she knew her old tricks wouldn't be enough. The short time they spent at the wine bar proved that without any doubt. To get anywhere with Belle she needed to change her strategy.

She pulled into the dark parking garage and swiped her keycard at the guard station. She gave a friendly nod to the officer and continued through the automatic gate and up to the top level.

"Where are we? Am I about to be murdered like some serial crime drama?"

Tara laughed. "Well, I'd be the worst serial killer ever since I just swiped my parking card and registered with security. But I guess you never know."

"Yeah, I think I saw this episode on *Criminal Minds*."

Tara drove to the topmost level and pulled into the parking spot. She cut the engine and turned toward Belle. "I've seen all of them, and I'm almost certain that was not an episode."

"Uh huh. That's what a killer would say."

Tara rolled her eyes and laughed as she got out and opened Belle's door for her. "True," she said as she helped her out of the Jeep and grabbed the bottle of wine from the backseat. Tara took Belle by the hand and led her to the elevator. She pressed the button for the top floor. The elevator chimed and opened to a dim space.

Belle read the sign above the reception desk. "Hicks Architecture Group. What are we doing here?"

"I need to grab something. Wait right here." Tara stepped into an office and came out with two glasses. "Can't drink wine without these."

"Tara, you can't take those. What are you doing?"

Tara grabbed her hand and pulled Belle back into the elevator. As the doors closed, she fished a key from her pocket and inserted it into the control panel and turned it. The elevator rose to the final level, the roof.

When the doors opened, Tara stepped out into the balmy Florida air. The sky was clear and thousands of stars sparkled in the deep blue night. She turned to take Belle's hand, but she hadn't yet gotten off the elevator. "What are you doing?"

"What are *you* doing? I doubt we should be up here."

"It's fine. I know people." Tara smiled and reached out for her.

Belle took Tara's hand and let her pull her gently out of the elevator. "No kidding. Who don't you know?" Tara pulled her to the side of the building and Belle gasped. "Wow! This is amazing."

Tara pointed to the ground twenty-three stories below at a couple walking in the park. "I don't know them. I don't think."

Tara watched Belle as she stared out over the downtown Orlando skyline and Lake Eola. Strands of hair that broke free from their arrangement and blew in the breeze that swirled around them. Belle's eyes were wide with amazement and the shimmering city lights reflected in them. She was beautiful, and by far the most intriguing and intelligent woman Tara had ever met.

She opened the wine, poured two glasses, and handed one to Belle. "Here's to ending this night far better than it began."

"Mission accomplished," Belle said as she gently tapped her glass to Tara's.

"The view is so much better from up there," Tara said as she pointed back toward the top of the elevator.

"Are you serious?" Belle's mouth hung open in shock.

"Yeah. But we're fine here. You're in a dress and heels. You don't need to be climbing—"

Belle cut her off in mid-sentence. "Well, now we are doing it."

Belle took her wine glass and marched over to the scaffold ladder on the side of the mechanical room. She slipped off her shoes, held them and her glass in the same hand, and stepped onto the first rung.

"Holy shit!" Tara ran over to the ladder. "Belle. No. Come down. You're going to fall." Either Belle didn't hear her or she wasn't listening. Tara's money was on the latter.

"Hold these." Belle tossed her shoes to Tara. "I don't need them. Just put them down there." Belle raised the tight skirt of her dress high up her thighs. Tara couldn't help but graze her eyes up the smooth exposed skin. Her pulse quickened and her body thrummed with fear and desire as she watched Belle make her way up the ladder.

When Belle reached the top, she stared down at Tara. "Haven't you learned never to tell a lady she can't do something?" She straightened her skirt and took a prideful sip from her unspilled glass.

"Well, I've never met a lady quite like you before."

"Are you coming?"

Tara's mind flashed to a vision of Belle's body pressed against her as her fingers coaxed those very words from her lips. She thought, *not before you do,* but said, "Absolutely."

CHAPTER SIXTEEN

W hat am I looking at?" Roz asked impatiently as he stared at a wall of monitors.

"This, sir, is a live feed of every surveillance camera in and around the museum," Jesse said.

"Well, I'll be damned. It is." Roz stood and leaned in to one of the screens. "Will you look at that? You dumbasses did something right for a change."

"I did it, sir. I figured that we could use a little more sophistication, seeing as how the brute force tactics weren't getting us very far. I'm working on hacking into the proximity card server so that we can gain access without needing an employee or their badge. But so far I'm not having much luck. But I did manage to hack some of the locking mechanisms. That might come in handy."

"I prefer taking things by force. Not with this pansy ass computer shit." Pete added his opinion.

"Nobody asked you, did they?" Roz shut him down. "I don't give a rat's ass how we get in. You just better get us out."

"I might have a way to disarm the entire system before we breach the doors and disable the guards so they can't activate the alarm."

"What about the manual switch or exterior doors?"

"Since that one isn't connected to the system I won't be able to deactivate them. But since it isn't, the alarm is strictly audible and does not connect to police dispatch. Even if it's triggered, we still have time before it's called in."

"And there is your brute force." Roz looked to Pete. "You will make sure that alarm is not triggered, by any means necessary." Pete grinned devilishly. "I like the sound of that."

❖

Belle's heart pounded and her hands shook. She couldn't believe that she had just scaled the side of an elevator shaft and stood barefooted overlooking the glittering lights of downtown. She was as exhilarated as she was frightened. Never in her life would she have imagined herself there, either alone or with someone like Tara.

She looked down the side and watched Tara make her way up the ladder. Now that she was up there, Belle couldn't believe that she'd went through with it, dress and all. She realized that there was no way she had gotten away without showing her ass, literally. As soon as Tara reached the top, Belle asked, "Have you ever seen something so ladylike?"

Tara laughed and wrapped her arms around Belle. "That was the best thing I've ever seen in my life."

Belle blushed and buried her face in Tara's shoulder. "You saw my butt, didn't you?"

"Maybe a little."

Belle was embarrassed, but there was something so comforting about the way Tara held her. And the scent of Tara's cologne intoxicated her. "You smell so good." As soon as she said it, Belle grunted in regret.

Tara chuckled. "Thank you."

Belle pulled away and looked up at Tara. She was curious. "What did Cate say to you earlier?"

"Oh, nothing."

Belle didn't buy it. She stepped out of Tara's arms and backed up against the railing. "I call bullshit!" Belle turned around, lowered herself down, and hung her legs over the side of the building.

Tara laughed at Belle's familiar words. She sat next to Belle and swung her legs over as well. "Okay. You want to know?"

Belle wasn't sure she did after she'd said it like that, but she still said, "Yes."

Tara rested her hands on the bar above her and turned her head toward Belle. "Honestly, she asked me why I brought you to the same place I bring all my dates."

Belle was right. She could've done without the answer. "Oh. Wow." Belle sat and looked out over the city. The fountain caught her attention as it began its evening show, a beautiful choreographed spectacle of lights, water, and music. She couldn't hear anything except the sound of her beating heart and the rush of wind around her. "Have you always been this way?"

Tara dropped her hands into her lap and looked at Belle. "What do you mean?"

Belle was coming to the conclusion that no matter how attracted she was to Tara or how unexplainable her feelings were, Tara wasn't the right woman for her. "You, with your aloof attitude, noncommittal lifestyle, and carefree personality. I mean, how many jobs do you have?"

"Oh. That."

Belle couldn't help but laugh at Tara's detached response to her question. "That's what I mean."

"Is this about what Cate said? Yes, I have a lot of dates. Many of them are just casual acquaintances that I spend time with, nothing serious."

"It's not the number of dates. It's that none of them are serious. Do you have anything in your life that is constant?" Belle knew too well what it was like to live without structure and continuity. She couldn't imagine someone choosing that life on purpose.

"My family, I suppose, but someone can only take so much of it. My whole life my parents have had everything planned out. My life, my education, my career. Hell, they'd have had me in an arranged marriage if I wasn't a lesbian. Until I turned twenty-one, I did everything I was supposed to. But then I couldn't do it anymore. I was suffocating. I felt like if I didn't get out I was going to be crushed. So I did. I quit school, I traveled, I worked any and every odd job I could, and yes, I slept with a lot of women."

Belle was speechless. The very thing she had spent her whole life wishing for was the exact thing that Tara was running away from. "I didn't know."

"I know. It's okay. So, no. I haven't always been like this. Just since college. But I can't imagine ever going back to the way it used to be."

Belle's heart squeezed in her chest. "I see." Tara all but confirmed that she would never be what Belle wanted her to be and she was just another jaunt in Tara's quest for freedom.

Tara brushed her hand across Belle's cheek and looked into her eyes. "But right now I don't feel any of those things here with you."

A knot tied itself in Belle's throat, and she couldn't speak. Tara leaned in, and Belle held her breath. Her lips parted and her eyes closed as Tara's soft lips pressed to hers. A fire sparked to life inside her and spread through her body. Belle slid her hands up Tara's arms and around her neck. She felt Tara's tongue flick at her bottom lip, and Belle opened her mouth for her. Their kiss deepened and Belle lost herself in Tara's taste and touch.

Belle pulled her close and leaned back bringing Tara with her. She felt the weight of Tara press against her, and a low heat built between her legs. Tara pulled back from their fevered kiss and stared at her. Belle watched as the desire she felt was mirrored in Tara's wild eyes. She had never wanted someone so badly. She throbbed with a need that took over her logic and sense.

❖

Tara looked down into Belle's darkened eyes. She knew she could so easily get lost in them, and the thought frightened her. Tara had just finished telling Belle that she wasn't the type to wrap herself in a single woman. She couldn't help but think that she was telling herself as well as Belle. Tara stroked away the strand of hair that blew across Belle's forehead, and her eyes fluttered closed. She was so beautiful that Tara ached to kiss her. But she feared that if she began again she would never stop.

Against the warning signs that her head threw out at her, Tara leaned down and pressed her lips to Belle's once again. Their soft and languid connection turned into a voracious need for more. Tara ran her hand up Belle's arm and gripped her shoulder. Belle moaned, and a surge of heat moved up Tara's thighs. When Belle twisted her hands into Tara's hair, an intense desire jolted through her, and she pulled away. While she had the desire and the ability to take Belle right there on the top of the building under a clear night sky, she couldn't.

Tara sat up and stared at her legs that dangled over the side of the mechanical building. She wanted her, without a doubt; it just didn't feel right. Not there, and not that way. Belle deserved something far more meaningful and passionate. The problem was, for the first time, Tara didn't think she was the one who could offer her that.

"Are you hungry?" Tara asked Belle who had sat up beside her. She couldn't look at her because she was afraid of what she would see, whether it was disappointment, frustration, or hurt. In spite of how much she wanted Belle and how relentless she was pursuing her, Tara found herself in an unfamiliar place. A place she had spent the last decade of her life avoiding.

"You know, I think we should just…maybe we should just call it a night."

Tara was right. She could hear the emotion in Belle's voice. She looked over at Belle to see her face, but she had already turned away and was pulling herself to her feet. "Okay." It was all Tara could say as she watched Belle grab the railing of the ladder and climb down the side of the building.

Neither of them spoke as Tara drove Belle home. Tara didn't know what to say to explain herself so she said nothing. She wasn't certain that it was the best course of action, but in her head it sounded better than any *I want you, but I don't want to be tied down* speech she'd used a thousand times before. Yet unlike those times, Tara was afraid that it wasn't the complete truth anymore, at least not where Belle was concerned.

She pulled up to Belle's house and killed the engine. Nothing about the night had gone right, and she needed to tell Belle she was sorry for that even if it wouldn't do any good.

"All right, well, I'll see you," Belle said as she pulled the door handle.

Tara reached across Belle's lap and stopped her from getting out just yet. "Belle, wait a second, please."

Belle looked down at the arm that held her and Tara withdrew. "I just wanted to tell you that I'm sorry."

Belle looked over at Tara. "For what?" Belle asked.

"For this pretty disastrous evening I made here."

"It's not your fault, Tara. I think both of us put too much into making it something bigger than it was. It happens. I wouldn't call it disastrous, just misguided. You are a great person, and I'd like to be your friend."

"Friend?" Tara had friends. Hell, she had more friends than she could count. Why did such an innocuous word sound so final, so nonnegotiable?

"Yeah." Belle looked away from Tara and stared out the window.

Tara thought she heard the faint sound of a breathy sigh. "Belle?"

Belle cleared her throat and looked over at Tara. "Yeah?" Her tone was upbeat, and she beamed, as if a switch had been flipped.

"Uh, nothing, I guess."

"Okay. Well, I had a nice time tonight, in spite of the few glitches. Thanks!" Belle leaned over and kissed Tara quickly on the cheek. She paused for a split second after, and Tara thought she saw a flash of disappointment. But it disappeared, replaced by one of Belle's beautiful smiles. "Good night, Tara."

Tara didn't even have the chance to help Belle out of the Jeep. She was out and halfway up the steps when the soft burn of Belle's last kiss faded away.

Chapter Seventeen

The next morning, Belle wandered over to Kyle and Andrew's. As always, the door was unlocked in anticipation of her arrival. It was one of the first things they did as soon as they came downstairs each morning and before they started the coffee. Belle let herself in and headed back to the kitchen. Andrew stood at the stove attending to breakfast. She kissed him on the cheek.

"Good morning, sunshine! How was your da—oh Lord." He stopped mid-sentence when he got a good look at Belle's appearance.

Belle hadn't even bothered to change out of her pajama pants, and her hair was in a ratted nest on the top of her head. "Hey." She grabbed a cup and poured herself some coffee.

"Babe! Kyle? Will you come in here for a sec?" Andrew hollered out the patio door to Kyle who sat reading the paper.

Belle added too much sugar and milk to her coffee, but she needed it. When she turned around, Kyle and Andrew stood side by side and stared at her. "What?"

"Um, sweetie. Did you even attempt to wash your makeup off last night?" Kyle asked.

"Or this morning?" Andrew added.

Belle swiped under her eyes, and only when she pulled back black smudged fingers did she realize that, in fact, she hadn't done either. "It would appear not."

"Oh wow. Okay. Why don't you go get one of my Olay wipes and take care of that while I put breakfast out?" Andrew said as he took her by the shoulders and pointed her toward the bathroom.

"It's not that bad." Belle wasn't used to wearing makeup, or at least enough to worry about if she forgot to wash it off before bed. When she got to the bathroom, she changed her tune. "Holy crap! I'm a wreck."

She washed and dried her face, then took her hair down and gave it a good brushing before she smoothed it back into a neat ponytail. Human again, she went back out to the kitchen. Belle grabbed her cup off the counter and went to sit at the patio table with Kyle.

"It's alive." Andrew kissed her on the forehead before he set her plate in front of her.

"Sorry about that. I just sorta stumbled over here as soon as I got out of bed. I didn't even brush my teeth first." Belle covered her mouth in disbelief.

"Well, we know you weren't out late. So what happened?"

What happened? Nothing. That's what happened. "Oh, you know, turns out I should've trusted my instinct."

"What?" Kyle asked.

"We're too different. She just wants a good time, no commitment. Just like I figured."

"Okay. So what's the problem with that?" Andrew asked.

"That's not what I want. At all. She is the complete opposite of what I want."

"In what way?" Kyle asked.

Belle laughed. "Every way? Let's just say she isn't the settling down type."

Andrew groaned and Kyle rolled his eyes. "Seriously?"

"What? Yes, seriously! That is a problem. I don't want someone whose one goal is to sleep with every woman in Orlando. And besides that, she has zero ambition, unless you count her endless odd jobs and dedication to avoiding commitment."

"We all have those exact same goals at some point in our lives, although my penchant for the ladies shifted to men somewhere in the middle." Andrew grinned and winked at Kyle.

"Right. But you weren't against settling down. She is. I think her exact words were 'I can't imagine it, ever' or something like that."

"I wasn't. But he was." Andrew pointed to Kyle.

"No way!" There was no way that Kyle was anything like Tara. He was born to be married and wanted a family almost as much as Belle did.

"It's true," Kyle admitted. "I had no intention of being with one man for the rest of my life. The thought of it scared me to death."

"And then you met Andrew and everything changed, right? You just knew?"

"No way. He scared me worst of all. He made me question everything I knew about myself, everything I thought I wanted, and I ran."

"Broke my heart into a million pieces, he did."

Belle couldn't believe that Kyle could've been that person. "Why did you change your mind?"

"I don't know. I think he drugged me." Kyle laughed and Andrew smacked him on the arm.

"I did no such thing. Now take your *vitamins*, sweetheart." Andrew gave Belle an exaggerated wink.

"Nothing is as it seems on the surface, Belle. Some things work out and some things just never do. But why not have fun with it while it does?"

"Have fun with it?"

"Yes. She is gorgeous, and you're attracted to her. So why not enjoy it for whatever it is for however long you can? She isn't the only one who can be a free agent."

"I can't do that. I already told her I just wanted to be friends."

"Sweetie, I've seen the way she looks at you. I doubt she heard anything you said about just being friends."

"I know!" Andrew said. "I have a fundraising gala performance next weekend. Invite her as your date, uh, I mean friend. We can all go together."

Belle wasn't sure any of that was a good idea. She tried to avoid putting herself into situations where she knew there would be no good outcome. However, she didn't know why women like Tara were the only ones who could enjoy the benefits of noncommittal relationships. Plus, she did want to try to be friends with Tara if nothing else, and it would be a nice change to have an actual date to one of Andrew's awkward social gatherings. "Okay, I'll ask her." Both of them looked at her as if she had two heads. "You will?" Kyle asked, confused by her uncharacteristic answer.

"Sure. If it means I don't have to go by myself again, then what would it hurt?" It was a rhetorical question, because Belle knew what.

"Well, all right then." Kyle looked at Andrew and shrugged.

❖

Tara slipped her bag under the desk and clocked into the system. As she checked the logs for the shift change, she began to grow anxious. She hadn't seen or heard from Belle since their train wreck of a date several days earlier. Tara had thought about calling or texting her, but nothing she could've said would have changed that night, even if she wanted it to.

As she began her rounds, she felt someone watching her. She looked around and saw a man in a hooded sweatshirt pacing in front of Gustav Klimt's *Portrait of a Lady*. He glanced around at the others in the room before he made eye contact with Tara. He pulled his hood lower over his face and crossed the room toward the other exit. Tara radioed for assistance to the European art exhibit and headed around to cut him off on the other side.

Tara's heart pounded and her body flooded with adrenaline. As Tara rounded the corner, the man bolted toward her. She yelled for him to stop, but he didn't even slow down. From the corner of her eye, she saw Belle pushing her cart across the hall right into the path of the man. "Belle! Stay there!" But she didn't hear her. Tara saw the cords of her earbuds hanging down and realized why. "Shit!"

Tara ran with all her speed but was still too far away, and she could only watch helplessly as he plowed right into the cart and pushed it back into Belle. The handle of the cart slammed into her and she clutched her stomach. Without losing stride, he continued toward Tara who watched as Belle collapsed onto the marble floor in a heap. First her stomach turned, and then she became enraged.

Two other guards ran after the thug as he continued toward her. She warned him once more to stop, but he didn't. When he was within reach, Tara lunged at him. She wrapped her arm around his neck, and with all her body weight, forced him to the ground. The other guards were a second behind. The suspect struggled beneath her and begged to be let go. Tara wrestled against him until she had him restrained. She pushed back his hood as they pulled him upright. He was just a kid, no more than fourteen.

"Let me go! I ain't doin' nothin'. I ain't breaking no rules, man."

"Then why are you running?" Tara panted.

"Cause y'all will make me go back there. I ain't going back there."

Tara didn't care what he was talking about. She saw several people crowding around Belle, so as the other guards attended to the truant, she rushed over to her. "Are you okay?"

Belle gave a small nod.

Tara helped her up and sat her on a bench along the wall. Kyle, Joseph, and several other managers came running up the hallway toward them. Tara checked Belle for injuries as Kyle skidded to a stop in front of them.

"What the hell happened?"

Belle struggled to catch her breath. "I can't breathe," she said as she clutched at her sweater and ripped it off.

Tara saw the scrape on Belle's elbow, but she was more concerned about her chest. She'd seen the impact it made with the cart and thought there might be broken ribs.

"It's fine. Just need to catch my breath," Belle said between gasps for air.

"Where does it hurt?" Tara asked as she raised Belle's shirt to get a better look.

"Right here." Belle pointed to the center of her abdomen and sucked her teeth.

Tara saw a clear red imprint of the cart handle across her midsection. "Ouch! That cart hit you straight on." Tara looked around at the people standing around when she saw Kyle. "It could just be a bruise or she might have cracked a rib."

"They called nine one one already."

Belle looked toward the kid in the hoodie and the handful of guards and staff that surrounded him. "What the hell is it with these crazy people in hoods? Who is he? Do you think he's one of those guys?" Belle asked breathlessly as she pressed her stomach and then grimaced.

"I don't think so. This kid can't be more than fourteen. Probably a runaway or truant. You shouldn't push on it."

"He's just scared. That's why he ran. What was he doing before he spooked? Oh, man, why can't I catch my breath? It feels like someone is squeezing me around the middle."

"Don't worry about all that right now. Stop talking and just sit." Tara wasn't surprised that Belle was more concerned about the boy and his situation than about herself. The same couldn't be said for Tara.

Kyle's face was ashen as he sat next to Belle and grabbed her hand. She patted his with her other. "I'm fine, Kyle. Go check on that kid for me, please."

"Okay," he said.

Tara took another look at Belle's chest and lowered her shirt. "Okay, sunshine. You might need a couple of x-rays."

"It barely hurts. This hurts worse." She held up her arm and showed Tara a large bloody scrape on her elbow. "I think my arm is on fire."

"That's the adrenaline. Trust me, you won't be saying that in a few minutes." Belle's face turned white. "Are you okay?"

"The few minutes is up. I think I'm going to be sick." Belle covered her mouth.

"Shit!" Tara grabbed the first thing she saw, a large trashcan, and pushed it in front of Belle just in time.

Belle sat with her head hung over the can as Tara rubbed her back. When two paramedics arrived, Tara moved away and let them assess the situation. She watched intently over them until Joseph called her name. She left Belle's side and went to debrief her boss.

By the time she had explained to him what had occurred, the paramedics had finished. When Belle let out a shout, everyone turned toward her. Both Kyle and Tara went to her.

"What's wrong?" Kyle asked.

"I'm not going to the freaking hospital."

One of the technicians spoke up. "I think she just had the wind knocked out of her and has a bit of bruising. If you want, she could get her chest scanned just to be sure."

"Does she have to go to the hospital for that?" Tara asked.

"No."

"Okay. Then we can take her to an urgent care or whatever."

"Do you want to do that instead? The hospital might be better though. Just in case," Kyle suggested.

"I'm fine. If it gets worse, I'll go to the doctor."

"All right. But maybe you should go home for now. I'll drive you. Come on." Kyle helped Belle up off the bench.

Tara couldn't help but think that she could just pick her up and carry her if she had to. Much better than Kyle could. She surprised herself with the unexpected jealously. "Should I go get your wheelchair?" Tara asked Belle.

Belle looked up at Tara and smiled. "At this rate we should put my name on it."

"I'll work on that."

"What are they going to do with that boy?" Belle asked as they walked by. "If he didn't harm anything, maybe we can just give him a warning?"

"What?" Tara couldn't agree that what had happened to Belle was harmless.

"He was scared. I'm sure he didn't mean it. You startled him. Please?"

The look in Belle's eyes was sweet, concerned, and caring, and Tara fell right into them. "Okay. I'll see what I can do."

"Thank you." Belle smiled. "Hey, I was coming to ask you something before all this, but now I can't seem to remember what—" Belle groaned.

"Fundraiser," Kyle whispered.

"Oh right. Saturday, Andrew is having a fundraiser thing. Would you like to come with me? Be my date, uh, or whatever?"

Tara was speechless. Did she just ask her out on a date? She leaned in close to Kyle. "I think she might have hit her head as well."

"I'm not deaf, and I am well aware of what I am asking. It's a simple yes or no question." Kyle chuckled and looked away, pretending he wasn't standing between them.

"Uh, I know. I mean after..."

"Yes or no, Tara? Preferably before I get sick again."

This was a new side to Belle. And whether it was brought on by the trauma or something else, Tara was hooked. "Yes. Of course I will."

CHAPTER EIGHTEEN

When Tara arrived at Belle's, she was once again floored by her beauty. Belle came down the stairs with Andrew as she waited with Kyle in the foyer. For someone who expressed such a dislike for pretentious social gatherings, Belle could have fooled even the most elitist of them all. Her everyday appearance was casual and simple. A clean and comfortable attractiveness that Tara found both refreshing and charming. However, she became another creature when night fell and she exposed something far more alluring and seductive.

"Hi," Belle said as she slid to a stop in front of Tara.

"You look gorgeous."

Belle blushed. "Thank you. You look amazing as well."

Tara hadn't thought twice about how she looked. She'd worn the same black Armani suit to every event her parents insisted that she attend. But for the first time, she was glad she was wearing it as she watched Belle's eyes rake shamelessly over her from head to toe. "Thanks."

"No. Thank you," Belle said in a drawn-out manner. When Kyle chuckled, Belle corrected herself. "I meant thank you for coming."

Kyle said, "Yeah, right," at the same time Tara said, "I know."

"It's nice to not have to attend one of these things as the third wheel. These things make me crazy uncomfortable when I'm standing alone in the corner while these two schmooze with the muckety-mucks."

"Muckety-mucks, huh?" In spite of Belle's rumblings, Tara thought Belle would fit seamlessly into that world, or her world, as it were. "Where are we going?" Tara slipped Belle's shawl over her bare shoulders and reveled in the scent of her sweet perfume.

The four of them headed out to the cars. They were going to follow Andrew and Kyle, as Belle always did. Tara helped her into the Jeep and closed the door.

"It's a ballet fundraiser at some mansion in Winter Park. Like I said, muckety-mucks."

Tara's heart stopped. "Winter Park?"

"Yeah. Just follow them. They know the way."

It wasn't the journey that had Tara's stomach in a knot; it was the destination. She scanned her memory for any recollection of an event at her parents' house that evening, but she came up empty. It couldn't be at their place. "Do you know who's hosting?"

"I don't, no. Andrew said they are huge donors and something about designing the new performing arts center."

Tara's stomach leapt into her throat. It was her parents. What the hell was she going to do? It was too late to back out of the night, so she would have to tell her. But how? It wasn't the way she had anticipated telling her, if she'd ever planned on it in the first place. Her mind spun with explanations and excuses. "Hey, umm…"

"You know, I don't know how anyone could live like that," Belle said as they drove along the manicured tree-lined streets and past the iron-gated driveways. "I mean, their houses are so big they never even see each other. With nannies for the kids so they don't have to be bothered."

"Well, I'm sure it's not quite that bad." Tara could tell her from experience that she'd had no nanny and her family ate dinner together every night. "I'm sure some of them would surprise you."

"I doubt it."

Tara was a little surprised by Belle's biased opinion of the types of families who lived in these homes. "Well, maybe the family who lives there spends each Christmas volunteering at a children's hospital," Tara said as she pointed to a massive Mediterranean style villa. In fact, Tara knew for certain that was how the Manshone family of doctors spent their holiday.

"It would be nice if that were true."

"It is," Tara mumbled under her breath. "I bet if you gave them a chance you'd change your mind." Tara felt the ever-increasing sense of doom close in around her. No matter how she tried, there was always something that wedged itself between the two of them. She couldn't understand how she could continue to feel so drawn to someone so very different.

"Maybe. Giles was a very kind and generous man, so I know it's possible. And you have to admit, it would be something to call one of these places home."

"See. It's not so bad." Tara felt hopeful as Belle opened herself up to the possibility that not all millionaires were pretentious pricks.

"You've got to be kidding me!" Belle said as they pulled up behind Kyle and Andrew. "I won't be mad if you back up right now and drive away."

Tara looked over at Belle whose mouth was agape with shock. Granted, the Hicks estate was exceptionally grand. But it was a showpiece of pure love and devotion that her parents had created together. Tara contemplated taking Belle's out, but before she could shift into reverse, a line of cars appeared behind them. Tara's heart raced. There was no way in hell she could tell Belle right at that moment that she was Tara Hicks, daughter of the evening's *muckiest-mucks*.

She averted her eyes as the gate attendant asked for a party name. Thankfully, Belle answered for her so she didn't have to. He checked off their names and directed them forward. They parked and followed the crowd of people into the house. Tara kept her head down and tried to keep herself hidden in amongst the herding guests. Once they were inside, Tara scanned the room for familiar faces, and to her dismay they were everywhere. She had never before felt so visible at one of her parents' events. Kyle and Andrew excused themselves to meet up with the other members of the company while Belle stood close by.

"Let's get this party started," Belle said as a tray of champagne floated by.

Tara grabbed two glasses from the tray. She spotted a quiet opening next to the far wall of the foyer rotunda and grabbed Belle's hand. She led her along the perimeter of the room. When they stopped, she downed the entire glass and picked up another from the passing server.

"This place is even more impressive than I expected." Belle turned in a complete circle.

"It's all right," Tara said without taking her eyes off the crowd.

"Are you kidding me? I'm almost certain that is a Ming dynasty moon flask vase worth something like six hundred thousand dollars," Belle proclaimed in a failed attempt at a whisper.

Tara had no idea, but she knew her mother had once threatened her with boarding school when she caught her trying to sneak it out of the house for show-and-tell. "So they have expensive stuff. Don't most of *these* people?" Tara noticed a man squinting at her from across the room, and she grabbed Belle by her shoulders and turned their backs to him.

"Oh my, is that a Rembrandt?" Belle walked away and disappeared into the library.

Tara felt more comfortable in this room, as it was void of people and she had no chance of being recognized. She closed the door behind them. Belle was so caught up in the painting that she didn't even notice.

"A what?"

"A Rembrandt! Rembrandt Van Rijn, only the greatest Dutch painter in history. *The Night Watch? Storm on the Sea of Galilee?*" Belle listed off the paintings, but they were lost on Tara. "No?"

"Sorry. No." Belle moved in so close to the painting it was as if she were trying to smell the paint. "What are you looking at?"

"I think this is the real thing, Tara. And if it is, it's worth millions!" Belle looked at her and her eyes sparkled with excitement.

Tara watched as Belle's body vibrated with passion. "Millions, huh?" Tara was certain her parents had spent at least one or two on it. She remembered not being impressed when they brought it home. Certainly not like Belle was at that moment.

"Yes, Tara. Like thirty million!"

"What the hell!" Tara said.

❖

"Yes! Maybe even more." Belle's skin buzzed. "Look here." Belle pulled Tara in close to the painting. "Look at the detail around the eyes. It's his classic style. He put all of the detail here in order to draw us in."

"I see."

"I wonder if they've had this analyzed by the Rembrandt Society? They should for insurance purposes alone. But how much do you want to bet they don't even know what they have here? The rich buy art because someone tells them they should. I'd say most of them have no idea what they even have hanging around. Giles was different. He knew what he had, and he appreciated it."

"As a matter of fact, that is a 1635 Dutch painting on a beechwood panel painted by a student in the style of Rembrandt," a tall, elegant woman with dark hair said as she glided toward them.

"It can't be a pupil," Belle said.

"Belle, let's go." Tara grabbed her by the hand and tried to pull her away.

The woman approached and smiled kindly. "It's okay. Stay. I'd like to hear what she has to say."

Belle cleared her throat, attempting to hide any discomfort or intimidation. "I was just saying that I don't believe this was done by a Rembrandt student, but by the master himself."

The woman looked from Belle to Tara and back. "How so?"

"Okay. Well, here for example." Belle motioned for the woman to come closer as she had done for Tara. "Unfortunately, the years of varnish obscure the true color and intricacies, but you can see the detail around his eyes. And right here, in the fluidity and texture of the fabric. And you said beech. During the 1630s, Rembrandt's canvas of choice was beech, not oak like most."

"Interesting," she said as she backed away from the painting and smiled.

"Can I ask you why you haven't had the piece restored?" Belle found it peculiar that the piece hadn't been cleaned, nor had the aged and yellowing varnish been removed.

"I wasn't aware it hadn't been done. I expect that my art dealer should have advised me to do so had he thought it necessary."

"Any dealer worth a shit would have." Belle regretted her candor when she heard Tara's quiet gasp. "I apologize for that, ma'am."

The woman laughed. "Oh my dear, never be sorry for speaking the truth. So, what else should my shitty dealer have told me about this piece?"

"Well, first of all, if he sold you this unrestored painting for anything less than four million without an appraisal by the Rembrandt Society and a Dutch art expert, then I would question him about it. Can I ask who your dealer was?"

"Certainly, if I can ask a question first."

"Of course."

When the woman turned to Tara, Belle watched curiously. She wasn't sure why she would ask anything of her since she'd not said a single thing the entire time. "What are you hiding this intelligent and beautiful creature in here for, Tara?"

Belle's stomach turned over. "What?" Tara looked at Belle with wide eyes.

"We're not hiding, *Mother*."

"Mother? This is your...oh my God." Belle felt sick. She had gone on and on about the pretentious rich people who lived in the house and the whole time that was Tara's family.

"Belle, this is my mother, Mrs. Linda Hicks."

"Hicks? Hicks Architecture Group." It was all coming together. The ballet in honor of the architect and design firm, the building Tara took her to on their date, the fundraiser for the company. "You knew where we were coming tonight and you didn't tell me?" Belle backed away from Tara and her mother. "Ma'am, I am so sorry for everything I said. I didn't know. I should go. I have to go."

"Belle, wait!" Tara called out to her, but she didn't stop.

When Belle got out to the driveway, she realized that she had no way of escaping. She hadn't driven; Tara had. Tara Hicks, daughter of the prominent millionaire Hicks philanthropists, architects, and patrons of the arts. "I made a complete fool out of myself again!" Belle tried the door on Kyle's car, but of course it was locked. "We are on an armed and gated millionaire compound and you lock your fucking car!" she said as she slammed her hands onto the roof.

"Belle!"

She looked over and saw Tara coming toward her. "Just don't. What the hell are we doing, Tara? We are driving ourselves crazy trying to make something of this—whatever this is. And the whole time you're lying to me."

"I didn't mean to lie to you. But I guess I didn't mean to *not* lie to you either. I just…I don't know what we're doing, but I don't want to stop. No matter how messed up it is, when we are together, I can't stop thinking about you." Tara moved toward her, but she backed away.

"What does that even mean, Tara? You didn't mean to lie? So while we were sitting in your parents' driveway at the gate it just slipped your mind?" Belle took several deeps breaths. Her heart and mind were in a race of anxiety.

"It wasn't a lie. I just didn't know how to tell you. And when you started making all those assumptions about people, like me, I guess I panicked."

"Panicked? You?" Belle had a hard time believing that the suave, smooth, and blindingly rich Tara Hicks ever panicked about anything.

"Yes. I'm not a robot, Belle. I have anxiety and fear, like anyone else. And right now, I'm afraid that if you leave, I'll never see you again."

The expansive yard was dark and dotted with massive live oaks that hung with Spanish moss. "Tara, we just don't work. It shouldn't be this hard, should it?"

"I don't know, Belle. I've never cared enough to find out until now."

That had to mean something, right? For Tara to admit that she might care about Belle, even a little? And if she was just playing the game like Tara, did it even matter? "So, do you even have to work?"

Tara picked at the bark on the tree. "No. Well, not really."

"Not really? That's not an answer." In Belle's world, you either had to work or you didn't. There was no not really. "Tara, no more lies or secrets. Just be honest with me."

Tara turned toward her. "Fine. No. I don't have to work. I have a trust fund."

Belle sighed. *Of course she does.*

"Don't do that. If you want me to be honest with you then you can't roll your eyes, or sigh, or give me that bullshit 'of course, you do' look."

Belle was scolded. She didn't mean to do those things, but she couldn't deny that she had every time Tara told her something about herself, as if she already knew her. When the truth was she only assumed to know who Tara was. "I'm sorry."

"It's okay. Come over here, please." Tara motioned in the direction of the line of trees that disappeared into the night. When she held out her hand, Belle took it and followed.

"Okay."

Beyond the last tree in the line was a small white gazebo on the edge of a lake. The full Florida moon reflected off the smooth surface of the water. "Wow."

"I know, right? It's my happy place."

Belle and Tara sat side by side and faced the lake. Their hands remained linked as they sat in silence for several long minutes. Tara's hand was soft and warm, and it held Belle's fast. It was a secure anchor in a moment where Belle felt like her world spun around her. "Tara, I am sorry. I don't know you. The real you that is. Since the moment I saw you that night at the ballet, I'd made up my mind about the kind of person you are."

"That soon, huh?"

"Yes. And then I saw you at the bar, and Hazel took you home."

"What? Hazel from the bar? No way. I so did not go home with her."

Belle was surprised. She'd been certain that Tara had slept with her. "Oh. You didn't?"

"Belle, do you know why I work at the museum even though I don't know the first thing about art?"

"I don't know, to save me from men in dark hoodies?"

Tara laughed. "Well, it would seem so now, but before that. I saw you there one morning after weeks of seeing you in my head wearing that stunning red dress. You were standing in the middle of the de Lempicka exhibit dancing to some Disney show tune."

"No, you didn't!" If Belle could have been more embarrassed, she would have.

"I sure did. And I knew right then that I couldn't let you walk out of my life a third time."

"So you applied for the security job just so you could see me again? You could've just come back to the museum."

"That wasn't enough. And even now, the few times I see you during the week still aren't."

Belle didn't know what to say. Tara had made it clear on the rooftop of her parents' building that she wasn't this woman she now confessed to be. "I don't understand."

"What?"

"Why are you putting so much time and effort into this? Me? Surely there are a few women left you haven't slept with in this town. And far easier than I am."

"True. You are proving to be more difficult than I expected."

"Oh my gosh." Belle pulled back her hand and swatted Tara in the arm.

"No. I don't think about it like that. I just enjoy spending time with you, even if it always ends with a train wreck. I just can't look away."

"I know what you mean. And that doesn't bode well for us, you know that, right?"

"Eh, who can say?"

Belle could say. No matter how much she wanted Tara to be the one, she knew there were just too many things working against them. In the end, Belle longed for a family, a wife and children to love and cherish the way she never was. Tara wanted everything but, and it wasn't something Belle could compromise on. But for now, she wanted to take Kyle's advice for a change and enjoy whatever the moment had to offer.

"You know, I didn't mean to ruin this night for you."

"I think I already told you that I hate these pretentious social gatherings of—"

"Muckety-mucks, right."

"Right. But seeing as how that now includes you, I might have to review my stance."

Tara stood and helped her up. Their bodies pressed together, and Belle's skin ignited. Tara leaned down and brushed her lips over Belle's and whispered, "Is there anything I can do to assist you?"

Belle thought of several things she could do in that moment. She just had to decide which one to try first. And if she was going to listen to Kyle, this was her one and only chance. "I have a few ideas."

❖

Tara wrapped her arms around Belle and held her close against her. She watched Belle's eyes darken with desire, and Tara felt a rush of need surge through her body. They had been in this same position before, on the edge of fevered passion when something always pulled them apart. Tara prayed this time was different.

"Have you ever *been* with anyone out here?"

"You're the first woman who's ever even been to my parents' home, Belle." Granted, it was under unexpected circumstances, but it was true. Tara had never brought a woman home before and never to her favorite place on earth.

"Good." Belle wrapped her arms over Tara's shoulders and closed her eyes.

Tara took the cue and pressed her lips to Belle's. In an instant, the gentle kiss turned into an intense fervor. Tara's tongue tangled with Belle's, and she delighted in the sweet taste of her. Each time they had kissed, Tara felt a deepening connection, but this time it was even more profound. Belle had never before seemed so present in the moment, and Tara was drunk on her.

When Belle pushed her back, Tara's knees buckled beneath her and she landed on the bench behind her. She only had a second to be stunned by the jolt before Belle climbed onto the seat and straddled Tara's lap. "What are—"

"Shh." Belle hushed her with a sensuous suck on her bottom lip. Tara's legs turned molten and a fire burned low in her belly.

Belle ran her fingertips up the side of Tara's neck. She felt her own pulse pounding under Belle's touch. It thrummed in cadence with the throbbing between her legs. Belle pulled her skirt high on her thighs so she could press herself down onto Tara's lap. Tara felt the heat from Belle's core push down onto her own. The seam of her slacks pressed into her clit, and she throbbed against the pressure. Tara gripped Belle's hips and held them as she bucked her own upward. Belle moaned, and Tara's center liquefied. Tara fervidly claimed Belle's mouth with her own. She needed to be inside her. She needed to feel Belle's smooth, wet heat against her hand.

Belle fumbled with Tara's tie until she had it loose and tossed it to the ground. She flicked each button of her shirt open and then pulled it free from her waistband. Belle growled at the undershirt that prevented her from accessing Tara's breasts.

The ravenous sounds Belle made fueled Tara's own primal need. She needed her, now. She reached behind Belle and unzipped her dress to her waist. The strapless gown slipped down and exposed Belle's pink nipples and voluptuous breasts. Tara's mouth watered, and she bent her head to take a firm nipple into her mouth. Belle's head fell back as she offered herself to Tara. Tara flicked and twisted the other nipple between her fingers as her tongue danced over the one in her mouth.

Belle writhed and squirmed on Tara's lap, pressing herself down onto Tara's leg. Tara's thigh was wet from Belle, and she couldn't hold back any longer. Tara slid her hand up Belle's smooth thigh toward her hot, wet center. She shuddered with anticipation as she pushed aside Belle's panties and brushed against her swollen clit. Belle's body shook from the contact.

"Please. Touch me," Belle begged.

Tara didn't wait and slid her fingers through Belle's satin folds. Tara moaned in pleasure at the feel of Belle's beautiful body in her hand. She unbuckled Tara's belt and slid her hand into her pants. Just as her finger flicked across her pulsing clit, Tara pulled Belle's hand free. "Just let me touch you." Tara slipped two fingers inside Belle, and she gasped. Belle rocked and bucked on Tara's hand as she pushed her fingers inside her. "Oh God, Tara."

Tara pressed her hand to Belle's shoulder and leaned her back to access more of Belle. Belle grabbed Tara's arm for balance as she leaned back and opened herself up for her. Tara thrust her fingers in and out as Belle moved in rhythmic unison. She was close. Tara could feel Belle begin to tighten around her fingers. Belle shook and squeezed herself around Tara's hand as she pulled every ounce of pleasure from Belle's body. Belle cried out in ecstasy and fell in sated satisfaction onto Tara's shoulder.

As Belle lay on her shoulder, Tara pulled her dress up and zipped it for her. Belle's laugh was muffled in Tara's neck. "Umm..." she said as she sat up and looked down at her chest. Tara had succeeded in zipping her up. The problem was that she wasn't in it. Belle's breasts had both managed to get left out of her dress.

They laughed as Belle reached around, unzipped, and re-zipped her dress with all of her body parts inside. "I liked it better the other way." Tara smiled.

"Of course you do." Belle stood and pulled down her dress. It was wrinkled and disheveled. She smoothed down her dress and said, "All right, well, we can't go back in there like this, so I guess you can just take me home." Had Belle had her own vehicle, Tara was certain this was where she was supposed to walk off into the night and leave Tara in awe of their encounter. But alas, Belle was not that smooth.

Tara would've taken Belle anywhere looking like anything, if she'd wanted to go. She just wanted to be with her. "So how about some dinner?" She looked at herself and then at Belle, "Drive-thru?" Tara reached out for Belle's hand.

"Sure." Belle smiled, but she didn't take Tara's hand. Instead she spun around as she remembered something. "Oh crap. I forgot to get the name of that art dealer from your mother."

"No worries. It's Otto Rosenberg." Tara's hand dropped down to her side.

"Great. Thanks."

CHAPTER NINETEEN

Tara had tossed and turned the entire night as her mind replayed every detail about the night before. After she dropped Belle off, Tara drove aimlessly around town for almost two hours before she found her way home. As she closed her eyes to sleep, she could still feel Belle's kisses and her soft body pressed against her. Tara had gone to bed, but her head refused to let her sleep. Tara watched the time change from 5:59 to 6:00 a.m. She decided after five hours of restlessness that she just needed to get out of bed.

She padded across her room to the bathroom and started the shower. She stripped out of her tank and shorts and stepped into the hot spray. She let the water sluice down her body and rinse away the tension that knotted inside her. The more she thought about it the more discontented she became. Belle had her in a clashing whirl for weeks, struggling with their undeniable differences and independent outlooks. Belle was confronted with truths about Tara that should've sent her running, but hadn't. It was clear to Tara that Belle was not impressed by her social status or wealth even before she'd found out. So she didn't understand why, if Belle was turned off by Tara's honest avoidance of commitment, she still gave herself to Tara.

The thought that Belle had decided to take advantage of Tara in a strictly physical way made her uncomfortable. The thought that she even cared surprised her more than she anticipated. Sure, plenty of women had done the same, and Tara couldn't have cared less; it was her free ticket. But she never would have pegged Belle as being one of them, and it bothered her.

Tara got out of the shower and wrapped herself in a towel. Without drying off, she walked to her nightstand and picked up her phone. As her wet body dripped onto the floor, she sent a text to Cate and Lucy.

Available for a girls' meeting? I need to talk.—T

Tara sat on the bed in her wet towel and held her phone in her lap. *I think she used me.* The idea left Tara rattled. Her phone chimed and two messages popped up.

My place. Now!—Lucy

Are you okay? On my way—Cate

Tara wasn't certain what she was.

See you then.—T

Tara slipped on a pair of jeans, a T-shirt, and a pair of flip-flops, and headed out the door. It was a cool morning, but Tara slipped the cover off the Jeep and tossed it onto the ground near the garage. She needed the breeze and loud music to shake her mind loose.

Twenty minutes of hard rock later, she pulled up to her sister's house. It was barely after seven a.m., and she couldn't remember the last time she had seen that time of the morning. It was refreshing considering that she was running on zero hours of sleep.

Cate pulled up as Tara climbed out of her Jeep.

"What the hell? Are you okay?" Cate asked as she trotted up to Tara. "Yikes, you look like shit."

Tara chuckled; she knew that much. "Yeah, no sleep. What's your excuse?" Tara asked as she motioned to Cate's frumpy pajama pants and cow slippers.

"I was sleeping. Come on then." Cate linked her arm with Tara and headed into the house.

The smell of fresh brewed coffee drew them toward the kitchen. Three steaming cups sat on the table in the breakfast nook, and Lucy carried a tray of cream and sugar in from the kitchen. "Hey." Lucy said, still in her nightgown and robe.

"Did I wake both of you up? You didn't have to—"

"Shut the hell up. When do you ever send an SOS?" Cate said as she slid across the bench and cupped the mug in her hands.

"No kidding. Sit." Lucy directed her.

Tara felt that maybe she had overreacted about the whole thing and calling a "meeting" was overkill. "You know, it's not a big deal."

"Bullshit. I talked to Mom last night after the party. So, out with it. What happened after you chased after her?"

"Hold up. What happened?" Cate said.

Lucy sat up straight and turned to Cate. "Oh. Okay, so Tara took Belle to the ballet gala last night, and after Belle schooled Mom about the painting in the library—"

"She didn't school her, Luce. She—"

"Shhh, Tara. I need to give the back story." Lucy tapped her hand on the table in front of Tara.

"Fine." There was no use in Tara trying to correct her sister. She was going to tell her way no matter what.

"Thank you. Okay. So Belle gives Mom a lecture on Rembrandt and even calls Mr. Rosenberg an ass."

Tara interjected. "No. She called him shitty."

"Will you let me tell the story? You know the rules."

Yes, she knew "the rules." She made them up. But it was to her advantage since she was always the one to get to tell the story about how Cate flashed her boobs at the bus driver or how Lucy stole the *Lion King* collector's cards from the flea market. She wasn't appreciating "the rules" from this side of the table. "Meh, fine."

Cate leaned forward and rested her chin in her hands. "This is more fun when it's not about me."

"I know, right? Okay. So, Tara never told Belle who she was or where they were going last night because when Mom introduced herself, Belle freaked and ran out! Tara followed her and neither of them came back."

"Oooh! Really?" Cate raised her eyebrows and turned her head toward Tara.

Lucy did the same and said, "Yup."

"I officially regret this." Tara flopped her head into her hands.

"Aww. Come on! You've been doing this to us since we were nine years old. It's our turn."

"She's ruining this for us."

"All right, fine. What happened after you went after her?" Lucy patted Tara on the thigh.

Tara told them how she followed her to the car and then to the gazebo. "First she told me that it was never going to work between us, and then the next thing you know she…we…right there by the lake." Tara left out all of the wonderful and vivid details that flashed in her mind.

"So what's the problem? That's what you wanted all along, remember?"

"No. Well, yes, kinda. But it was different. She went from no to go in mere seconds."

"Maybe she turned the tables on you."

"What? How's that?"

"She assessed the situation and took what she could get from it. She knows that you won't ever give her more than that, so she figured she'd enjoy it for what it is. A good time. No attachment."

Tara couldn't imagine that Belle was that type of person. She was too passionate and connected to everything around her to be able to give herself to someone like that without any feelings. "No. She isn't like that. Belle Winters doesn't open herself up like that to people."

"How do you know? We all have times of weakness and make poor decisions. Or we just get caught up in the moment."

Tara thought about it for a moment. "So I was right."

"About what?" Lucy asked.

"She used me."

Lucy and Cate looked at each other but said nothing.

"Don't do that shit. What?" Tara said.

"It's nothing you haven't done to all the girls before her," Lucy said and Cate reluctantly nodded.

They were right, and Tara couldn't even defend herself against it. "Maybe she did. I guess I deserve it."

"I didn't say that. I'm just saying that it was bound to happen eventually."

"We just don't go together. You know. She's right about that. We couldn't be more different. She's more passionate about one painting than I've ever been about any single thing in my entire life."

"That's not a bad thing, Tara."

"Sure, I've done things, but nothing that ever meant anything. You should've seen her face the night I told her that I'd never settle down. How do you disappoint someone you don't even know? Because I did. Now she thinks I'm just a spoiled trust-funder without any goals or responsibility. And she's right." Tara twisted her cup in her hands.

"That doesn't make you a bad person, Tara. You are kind, generous, and loving. You're a wonderful person." Cate reached across the table for Tara's hand. "You're still searching for your place, and that's okay."

"Is it?"

"Sure. You'll find it, or her, soon enough. Speaking of, what are you going to do about Belle?" Lucy asked, changing the subject back to the reason Tara had called the meeting in the first place.

"I don't know. I don't think I'm in control of that situation anymore."

"Aww. That's cute. She thinks she was in control at one point." Cate winked at Lucy.

She would never say it out loud, but Cate was right. When it came to Belle, she never did have any control.

❖

Belle rolled over and opened her eyes. Her first thought was of the night before and how Tara had touched and pleased her. She smiled, and then the truth set in. She covered her face with her pillow and screamed. She laughed and kicked wildly under her covers. *I cannot believe I did that.* Belle touched her lips that were still raw from their fevered kisses. She grabbed her phone and hoped that Tara might have sent her a message. Although she wasn't surprised, she was disappointed that there were no texts.

The night had ended after they'd swung through a drive-thru for fast food and ate it on the way back to Belle's. She had decided not to ask Tara to come up. Her reason had been twofold. She didn't want Tara to feel obligated to say yes or complicate Belle's decision to keep herself detached. It was just sex. That's how it was supposed to be with one-night stands, after all. It was her first though, so she was still new to the game and didn't know all, or any, of the rules.

Belle had fallen asleep to the echoes of Tara's quiet moans and quick labored breathing in her ears. And now that she was awake, they were no less intense. She needed to get out of bed and find something to distract her so she could stop replaying every hot and delicious detail.

Belle stumbled out of bed and went to the kitchen to make coffee. On most Sunday mornings she went next door, but she was in no mood to discuss her night with them. It was then that she remembered the rest of the evening and how she ended up half-naked in Tara's gazebo in the first place.

Belle groaned. How ridiculous and immature she must've looked to Tara's mother after she unknowingly schooled her on the Rembrandt and then ran out of the room like a child. "Oh! But that painting!" It was so exquisite in its current state Belle couldn't imagine how remarkable it would be when restored by a professional. "Why wasn't it restored?" she asked herself as she poured her cup of coffee. It didn't make any sense to her. Even if this Otto Rosenberg person was the worst art dealer around, he should've at least done that much.

Belle carried her mug to the couch and pulled her computer onto her lap. She opened up the browser and ran a search for his name. She scanned through the first few entries but stopped cold when she recognized another right away. The last entry on the page read *Florida art dealer Rosenberg sues multi-millionaire Grayson for collection ownership.*

"What the hell?" Belle said as she clicked the link.

A picture of a handsome middle-aged Giles and an attractive younger man loaded at the top of the page. Belle scrolled down to read the article.

Private art dealer Otto "Roz" Rosenberg has filed a lawsuit against millionaire Giles Grayson alleging that he is owed no less than half of the net worth of the massive art collection that he amassed for the Grayson estate.

"Roz?" Belle knew the name. She had heard it once many years earlier before Giles had died. He'd told her that there was only ever one man in his life that he'd ever loved and his name was Roz.

He'd spoken of him just once and only for long enough to say that of everything that he'd done in his life, he wished he could've done that part over again. Belle could remember the heartache in his eyes as he told her about the man he loved in private, away from the prying eyes of society. But he had loved him with everything he had until the day Roz broke his heart and his trust. She never knew how, but she feared that the article open in front of her would fill in all those blanks.

Belle flicked her nails against her teeth as she read the story.

Court filings by Rosenberg allege that the two men were in both an intimate domestic partnership for six years as well as a business during the time the art was acquired by Rosenberg for the millionaire's extensive collection. A claim that the Grayson camp has not acknowledged beyond the fact that Rosenberg was under employ as Grayson's personal art dealer and purchaser.

As Belle read the story, she felt sorry for Roz. She knew Giles had loved him but not that he had publicly denied or omitted the importance of their relationship. It was something that must have devastated the young Roz.

While the Grayson counsel did not comment on the alleged relationship, they did bring forward their own accusations of impropriety on the part of Rosenberg and his subsequent dismissal from Grayson's employment. The Grayson camp claims that Rosenberg used approximately $125,000 of unapproved funds to purchase a Jasper Johns painting that he resold for a personal $72,000 profit.

Belle's sympathetic feelings for Roz vanished when she read that he had stolen money from Giles and turned a profit right under his nose. She knew then what Giles meant about his broken heart and broken trust. She was ill to know that someone had betrayed him in such a way—to steal and trick someone by using their love and trust against them was reprehensible. But it was the last part of the story that surprised her even more.

While Giles had won the lawsuit, he never made Roz pay back any of the money he'd stolen or the profit he'd made from it. She wondered if his decision was done out of guilt or love, maybe both, but she loved him nonetheless. She did have a new and nagging suspicion that Mr. Otto Rosenberg was dealing in the shady world of black market art.

She grabbed her phone and sent a text to Tara.

Good Morning. Sorry to bother you, but I've got something to tell you about Otto Rosenberg.—B

Good morning to you! You are no bother to me. Really?—T

Belle blushed and then responded.

Do you want to meet later?—B

Sure, but I got called in to cover for Scott at the museum until 11. :(

No problem. Why don't I just meet you there?

Okay. :) I'll see you then, sunshine.

Belle's cheeks burned and she smacked herself in the head with her phone. "Eleven o'clock at night? What were you thinking?" she asked herself sarcastically. She knew what she was thinking; she wanted to see Tara, no matter what time it was.

Chapter Twenty

Tara never had a problem getting called in to work at the museum. It was an easy job, and she could spend the time she took doing her rounds to appreciate all of the things that reminded her of Belle. But this night was different because she could've already been spending it with her instead of waiting until eleven p.m. She was a little surprised that Belle had agreed to meet so late that night. Tara wondered what information could be so urgent that she couldn't wait to share. Of course a part of her hoped that it was so that they could relive a few of the better moments from the night before.

Out of all her coworkers, Xander was by far her least favorite to work with. Thankfully, she only had to cover for a couple of hours until her relief arrived at eleven. At ten p.m., Tara prepared for her last round and checked the internal and external camera feeds. As expected, the halls were clear and the perimeter cameras showed two OPD officers that made their own evening rounds. Tara tested her radio and headed off down the hall with her checklist.

Without Scott to entertain her with his shenanigans and challenges, patrol was dead silent and boring. Every crack and creak in the building was amplified by the tall ceilings and stone floors. She made her way through the gallery and down to the vault corridor. She walked along the glass wall and imagined Belle standing on the other side smiling at her as she always did. When her radio crackled to life, she all but jumped out of her skin. "Tara, you there?"

Tara cursed at him under her breath. "Yes. What's up?"

"Uh, the PD is at the door saying they got a call of an alarm in the building. I don't have any indicators on my panel. Should I let 'em in?"

Tara wondered if she'd tripped a sensor and he didn't cancel it out in time. "Where at?"

"They said in the west vault."

Tara was in the vault. "Xander, that's where I'm at now. Don't let them in until we call dispatch." Something wasn't right. If there was a tripped sensor he'd have seen it. "Xander? Did you hear me?"

"I just raised the gate. It's all good. They showed me their badges."

"No, Xander, wait for me!" It was against protocol to disarm the entry gates without proper coverage and authorization; he should've known that. She'd learned it the hard way from Joe the night of Belle's attack. "Xander?" She took the steps two at a time and raced to the lobby. He wasn't responding. "What a fucking idiot, Xander!" She called his name as she ran up the hallway. Tara turned the corner, and she skidded to a stop. Her heart leapt into her throat.

Two masked officers stood near the door. The smaller one had Xander in a choke hold so tight his face had turned red. His eyes widened with fear when he saw Tara. She held her finger to her mouth and shook her head just as the second, and much larger, man turned toward her. She glanced in the direction of the desk and gauged her distance to the emergency call button. Without a second thought, Tara shot off toward the desk. Just as she reached out, he lunged at her and caught her legs. His strong arm swept them out from under her and she tumbled forward and struck the seat of the chair with her chest. Her breath was forced from her lungs, and she gasped for air. He grabbed her by the back of her shirt and tossed her onto the floor. She looked at him from her back as he pinned her down with one hand. She struggled and kicked under his weight, but he was too strong.

As she fought against him, he squeezed her neck. She gripped at his hand that clamped like a vice around her throat. Tara swung her arms at him until she landed one solid shot to his face. He slammed her head against the floor and her vision flickered. Out of the corner of her eye she saw the red button. She reached out for it as far as she could. A loud click of the handgun cocking next to her ear paralyzed her. She dropped her arms in surrender as the other masked officer threw a gasping and bloodied Xander down next to her.

A light flashed on the board, and Tara watched as the thugs spotted movement on the display. Tara recognized the figure, and to her relief it wasn't Belle, but the overnight guardsman.

"Third shift, right on time. Take care of it," the beast of a man ordered his partner.

"On it," he said before he ran off toward the west end entrance.

As he disappeared, the enormous goon leaned down to tie her up. Tara's head pounded and her vision blurred. She struggled to catch her breath, but her lungs were too tight. She gathered every ounce of remaining energy she had and took one last shot to kick the gun from his hand. He'd anticipated her move and swept his hand out of her reach just in time. The last thing Tara saw before darkness was his enormous fist and the gun as he swung them back at her face.

❖

Belle pulled into the lower level of the garage next to Tara's Jeep. She turned off the car and waited, not so patiently, for Tara's shift to end. She could see the street and sidewalk on the other side of the low barrier wall of the garage and noticed the eerie stillness of the neighborhood. There wasn't a single vehicle on the street or amorous couple exploring the shops. Belle hadn't ever noticed just how far the streets rolled up at eleven p.m. on a Sunday.

Belle was a fumbled mix of emotions as she sat tapping her fingers on the steering wheel. She was nervous as hell, but filled with an excitement that had her heart racing. Except for the time she spent diving into the life and times of the shady Otto Rosenberg, she'd done nothing but think about Tara.

That had pretty much been the case since the first moment she'd seen Tara. Since they'd begun getting to know each other, as sporadic and limited as it had been, she often found herself fantasizing and daydreaming about her. But nothing she could've imagined in those short random bursts of thought compared to the heat and pleasure that she'd experienced in those few passionate moments the night before. She had taken Kyle's advice and put herself out there to take advantage of the situation. She wouldn't say that it had been a decision that she regretted, but she should've thought it through a little more. Because she was certain that one-night stands weren't supposed to call the next day.

Movement in her rearview mirror caught her attention. She glanced at the clock: 11:15 p.m. It had to be Tara. She looked in each side mirror, but there was no one there. "Not funny." Her heart began to race. She turned in her seat to get a better look behind her, but whatever she had seen was gone. She double-checked her door locks and grabbed her phone. Once out of the safety of her vehicle, she was second-guessing all her most recent decisions, including the one to meet Tara at midnight in a deserted parking garage.

She sent a quick message to Tara. After a few minutes without an answer, she called.

After several rings, the voice mail picked up and Belle disconnected. If Tara was playing a trick on her, she was going to be so pissed. However, if it wasn't Tara playing a trick then things could be much worse than that. She called Tara again. It was twenty after eleven, and Belle's feelings of lighthearted nervousness and anxiety turned into something far more disturbing. The hairs on her arms stood on end. She wanted to start her car and haul ass out of there, but something told her not to. What if something had happened to Tara like what had almost happened to her? Belle clutched her phone and grabbed her pepper spray from her purse before she got out of the car and headed toward the museum.

The insanity of her irrational decision to leave the safety of her vehicle and cross the dark street alone wasn't lost on her. She moved toward the staff door when she heard a rustling behind her. She fumbled with her key card on the panel and typed in her number. A red light flashed at her. "What the hell?" A gust of wind blew past and sent a chill down her spine. Her hands were shaking as she swiped and entered her code again. "Come on," she said. She was relieved when this time it flashed green and the door clicked open. She rushed inside and closed the door behind her.

❖

Roz leaned forward in his seat as he watched the flickering screens in front of him. His men had breached the building and overpowered the guards. The plan execution was in full swing, and soon he would have what he was owed. Nothing and no one would stop him from getting what was his. He tapped his fingers together as he watched Pete and Jesse drag three limp bodies down the long corridor to the elevator.

Roz followed the men across the monitors as the guards were secured in the vault and they made their way back upstairs to begin the final phase. Pete and Jesse entered the Giles Grayson Gallery, and Pete pulled a large razor knife from his pocket. He approached the first painting on the list, *Poppy Flowers, Vase with Viscaria,* and Roz's heart raced. He stared as Pete ran his hand up the length of the piece, and with one swift move, stabbed and pulled the knife down the side of the painting. Roz's heart soared and he laughed out loud. There was once a time when just the thought of this destruction would've turned his stomach, but he was invigorated. They would be his.

Jesse yanked a large gilded frame from the hooks and smashed it to the floor. He kicked the shattered splinters of wood aside and ripped the rest from the canvas. Roz hadn't anticipated how much joy the moment would've brought him. He almost wished he was there to watch the destruction unfold right before his eyes.

Movement on a far screen caught his attention and drew him away from the action. A figure stood in the security corridor pressed against the door. Roz squinted at the monitor. His blood boiled when he recognized Belle Winters. He screamed and slammed his fists against the desk. As she made her way toward the lobby, he cursed and picked up his phone. She would not ruin this for him, again.

CHAPTER TWENTY-ONE

Tara's head throbbed and her hands were cold and numb. From her side on the hard floor, she looked around through blurry eyes and tried to get her bearings. The floor felt like ice. And considering how cold she was, she could have very well been in a grocery store meat locker. She pulled at her hands, but they were twisted and tied behind her back. Her left shoulder and hip ached from the pressure of her body lying on them for too long. She struggled to sit up but couldn't find the leverage with her legs tied together.

Tara took long, deep breaths and talked herself into staying calm. As her vision cleared, she recognized a faint and familiar scent. She looked above her and saw Belle's fluffy pink sweater hanging from the back of her chair. *I'm in the vault?* She had no idea how she or the men had gotten in there since she didn't have the card access or the pin code for entry. She listened through the ringing in her ears for the sound of movement in the room but heard nothing. If there had been anyone else with them they were long gone. Tara wriggled herself toward Belle's desk and used it to sit herself up. With the pressure off her side, her extremities burned to life as the blood flooded back into them. She twisted her hands, but whatever held her bound tightened the more she fought against it. When she heard a quiet groan from the other side of the desk, her heart stopped. "Belle?" Her first thought was that she'd also been attacked as she arrived to meet Tara after her shift. "Belle, are you hurt?"

"No. It's Xander."

Tara's heart sank, but she wasn't sure if it was from fear or relief. Because if Belle wasn't captured as well then she was still waiting upstairs for Tara while the men were still in the building. As she started to play out the worst-case scenario, her phone buzzed in her shirt. It did so only once which meant it was a message reminder. Someone had texted or left her a voice mail. She begged the powers-that-be that it was Belle saying she had left or changed her mind about meeting, but Tara's gut told her otherwise.

"Xander, can you get free?"

"No. My hands are tied so tight I can't even feel them anymore."

"Shit. Mine, too." The helplessness she felt only increased the anxiety she had as the feeling that Belle was in danger grew stronger. Making it worse was the growing anger inside her for Xander and his stupid mistake. She didn't know what she would do to him if his actions caused her to get hurt. "Damn it all, Xander! What the fuck did you let them in for?" Her anger burst out before she could stop it.

"I'm so sorry, Tara. I wasn't thinking."

His response sounded like a whimper, but she was so pissed she didn't care. She said nothing else to him. The angrier she became, the more her head pounded in her skull. As her body warmed from her increased heart rate, she began to feel the throbbing in the rest of her body. It felt like she'd been hit by a truck, and the pain had her feeling nauseous.

"Where's Alan?" She hoped that the guard had gotten away and warned the police and, with any luck, Belle.

"He's here. But I don't…I don't think he's breathing, Tara."

Her heart felt leaden. She took several deep breaths through her nose to keep herself from being sick. Weak, Tara slid down the side of the desk and rested her face on the ice-cold concrete floor. Her phone buzzed again, and her heart twisted with powerlessness. She hoped with everything she had that Belle was safe somewhere far away from danger.

❖

The eerie feeling Belle had on the street followed her into the building. She checked the door again to make sure that it closed behind her. She made her way along the corridor and past the security window. As expected, there was no one on the other side. She scanned her badge at the next door and entered her code. When the light flashed green, she hesitated. Belle couldn't shake the feeling that something bad waited for her on the other side, but with the dark night her only other option, she chose to enter. She pulled the door open and went inside.

Each step Belle made was cautious as she entered the hall. The stillness of the air was comforting although she wondered why neither Tara nor Xander had met her at the door to confirm her arrival. As she stepped into the lobby, a horrendous crashing noise broke through the silence and Belle yelped. Her heart pounded in her ears as she listened for voices. Hushed mumblings and curses echoed through the hall. She hugged the wall and moved toward the sounds. From behind a glass vitrine she could see through into the Impressionist gallery. Her stomach leapt into her throat and her heart stopped cold in her chest as she watched a tall uniformed man slice Matisse's painting *Pastoral* from its frame. She gasped and crouched down against the wall. Her eyes welled up with tears and the pain of what she'd seen cut through her like a canvas. As Belle fumbled for her phone with shaking hands, she heard it ring. "Shit!" she hissed under her breath. She yanked it from her pocket. The phone slipped from her trembling hands and slid across the marble floor several feet in front of her. But it wasn't her phone that was ringing.

"Yeah?" the man said as he answered it. "I'm on it."

As she reached out from behind the case, the man on the phone stepped out into the hall. Belle's eyes met his and they both froze for an instant. She had one option, to run. She wouldn't be able to grab her phone and make it to the emergency exit in time so she just had to run. As he lunged for her, she sprinted toward the exit. She didn't look back, but she heard him close behind, his boots stomping once for every three of her strides. She reached out for the bar on the door just as he snatched her hair and pulled her back toward him.

Belle screamed. "Please, don't." He covered her mouth and nose with one of his giant hands. She kicked at his legs and feet as he held her tight against him. She scrambled for the canister of spray in her pocket, but she couldn't breathe. Her nails gouged into the fingers that gripped her face. Her body flailed and she struggled for air until she grew weak. The room began to spin and dim into a hazy darkness. She heard him yell something to his partner, but Belle's head felt filled with cotton and all she could hear was the sound of her slowing pulse pump through her ears. When she could no longer fight, her arms dropped to her sides like rubber limbs. When the rest of her body went limp, he dropped her. She fell into a heap with a hard, crumbling thump onto the floor.

Belle was alive but too weak to move as she lay on the frigid floor and watched through heavy lids as the two men rolled and crumpled precious and priceless works of art under their careless arms. Belle tried to yell out, but she hadn't the strength to even open her mouth. Too weak to move, she cried in painful silence as they carried her life and love out the door and into the dark night.

❖

Roz watched Belle's body lay lifeless in the floor in the hall as his men carried his treasure out the front door. It took less than hour for him to resolve twenty years of injustice and restore what was rightfully his. He was elated, but his heart was cold. The damage or the value of his plunder was of no concern to him. All that mattered was that he had what belonged to him, and no one would ever again enjoy what had once filled him with joy. The loss of these works would leave an empty hole in the world not unlike the one in his soul. There wasn't a single thing anyone could do about it, and now that he had what he wanted, he would die before anybody got close enough to try.

Roz smiled as he shut down the monitors, sat in the pitch dark, and waited patiently for his rewards to arrive.

❖

Belle struggled with consciousness for several minutes. She had to get up and pull the alarm. She had to find Tara. She took a few deep breaths and pulled herself up. She was weak and lightheaded as she looked around the room. It took her more time than she would've expected to figure out where she was. Belle saw the remnants of wood scattered across the hall in the doorway of the Grayson Gallery and her heart sank. "Oh, God."

Above her head was the glowing sign for the exit, and she remembered where she was. She pushed herself up and leaned her whole weight against the steel door. When she caught her breath, she reached up with shaking arms and pressed the emergency exit handle. The door fell open against her weight as alarms blasted overhead. Her head rattled and she rolled herself off the floor onto soft legs. Belle clutched at the wall to keep herself standing. The police would be there soon, but she couldn't wait for them to find Xander and Tara. She stumbled along the hallway and called Tara's name over the mind blasting sound. The farther she went the harder her heart pounded. Fear and anxiety filled her as she searched. Her mind played out the worst scenarios, and she tried to push them from her head.

The quicker her blood pumped the faster she made her way through the building. When Belle got to the end of the hall, she called Tara's name again. She screamed over the blaring of the alarm, but even if Tara hollered back she wouldn't have heard her. The wings split in two directions, and Belle didn't know which way to go. If she chose the wrong way and Tara was badly hurt, she could be too late to help her. Her stomach turned at the thought of finding Tara in that condition. The man who had just suffocated Belle had no idea whether she was alive or dead when he'd tossed her to the ground. The same had no doubt been done with Tara, or worse.

Belle covered her ears from the howl of the alarm. She looked around for any sign of where Tara was taken. The front door at the end of the hall was open, as it had been when she arrived. Belle struggled to make rational thoughts. Had she and Xander escaped before Belle had walked in on the men? No. Those men never would've allowed anyone to walk out onto the street and alert authorities. They had to be in the building. Belle crouched down as she gripped her head tighter. Her attention was drawn to an unfamiliar long, dark streak along the floor. As she took a closer look, it resembled a black boot scuff like someone had been dragged along. She tracked the mark that led to the elevator. Belle prepared herself for what she was about to see inside. She held her breath and pressed the button. As the doors chimed and opened, she exhaled. They weren't in there. But the blood on the floor told her they had been.

Belle cursed at the slow moving car as it lowered her to the basement. She pushed at the doors and squeezed herself out before the doors opened. She searched for similar marks on the floor and ran the length of the hall along the glass vault, but there was no sign of them. Belle ran her fingers through her hair in frustration and turned in a circle, when she spotted Tara and Xander lying on the floor inside the vault. "How the hell?"

Belle ran to the door and scrabbled for her key card. She entered her code, pulled open the door, and ran to her. "Oh, Tara." Belle touched Tara's bloody face, and it was as cold as the floor beneath her. "Tara? Please, wake up." She stroked her hair and face as she leaned down close to her.

❖

"Baby, please wake up."

Tara heard Belle's soft distant voice calling her, and she groaned. "Oh! Tara, hey, open your eyes, sweetie." Tara was weak and cold, but she opened her eyes to Belle's sweet smile.

"Hey," Tara said and returned a feeble smile.

"Shh. Let me get this off of you." Tara watched Belle shuffle through her desk drawer for something. She found a razor knife and went to work cutting Tara's arms and legs loose.

"Xander. Alan." The new freedom of her cramped arms made her wince in pain.

Belle went to them. Tara couldn't see, but she could hear Belle cut them loose as she called their names. As Belle said Alan's name several times without response, her stomach twisted. She held her breath waiting to hear his voice. When she heard him groan, she breathed a sigh of relief.

"Alan's okay and Xander isn't as beat up as you. I think they're fine," she said as she returned to her side.

Tara didn't have the strength or full use of her muscles so Belle helped her up. The rush of blood to her head made her dizzy. "Whoa. Slow." Belle propped her against the desk, and Tara's entire weight leaned into it.

"You're hurt pretty bad. The police should be here soon."

"Did they hurt you?" Even through a haze, Tara could tell that Belle was out of sorts.

"I'm fine," Belle said as she fiddled and fussed with Tara's uniform. She reached up to her desk for a box of tissues and dabbed at the wounds on Tara's face.

"Belle, stop." Tara grabbed Belle's shaking hand. Compared to her own it was so very warm and comforting, so she held on to it.

"What? You're bleeding. We have to—"

"Just wait. Are you okay? You're shaking like a leaf, and I've seen more color on a sheet of notebook paper.

"I was so scared." Belle's eyes filled with tears.

"Belle, I'm okay, now. I've been cut and bruised before. Worse than this come to think of it."

"They…I thought he was going to kill me. And then I thought he killed you. I was so scared, Tara. I couldn't breathe. He left me there to die." Belle pulled at her shirt collar and gasped for air.

Tara's heart ached as she watched Belle fight to stay strong even as the fear washed over her face. "Shhh. Come here." Tara reached up for Belle, and pain shot through every part of her. "Ah, shit!" she said as she clutched her side.

"Tara?"

"I'm fine. Just sore." The pain she felt from her injuries was nothing compared to the hurt she felt as Belle looked at her. "Just come here."

Belle moved in closer to Tara and touched her face.

"I'm sorry I didn't get here sooner."

"No, sweetheart. This isn't your fault. I'm just glad you're okay." Tara cupped Belle's cheek and wiped away the tears that ran down her face.

"I am now."

Tara pushed herself up and kissed Belle's soft lips. Tara's lip was swollen and sore, but the contact sent a long absent heat through her veins, and her temperature rose as she fed off of her warmth. A tap on the glass made Belle jump away, and the loss sent a shiver of cold through her. A team of officers stood on the other side of the glass, and Belle left her to let them in. The blaring of the alarm stopped, and the pain hit her like a truck as she realized they were safe. She slumped over onto the floor with a grunt and closed her eyes.

CHAPTER TWENTY-TWO

As soon as Belle opened the door, the officers rushed in. The uniformed men pushed past her and secured the area. Belle returned to Tara's side and pulled her close. The fully armored tactical team swarmed through the entire vault with speed and efficiency. Once they declared the all clear the paramedics moved in on the injured. Belle was reluctant to move when they started to assess Tara's condition. She stepped away and watched as they helped her off the floor and into a chair. Tara winced and growled as they poked and prodded her injuries.

Belle leaned against the wall and braced herself. The sight of blood always made her stomach turn. She hadn't thought about it at all when she'd seen Tara crumpled on the floor of her vault bruised and battered, but now she was feeling queasy. Before she could stop herself, her knees went weak and she slid down the wall and landed on the floor with a thump. She felt the blood rush from her face and the cold of the room hit her.

"Belle!" Tara called as she attempted to jump up from her seat, but she was stopped by both the paramedics attending to her and the officer who placed himself directly between her and Belle. The look on the officer's face was stern and unyielding.

Another set of EMTs went to Belle's side. She saw the concern on Tara's face and attempted to comfort her distress. "I'm fine. Just a little woozy from watching them poke at you." She didn't feel fine, and it was more than just the sight of blood that made her feel that way. "I think I just need some air."

"Ma'am, once we assess you and get you stabilized we can begin transport to the hospital," one of the emergency workers said.

"What? No, I don't need to go to the hospital. I just want to talk to my friend," Belle said

Through the chaos of people and noise an officer approached her. "I'm sorry, ma'am, but we cannot allow you to speak with anyone until we've gathered everyone's statement."

"I can tell you right now what happened."

"Ma'am, I advise you not to say anything at this time."

"What?" Belle asked as they lifted her onto a stretcher. "No! I don't need to go to the hospital I said. Stop."

"That is your choice, ma'am, but we are recommending that you be seen by a doctor. You may be unaware of your injuries due to the shock and increased adrenaline in your system."

Belle was going to continue to fight back until she heard Tara's voice over the crowds. "Babe, just do as they say. It will be okay. I promise."

She watched as Tara was then lifted onto a stretcher as her face contorted with pain. Her heart ached as did her head as her heart rate began to decrease. "Tara? Are you okay?"

"I'm fine. Just a bloody nose and a few cuts and scrapes."

Belle pointed to the laceration on her cheekbone. "That looks worse than a scrape," Belle said as they pushed her past Tara. Her head spun a little until she set her heavy head back and twisted the sheet with her fingers.

"Eh. A few butterflies, and I'll be good to go."

"Are they all right? Where are they?" Kyle asked as he pushed his way toward them.

Everyone in the room turned toward the doorway as a frantic and disheveled Kyle ran in.

The look of distress on his face tore at Belle. When he saw her, his eyes teared and she responded in kind. When he pulled her into a tight embrace, the pressure of his hug caused a sudden panic within her. She pushed him away and gasped for air. "I...need...air."

"What's wrong?" he asked. He looked at Tara. "Damn, and your face!"

"It's fine. Superficial, for the most part. We're going to the hospital."

Belle began to breathe deeply and exhale through pursed lips in a steady cadence. "There are too many people in here. Please, can we go?"

Tara slid her hand across Belle's arm as she passed. "It will be fine, sweetheart." Kyle rushed along beside the gurney.

Belle felt odd and tingly. "She'll need butters for that," Belle mumbled.

"Butters?" Kyle asked.

"Butterflies. Steri-Strips, for this," Tara said as she pointed to her face.

"Wait! Are you sure you don't need stitches? Does she need stitches?" he asked over his shoulder to the EMTs as they left the room.

Tara waved them off. "I'm sure they'll know either way at the hospital, Kyle." The officer that accompanied them out of the vault stopped Kyle as they loaded Belle and Tara onto the elevator. "Sir, you're going to have to stay here to speak to one of our detectives."

"What? I can't. I have to go with them."

"No, sir, we cannot allow any of you to communicate until we have assessed the entire scene and eliminated the suspects."

"We are suspects? This is outrageous!" The shocked look on Kyle's face was clear even through Belle's fading vision. "I'll see you at the hospital, my love," he called out to her.

"It's okay, Kyle. We'll be fine," Belle told him as the elevator doors closed.

As they rode the elevator up in silence, Belle took those few moments to prepare herself for the worst. In her determination to find Tara, she looked past most of the damage the men had done. Quick flashes of gold shards and the sound of ripping fabric was all she could recall. She tried to steady her breathing that had already begun to speed up. She counted in her head, *in for four, out for four.*

When the doors chimed and opened, Belle was bombarded with the screeching of police radios and what sounded like a thousand voices all yelling at once. Small yellow numbered markers littered the floor where even the tiniest piece of debris was found. Shattered glass crunched under their feet as they traveled along the corridor. As they made their way past the galleries, Belle tried to see around the people and commotion to get a sense of the damage, but the paramedics kept them moving along down the hall.

"Please. I need to see." Belle said as she reached out toward the gallery as they passed.

"I'm sorry, ma'am."

When they reached the Grayson Gallery, her heart stopped. The smiling portrait of Grayson that always greeted her each day was lying on the floor. "Wait." She tried to sit up from the gurney, but a firm hand gripped her shoulder and pulled her back. Even from there Belle could see that the glass was smashed from the bent frame. Belle's eyes drifted from the portrait up to an opening of people who milled around in front of *View of the Sea of Scheveningen*. But to her horror, there was no Van Gogh, only an empty frame with its tattered remnants clinging to the gilt wood.

Belle covered her mouth. She tried to stifle the devastated cry, but it was no use. Her body shook with desolation and dismay. Had she been standing her legs would've given out on her. "They took it!" Belle screamed in pain, not from a physical pain, but from one deep within her soul.

"Shhh. Come on. Let's go outside," Kyle said as he rubbed her arm.

As they loaded her into the ambulance, she watched the lights flashing around her and got lost in their blinding cadence. The loud and bustling noise around her became muffled as she stared off into space.

❖

The ambulance sped into the bay and the doors burst open. The nurses and paramedics exchanged information as they pushed her stretcher into the building. Belle had hoped that she and Tara would've arrived at the same time so that she had a chance to see that she was all right. But as the second ambulance pulled in, Belle was already inside. They wheeled her into an examination cubicle, and she noticed the police and detective who had followed her in and were now camped out on the other side of the curtain.

Once the doctors were gone and Belle was comfortable, the detective entered. "Good evening, ma'am. My name is Detective Campbell. I'd like to ask you a few questions about the incident this evening."

"Hello," Belle said as she pushed herself up in bed.

"I know you must be exhausted, so I'll try to be brief."

Belle relayed her memories of that evening to the officer the best that she could. She didn't know if it was her exhaustion or her mind that were making it difficult for her to vividly recall what she had experienced. She could remember the sound of the siren, the man's choking hands around her neck, and Tara's bloody and battered face, but everything else seemed to be clouded in a fine mist. "I'm trying, but it's getting so hazy." Her head dropped back against the bed and she began to cry.

"I understand, ma'am. I think we have enough for this evening. I would like you to come down to the scene tomorrow for a cognitive interview." He took a card from his shirt pocket and handed it to her. "If you can think of anything between now and then, call me."

"I will." Before the officer left the room, Belle asked about Tara.

"She's stable and being questioned as well. Once we get her statement in hand, you're both free to go. We'll see you tomorrow, Ms. Winters."

Belle breathed a sigh of relief. "Thank you."

When Tara and Belle were discharged, they met Kyle in the waiting room. He was clearly relieved to see them up and walking out of the hospital on their own. "I'm so glad you are okay. I was scared to death."

"I know the feeling," Belle said.

She gave him a small smile. "I'll take you two home before I head back to the museum." He helped them both into the car to take them home.

"How bad is it, Kyle?" Belle asked.

"Don't worry about that right now, sweetie." Kyle tapped Belle on the thigh. "I want you to go home with Tara tonight. You can both keep an eye on each other for me. Okay? Tara?"

"That sounds like a perfect idea to me." Tara agreed without any hesitation.

"No. I can go home. I'm a big girl you know," Belle said.

"I know, but it would make me feel a lot better knowing that you two were together in case something happens."

"Seriously? You don't have enough proof of the shit that can happen when we're together? At this rate, I'd expect her damn house to burn down."

"I hope not. I love my house. But it's a risk I'm willing to take."

Belle didn't have the strength to argue any more than she already had. "Fine."

❖

The three of them were silent for the remainder of the ride to Tara's house. She was okay with that, however she was concerned about Belle. Tara hoped that once she got showered and changed she could begin to relax and hopefully get some sleep.

Kyle pulled up to Tara's house and let them out. "Take care of yourselves. I'll see you tomorrow."

Tara helped Belle up to the house and let her in. Belle stopped in the foyer and stared around the room in awe. "Wow! I almost said something stupid like, 'this place must've cost a fortune.' But then I just said it didn't I?"

Tara laughed. "It wasn't as bad as you'd think. It was in terrible shape when I bought it."

"That's even more impressive. Did you do the work yourself?" Belle asked as they made their way up onto the large wraparound porch and into the house. "Holy—" she said as she looked up at the vaulted ceiling and wooden rafters with a second story balcony overlooking the wide-open great room.

"I did some of it. I designed it myself, fixed the little things, but I hired contractors for the big stuff. Like those beams."

"And a crane."

Tara laughed. "Yes. Definitely." Tara showed Belle to the large sectional sofa. "Will you be all right here for a minute while I go clean myself up?" Tara's uniform was covered in blood, and what had dried to her face was pulling at her wounds.

Belle sat onto the couch. "Yes. I'll be fine."

Tara turned on the television and handed her the remote. "I'm not sure what's on at four thirty in the morning, but here you go. I'll be right back. Promise."

"I'll be here."

Tara leaned down and kissed Belle on the forehead. "Good."

Tara went upstairs to her room and picked out comfortable clothes for herself and for Belle. She carried her things to the bathroom and set them next to the sink. She looked between the shower and the bath and thought for a moment. Instead of starting a hot shower, she filled the tub. She exchanged her pile of clean clothes for Belle's and then gathered towels, washcloths, and soaps for her as well. Once the bathroom was set, she headed back downstairs to get her.

Tara chuckled at the home shopping station Belle was watching. "Hey," Tara said as she came around the couch.

"Hey. That was fast."

"I decided to run you a bath first. I can shower down here in the guest room."

"That sounds so amazing, but you didn't have to."

"I wanted to. Now come on." Tara grabbed Belle by the hand and led her upstairs.

Once Belle was settled, Tara grabbed her things and went downstairs to shower. She turned the water as hot as it would go and then dialed it back a little when the room filled with thick steam. She stepped into the spray and sucked her teeth as the water washed over her wounds. Tara pressed her hands against the wall and let the heat soothe her sore and bruised body. She was exhausted. Her mind and body had been vibrating for hours, and the adrenaline was wearing off. She washed her hair and body and then forced herself out of the shower.

Tara sat on the couch and flipped blindly through the stations on the television. She had almost drifted off to sleep when Belle slid down next to her on the sofa.

"Hey. How are you feeling?" Considering what they'd both been through, Belle looked beautiful.

"Better. Had the water not cooled off I might still be in there." Belle slumped into Tara's side.

Tara wrapped her arm over Belle's shoulders and pulled her in close. She ran her fingers through Belle's hair and she shivered. "Are you cold?"

Tara slipped the blanket from the back of the couch and covered them both with it. Belle slid her arm around Tara's waist and settled into her side. Tara's skin tingled under the intimate contact of Belle against her body. When Belle's hand moved down to the top of her thigh, Tara felt a heat rise within her and her tired muscles tightened. She pushed it to the back of her mind and tried to focus on anything else. She clicked the buttons on the remote and flipped through the stations.

"How do you even know what you're looking at?" Belle whispered into her ear.

Tara's stomach fluttered as Belle's breath brushed over her neck. "I don't know. I'm just flipping."

Belle ran her finger along the outside seam of Tara's pants and her leg shuddered. "What are you doing?" Tension and desire was building deep inside Tara.

"I was so scared, Tara. While I was lying on the floor in the lobby all I could think about was you." Belle ran her hand from Tara's thigh to her side. She slowed around the outside curve of Tara's breast, and her nipple tightened. Belle's thumb flicked over it as she moved her hand up to her neck. "I had to find you. I had to know if you were okay." Belle drew a finger over Tara's swollen lip.

"Belle. I…" Tara fought the need that burned in her belly. Her breaths grew quick and shallow as her pulse throbbed between her legs. "I don't think we should."

"Tara, I don't want to think." Belle cupped Tara's cheek. "Just kiss me, please," she whispered against her lips.

Belle's plea was irresistible, and Tara wanted nothing more than to give her what she asked for. Tara turned toward Belle. She grabbed her hands, held them down between them, and looked into Belle's darkened eyes. "Are you sure?" Tara had to hear her say it.

"Yes. I want you, Tara."

It was all she needed. Tara released Belle's hands and slipped hers under the hem of Belle's loose nightshirt. Her palms slid up Belle's smooth skin and grazed the side of her soft breasts as she brought the shirt up. Belle lifted her arms and Tara raised it up and over Belle's head, then tossed it to the floor. She ran her palm down the center of Belle's chest and pushed her back.

As Tara stared at her beautiful body, Belle took her hands and moved them from her belly to her breasts. Tara took a nipple in each hand and twisted them into two hard peaks between her fingers. Tara's mouth watered. She bent down over Belle and wrapped her legs around Tara's hips. Tara teased the rosy pink nipple with her tongue before she took it into her mouth. Belle clutched Tara's head as she pressed herself up into her mouth. Belle's whimper of pleasure fueled Tara's desire. Belle ran her hands down Tara's back and pulled her shirt up and over her head.

Tara sucked and teased Belle's breast with her mouth as she slipped her hands down into the waistband of Belle's pants and pushed. Belle raised her hips and kicked out of them. Tara removed her own and pressed herself into Belle. Tara groaned at the pure pleasure of Belle pressed into her. Belle grabbed her hips and pulled her down hard. The pressure on her clit made her cry out.

Tara cupped Belle's face and pulled her up. She licked her lips, and Tara needed to taste them. Tara took Belle's mouth ravenously with her own. Their tongues tangled together as Tara thrust her hips into Belle.

She had to feel her. She needed to be inside Belle drawing out every ounce of pleasure from her body. She slipped her hand between Belle's thighs and dipped into her. Tara groaned and Belle cried out. She circled her clit, and Belle bucked under her touch.

"I need you inside me," Belle said breathlessly.

Tara gave her what she wanted, and she slipped her fingers deep inside Belle. Belle opened herself up for Tara, and she took it. Tara thrust in and out of Belle as she stroked her clit with her thumb. Tara set her head on Belle's belly as she watched herself bring Belle to the brink of ecstasy.

"Oh God, please, don't stop."

Tara could feel Belle tighten around her hand. She was close. "Come for me."

Belle's whole body bucked and shuddered beneath her as Tara pulled her to the edge. Just as Belle reached the peak of pleasure, Tara took Belle into her mouth. Belle raised her hips and stiffened around Tara's hand as she cried out her name.

Belle pulled Tara up and kissed her. First sweetly and then with a renewed heat as Belle slid her hand down between Tara's legs. Tara bucked as Belle slid her finger over her throbbing clit. Belle stroked several times before Tara stopped her hand.

"I want to touch you."

"I know. I'm tired, though. We should get some sleep, sweetheart." Tara spread the blanket over them as she pulled Belle close.

"Oh, okay." Belle settled into Tara's embrace.

Tara stayed awake long enough to hear Belle's breathing slow to a soft and gentle cadence.

CHAPTER TWENTY-THREE

Belle woke to the fresh scent of brewing coffee. She opened her eyes and stretched her arms and legs. She blinked the sleep from her eyes and focused on the ceiling. It took her a moment to realize that she was not in her own bed. Confused, Belle rolled over, and before she could stop herself, she tumbled off the couch onto the floor. She hit the floor with a thud. It was then that she remembered where she was, and why she was stark naked save for the blanket that she landed on.

"Ow. Shit!" She struggled to roll herself off of the blanket, but found it easier to roll up into it like a burrito. She wrapped the blanket around her body and squirmed into a sitting position. She could imagine how entertaining and embarrassing that scene would've been for herself and anyone watching. For a brief instant she was thankful no one had, until she saw Tara standing over her with two cups of coffee and a face red with stifled laughter.

"Everything all right down there?" Tara smiled.

"Yes. Just showing my ass." Belle was officially the most awkward person on the planet.

"Literally."

"Kill me." She covered her head with the blanket and smooshed her face into the couch. She thought she might die of embarrassment that time.

Tara set the cups on the table and knelt down beside her. "It's a beautiful ass, if that helps."

"No," Belle said from her muffled cocoon.

"Come out. Or I'm coming in." Tara peeked through the blanket as Belle looked up at her.

"Can I have my clothes?"

Tara raised an eyebrow and appeared to contemplate the question for a moment. She smiled and said, "Okay, if you must." Belle stuck her head out and watched Tara gather Belle's clothes from the floor and set them next to her. "The bathroom is right over there. I'm making breakfast. Is there anything you don't like?"

"I don't care for embarrassment, but I got a full helping of that already this morning."

Tara leaned down and kissed Belle on the lips. "Don't be embarrassed. It's you. And you are beautiful."

Belle blushed, and her stomach fluttered to life. She wriggled herself up onto the couch and headed off to the bathroom.

Tara cleared her throat, and Belle turned around to see her holding out the pile of clothes that Belle had forgotten to take with her. "Right." She reached back for them and then shuffled off to the bathroom.

Belle washed up and got dressed. Every muscle in her body ached and she noticed several bruises the size of fingers on the side of her face. She remembered vividly how tight the man had gripped her face, and now she had the physical signs as a reminder. She hoped makeup would cover the outward marks of the attack. She pulled back her hair into a long braid that fell loose at the end. Without a hair tie, it would work its way out, but it would do for a bit. The scent of bacon wafted in from the kitchen, and Belle's stomach rumbled. She folded the blanket on her way out and set it on the couch before following her hunger to the kitchen.

Belle had seen Tara during their awkward morning moment, but she hadn't noticed her face until she stood and stared at her from the doorway. Tara was black and blue from her lip to her right eye that was spreading like a watercolor toward her left. The red and swollen gashes crisscrossed with white Steri-Strips made Belle's legs wobble as the memories of the night before came flooding back. Tara looked over and smiled. Even battered and bruised, Tara could melt Belle's heart. "Shouldn't you have ice on that?" Belle asked as she sat on a stool on the other side of the island.

Tara turned out the bacon from the pan onto a plate and paper towel before she grabbed an icepack from the countertop and held it up. "Right here."

"Lotta good it does *not* on your face." Belle grinned slyly.

"It's fine. Besides, I heard battle scars were sexy."

Belle couldn't deny that. Tara was always deliciously handsome, but knowing what she'd gone through to get those injuries did add an extra level of allure. "I suppose so."

Tara rounded the island and pressed herself against Belle. "You should see the other guy."

Belle had seen him, and the memory of his face was still fresh in her mind. "I did."

"Oh, Belle. I'm sorry. I didn't mean it like that."

Belle knew what she had meant by it and she brushed it away. "I know. It's okay. But did you get any hits in, because from what I remember…" Belle found it not so hard to make a joke of the scariest moment of her life.

"Hey! Yeah, not so much. He was a huge bitch."

"You're not kidding." She needed to be grateful that she and Tara were still alive and able to make light of what had happened, even if she knew nothing would ever be the same. "How bad do you think it is?"

Tara stroked Belle's arm. "I'm not sure. But when we head over there in a bit we'll find out."

Belle took a deep breath and exhaled slowly. "I don't know if I can do it alone."

"You won't. I'll be there, and I'm sure Kyle will be there. I'm here for you, Belle. We can deal with this together." Tara reached out for Belle's hand and held it against her chest.

Belle looked up at Tara with surprise. *Together*? No one except Kyle and Andrew had ever offered such a thing to her, not family, friend, or past lover. It was just a word, but to Belle it was more than that, and something she never expected from anyone, least of all Tara. "Um. Okay."

"Whatever happens, I'm here."

If Belle thought she could be any more overwhelmed she was wrong. Tara's unexpected offer of *togetherness* was more than she was ready to deal with. Belle pulled back her hand and offered a simple, "Thank you." A part of her wanted to jump into Tara's arms and spew promises of her own devotion, but it was not the time or place when in reality her entire life had just been trashed and tossed on its side. Reading too far into Tara's spontaneous words was reckless and imprudent, and no one could be held accountable for the things they said or did in times of trauma. Belle had proven so with passion a few hours earlier.

They ate, dressed, and headed over to Belle's apartment so she could change into her own clothes before they drove to the museum for a heavy dose of heart wrenching reality.

❖

Tara waited in the Jeep for Belle to change. She had gotten enough of a look at the destruction the night before to know that Belle was going to need every bit of support that Tara could offer. And for once she was giving it without care or concern for what she could get out of it. Belle hadn't asked Tara for any help, which made it that much easier for her.

Tara looked at her face in the rearview mirror and lightly touched her swollen injuries. She was so thankful that Belle hadn't received the same brutal beating, but she believed Belle's might have been far more traumatic. Tara received her injuries from fighting back as he attempted to overpower and restrain her. She never believed his intention had been to kill her. However, she couldn't say the same for Belle.

Tara had seen the bruises on her face of the distinct hand- and finger-shaped marks. He had applied more than enough pressure over her mouth and nose to smother her. In mere minutes, Belle would've been unconscious, and he released her because he believed she was dead. Why had his attack on Tara shown more restraint than with Belle? If their intention had been to kill, why had they wasted time locking her and Xander up in the vault? Tara's conclusion was that Belle was an unexpected interruption, and he had reacted out of fear and instinct.

As Tara stared at her face, Belle returned and startled her out of her thoughts. She readjusted the mirror and smiled. "Hey. All set?"

"As I can be, I suppose. Is everything okay? Do you want me to go get you some ice or anything?"

It looked far worse than it felt, but Tara adored Belle's concern. "Nope. I'm good." Tara took Belle's hand and kissed it before she set it down onto her thigh and held it there. Only when they arrived at the museum did she let her go.

Kyle was waiting for them at the front entrance where various police and unmarked vehicles lined the block. Crime tape stretched from tree to tree around the front and side of the building. Belle stared in shock and stood paralyzed on the sidewalk. Tara interlaced her fingers with Belle's as Kyle approached. He saw the move and raised a curious eyebrow but said nothing.

"Hey. How are you doing, love?" he asked Belle as he kissed her hello.

"I was okay before right now."

"I know. And you? Yikes, girl, you've been in the wars."

"No kidding," Tara said.

"What did they get?" Belle asked as she stared past them both toward the front door. Men in fabric boots and gloves went in and out carrying bags and boxes marked "evidence."

"All right, sweetie. I need you to listen to me. Belle?" He waved his hand in front of her face to get her attention.

"Yeah," she said as she looked over at him.

Tara squeezed her hand as Kyle explained what she was about to see. "They haven't gotten the glass up, most of the frames are still hanging on the walls, but a few were smashed on the ground to get the canvas out. They seemed to have kept to a few rooms in the east wing, and so far it appears random."

"Okay," Belle acknowledged.

Detective Campbell and another man approached them. Tara recognized the second man as the agent who had questioned her the night before. FBI Agent Nicholas Gulker greeted Kyle and Tara before he introduced himself to Belle. "Good evening, I'm here with the FBI Art Crimes Division. We're going to take you through the scene step by step so we can piece together what happened last night. Hopefully, we can fill in some of the blanks that we are missing at this point."

Kyle and Tara agreed, but Belle said nothing.

"Ma'am?"

Detective Campbell handed them a couple of pairs of protective shoe covers and they slipped them onto their feet. "Do not touch anything, unless it's necessary. We need you to stay back away from pretty much everything."

Tara, Belle, and Kyle followed Campbell and Gulker under the tape and into the building. Belle's grip around Tara's hand tightened with every step. Tara could hear the intentional cadence Belle had set for her breathing. They skirted the edge of the room to keep out of the way. They stopped against the wall with a straight line view down the main hall. Belle swerved and strained her neck to see what was happening.

"Let's begin down that way, but I need you to stay close and don't touch anything."

Most of the activity was focused in the Grayson and the Impressionist galleries. When they stopped near the doorway, Belle gasped. "Oh God," she whispered.

"What is it?" Tara asked.

"They took them all." Belle's eyes welled with tears that threatened to spill over. She covered her mouth in shock and took off toward the other room. Tara couldn't hold her back as she ripped her hand away.

"Belle!" Kyle and Tara called after her as did the detectives. They all followed after her.

She skidded to a stop at the next room and cried out. "No. No!" She stumbled back against the wall, and the tears fell down her face.

Tara was awestruck by the damage. She couldn't believe how someone could have so little regard for the beauty and worth of the world's most priceless art. The paintings were cut and sliced so indelicately that pieces of the painting fabric were still attached where the men just ripped it away. A couple of original giltwood frames were smashed onto the floor in glittering fragments of their former glory. It made Tara sick to her stomach, so she couldn't imagine what Belle was feeling.

Tara looked at Kyle. It was clear that his heart was breaking the same as Tara's as they watched the understanding and acceptance wash over Belle. Belle stood up, cleared her throat, and wiped away the tears. "How many, Kyle?"

He didn't hesitate with his answer. He might have been just as surprised as Tara to see the instant change in her demeanor. "Eleven."

"Who?"

"Four Monets, two Van Goghs, one Matisse, Cezanne, Klimt, de Lempicka, and a Vermeer."

Belle's tears began again, but her expression remained unchanged.

Tara's heart dropped in her chest. She might not have known much about art, but that was an extraordinary amount of money. "How much is that?" Tara whispered.

"Between three hundred and four hundred and twenty million, depending on the market."

"Holy shit!" Tara was rich, and that number still astounded her.

"Did they take anything else?" Belle asked as she stared off into the distance.

"Not that we've discovered."

"Sunshine," Belle said under her breath.

"What?" Kyle asked.

"Those are the paintings in Giles's Sunshine Collection. *Les Barques de Peche, Auvers sur Oise, Charring Cross Bridge, Impression Sunrise, The Concert, Marina, La Musicienne, Portrait of a Lady, Pastoral, View of the Sea of Scheveningen,* and *Poppy Flowers.*"

Tara was in awe that Belle could name each of the missing paintings without batting an eye. "*Poppy Flowers?*" Tara knew that Eden and Olivia would be devastated. "Why would—I failed."

"What?" Tara asked.

At the same time Agent Gulker said, "Excuse me?"

"I failed. He asked me to do one thing and I let him down. I promised him that I would protect them."

"Sweetheart, you didn't fail. No one knew this was going to happen." Kyle stroked Belle's arm, and Tara put her arm around Belle and pulled her in.

"We should have. That's our job, Kyle."

"I know, sweetheart. But we have to be glad that you are okay."

"Okay?" Belle stepped forward and turned her face. "Do you see this? These are bruises from the fingers that held my face so tight that I couldn't breathe. He held me off the ground as I kicked and clawed at him. The harder I fought the tighter he squeezed until I couldn't fight back anymore. When my body collapsed in his arms, he threw me to the ground like trash." Belle's body shook as she cried, and Tara's heart shattered. She wrapped her arms around her and Belle buried her face into Tara's chest and sobbed. Kyle wiped at the tears that fell on his cheeks.

"Belle. Please, I didn't mean it that way. I'm so sorry." He reached out for her. "I just meant that as priceless as these paintings are, you are the treasure and I am grateful to the universe that you are still alive."

Tara had tried to imagine what Belle had gone through, and it tore at her soul to know that she had been right.

Belle pushed away from Tara and Kyle. "Is it okay if I go outside and get some air?" she asked.

"Yes, ma'am."

"I'll come with you," Tara said.

"No. Please, I just need to be alone right now."

Tara didn't care for Belle wandering off on her own. But she had to let her deal with the stress and reality of the situation in her own way. Tara watched as Belle walked out the front door and sat on the stoop just outside the entrance. Detective Campbell asked to proceed with the interview.

Tara led him through the night beginning in the lobby where she had come around the corner and saw the masked men wrestling with

Xander. A quick shot of anger rushed through her and she couldn't help but blame him for the events that had unfolded. "If I didn't know that Xander was just an incompetent moron I'd probably suspect he was involved."

A rumble of agreement went through the group of them. "Unfortunately, we looked into him. Other than his marijuana dependency, he's clean."

"Now it makes complete sense." While it explained a lot of his personality it did nothing to assuage her opinion of him. If anything, it had the opposite effect, yet her mind was too exhausted to cast anymore anger or blame on him.

Tara spent the next hour going through the museum step by step, recalling the sounds and scents of the night. He asked questions that drew out minute details like the beating of her heart and the rasp in the suspect's voice. When they returned to the lobby, she saw Belle standing near the entrance of the Impressionist gallery staring down at the shattered photograph of Giles. Tara, Kyle, and the detectives quietly approached her.

"Hey, sweetie," Kyle said as he wrapped his arm around her shoulder.

Belle looked over at Agent Gulker and asked, "Can I please have that?" She pointed to the damaged picture laying on the floor amongst the shards of broken glass.

Detective Campbell called over one of the crime scene technicians and confirmed that that area had been processed and cleared of evidentiary materials. "Yes."

Belle crouched down and picked it up. As she stood she stroked a gouge in the image and the tears welled up in her eyes. Kyle wrapped his arm around her and led her back away from the commotion of investigators. Belle clutched the shattered picture of Giles in her arms as the tears flowed down her face. "How did this happen? Why did they do this?" Belle mumbled to herself.

"I'm so sorry." Tara moved in close and wiped the tears from Belle's face.

"Shhh." Kyle consoled Belle as she wept.

"Ma'am, I understand that this is a difficult time for you but if we could get you to come along and walk through the scene with us you can go home and get some rest."

Tara wasn't sure that it was such a great idea for her to relive the evening in her state, but Belle wiped her face and nodded. "I'm ready." Tara should've known better than to think Belle was capable of any less.

An hour and a half later Belle had walked them through each and every moment of the night before in vivid detail. Tara was sickened by the pain she saw on Belle's face and the imagery of what she had endured at the hands of those men. She wanted to hold her in her arms and never let her go. She never wanted to see such sadness or agony on her face again.

Tara saw her own sadness reflected in Belle's eyes. Belle sobbed and threw her arms around Tara and tucked her head into her neck. Tara lightly caressed her back as her adrenaline high took a nosedive. Belle was exhausted and leaned into Tara's tight embrace. Tara needed to take her home. "Are we done here?" It pained Tara to continue standing around forcing Belle to endure the constant mental and physical torment.

Agent Gulker and Detective Campbell agreed that they'd everything they needed from them and were free to go.

Belle turned to Kyle. "If you need me I'll be at home, okay?"

"I think they have things under control here. I'll be leaving as well. So don't worry." Kyle gave Belle a long hug and kissed her on the cheek. "I love you, kiddo."

"I love you, too."

Tara was glad that Belle had someone who cared so deeply and unconditionally for her. She deserved nothing but that from anyone who knew her. "Ready?"

"Mhmm."

Tara took Belle's hand and led her out the way they came.

CHAPTER TWENTY-FOUR

Tara woke to the sound of Belle struggling to keep quiet as she clanked around in the kitchen. She listened as Belle cursed under her breath at the cabinet as it slammed closed. She laughed and sat up to look at Belle over the back of the couch. "Don't worry, it's almost eleven. I'm awake."

Belle screeched and dropped the handful of silverware that she had in her hand. She bent to pick them up. "I'm so sorry. I was trying not to wake you up."

"Well, you lost that battle when you kicked the couch on your way out to the kitchen."

Belle crossed her arms over her chest. "I didn't want to turn on the light and wake you. Had you just slept in my bed last night this wouldn't even be a conversation."

Tara had wanted to share Belle's bed with her, but she knew if she did, there would've been little to no sleeping. Belle was in emotional overdrive and she needed rest, not sex. And for reasons she couldn't explain, Tara opted for rest. "You needed to sleep. How do you feel?"

"Well, all things considered, I'm all right. Coffee?" Belle asked as she held up two mugs.

"Yes, please." Tara crossed the room toward Belle and took a seat at the kitchen table. "Belle, they will find whoever did this."

"Maybe, maybe not. Only about four to ten percent of stolen artwork is ever recovered. They still haven't found any of the paintings taken from the Stewart Gardner in Boston, and that was over twenty years ago."

Tara was surprised by Belle's complete one eighty from the day before. She was calm, relaxed, and rational. Just like the Belle she knew. It was comforting but also unexpected. "Oh."

Belle set the cups down on the table and slid the cream and sugar closer to Tara. "Many times the pieces are destroyed hours or days afterward. Sometimes they get paranoid and panic, or realize there's no way they'll ever be able to offload them without being caught."

"Who would buy stolen art? By now, the entire world knows what happened. They'd have to be as dumb as the thieves."

"You'd be surprised by the darkness of the black market in art. Shady dealings happen every day amongst even the most upstanding citizens." Belle raised her eyebrow at Tara.

"What does that mean?"

"It means that sometimes genuine pieces are sold as reproductions or copies of the original work. For example, let's say an original Rembrandt was stolen. It spends years traveling and traversing the art underworld, being bought, sold, and traded by criminals and billionaires alike."

"So, you're saying we bought a stolen Rembrandt?"

"I don't know. But there are only two reasons your art dealer would say that it was a 'student of Rembrandt' work. One is because he is an idiot and doesn't know the first thing about art, or two, because he knows everything about art including how to traffic stolen masterpieces."

"What if it is real and stolen?"

"If it's real, your family just became about thirty million dollars richer. If it is stolen, they will lose the four million they paid for it, plus the painting."

"Why would someone do that?" Tara never knew there was such a dark and sinister side to the art world. It took the beauty and talent of the artist and turned it into a seedy product of greed and corruption.

"People do all sorts of things for money, Tara. And the art world is the perfect front for the worst kinds of crime."

"I had no idea."

"Most of us don't. But it still surprises you even when you do. Even more so when you realize how connected it all is." As she talked it out with Tara, a nagging thought swirled in her head.

"What do you mean?" It was an odd and heavily veiled comment that Tara didn't quite understand. But she knew there was something more to it by the distant look in Belle's eyes.

"I mean, what if this heist and Rosenberg's shady dealing with the Rembrandt is related? What if he's the one behind this?"

"Otto Rosenberg?"

"Yes. After that night with the Rembrandt I did some searching on the Internet and found several articles about a lawsuit involving Roz and Giles and their claims on the collection. It can't be a coincidence that his name comes up in both of these situations."

"Well, that certainly makes a lot of sense when you stop and think about it. If we picked up on the connection wouldn't the FBI have as well?"

"I know, right? I would think so. Should we—" A knock at the door interrupted whatever Belle was about to say next.

Belle jumped up from her chair, and went to answer the door. Tara was relieved to see that Belle was dealing with the tragedy so well. And if she was acting or putting on a front, she was doing a damn fine job of it. Tara knew that everyone dealt with things in their own way, and if this was Belle's she would do whatever she could to support it. But she was also concerned that Belle's theory about Roz was about to open a very large and very dangerous can of worms. She would rather just let the FBI work it out than the two of them get involved at all.

Belle opened the door to Kyle and Andrew holding two plates of something that smelled like heaven. When they came in and set them onto the table, Tara came to the conclusion that her heaven smelled like cinnamon rolls. Her stomach growled so loudly that everyone in the room turned to stare at her belly. "It always does that," she said as she patted her stomach.

"Good. Because we made your favorite," Andrew said as he smiled at Tara.

Tara had no idea why he was looking at her that way. She smoothed down her shirt, ran her fingers through her hair, and smiled back at him.

"Hey. I'm gonna go change real quick. You guys get started." Belle motioned between them and the plates on the table.

Tara and Andrew sat at the table while Kyle gathered the plates and utensils. When he set them down he looked at Andrew. "Why the hell are you staring at her like that?"

"Like what?" Andrew smiled wider.

"Like she's a frickin' unicorn!"

"I don't know. Just look at her, here, with Belle."

"Oh, good grief." Kyle looked at Tara. "Ignore him. He gets a little dramatic sometimes."

Tara laughed. "It's okay."

"So, how is she doing?" Kyle asked as he sat at the table.

"She's all right. She seems to be handling things pretty well so far. It's a huge shift from yesterday."

"Hmmm, okay. That's good."

"Yeah. She seems to be dealing with it quite rationally."

"Yep," Andrew said.

"What?" Tara asked.

"Nothing. That's our Belle. Always the rational one."

"Not always, just when she needs to be," Kyle added.

"Always," Andrew said.

"I don't know. She seems quite passionate and unguarded when it comes to art and such."

"Ha! I knew it."

Kyle shot him a look, and Andrew grinned. "She is, yes. But that doesn't spill over into any other part of her life. Art is her job, but it's also her escape, so she can be free and expressive about it. In everything else she is much more complicated and cautious. Belle doesn't make decisions lightly even if she tries to. It's how she keeps herself safe."

"I see." It seemed to Tara that Belle was anything but complicated. She knew what she wanted and she went for it, including the nights they'd spent together. Which seemed neither guarded nor cautious. And this Roz situation was going to be anything but *safe*.

"I'm so grateful that you are here to help her through this." Kyle reached out and took Tara's hand. "Thank you."

"I wouldn't want to be any place else." Tara said it and meant it.

Belle came out and Kyle pulled his hand back. "We ate it all. You snooze you lose."

"Whatever. What's this then?" she asked as she dipped her finger into the frosting on his plate.

Belle sat in a chair across from Tara and pulled a plate toward her. Tara stared at her and was mesmerized by everything about her.

Kyle cleared his throat and broke through the silence. "So, Andrew and I were wondering if you two would like to come with us to lunch. Nothing special, just a nice casual thing."

Tara was up for anything if Belle was, so she waited for her to answer.

"Sure," Belle said with a smile.

"Great! We can all drive together. One o'clock good?"

"Works for me," Tara said. Her stomach growled again, louder this time, and everyone laughed.

❖

While Belle waited for Tara to return she spent the time scrolling through page after page of Web links. She searched for everything she could related to museum robberies and missing art looking for any similar link to Roz. But she found nothing that resembled this incident with any other. The longer she looked the more she thought she was trying to find a sinister connection that wasn't there. A knock at the door startled Belle, and she slammed the cover closed on her laptop. "Come in!"

"Hi. Are you ready?" Tara said with a captivating smile.

"Hi. Yep. You saved me. I was trying to convince myself that I was overreacting about the whole *Roz is a mastermind.* I just have so many things going on in my head I can't really separate fact from fiction anymore."

"Maybe it's worth telling Agent Gulker and Detective Campbell even if it's a long shot. Wouldn't hurt for them to check it out."

"You're right. But we're gonna be late. One sec."

"Let's run it by Kyle and see what he thinks," Tara hollered down the hall to Belle.

"Okay." Although Belle couldn't help but think she was on to something, she didn't want to be the one to destroy someone's career, no matter how incompetent he was at his job.

Belle freshened up and brushed out her hair again. From the darkness of her room, she looked back out into the living room and stared at the suave and delicious woman standing there. Even with her fading cuts and bruises, Tara was striking. Belle wished she could just blink her eyes and this whole frightening nightmare would be over and they could move on together.

Tara's hands were slipped into the front pockets of her fitted jeans that hugged her solid thighs and ass, and her pitch-black button-down was tucked in loosely. Belle let her eyes skim over Tara's entire body uninhibited. Since the moment their eyes met, she longed to feel her skin pressed against her own and taste her sweet kisses on her lips. Now that she had allowed herself to experience those things, she ached every moment for more.

She'd taken a risk when she opened herself up to taking whatever Tara could give her. She told herself to accept that she might only ever be able to give Belle fleeting moments of pleasure and nothing else. But still her heart hoped for more.

Belle dressed in jeans and a simple blouse in keeping with the declared casual theme of the afternoon. She was looking forward to a simple and enjoyable evening to allow her swirling mind a much needed break. She took one last brazen look at Tara before she strode out of her bedroom. "Ready?"

"For you? Always." Belle giggled out loud. She felt her face blush just as Tara grinned and took her hand.

They met Kyle and Andrew at the car and they all loaded in. The drive to the restaurant was short, but Tara held on to Belle's hand the entire way. She let go when Andrew opened the door and helped her out. They chose an outside table on the patio with a balmy Florida breeze.

Kyle and Andrew twitched and tossed peculiar glances back and forth as they all discussed random topics and interests. Finally,

Belle couldn't take it anymore. "Okay. What is going on with you two? First breakfast delivery, then a double date lunch invite, and now the two of you are being all squirrely over there." Belle flicked her finger and gestured all around them. "You're weirding me out."

"We have something we've wanted to discuss with you, but with everything that's happened, there hasn't been a right time."

Belle's heart started to beat a little faster. "Uh. Okay. Please tell me it's not anything bad."

"It's not bad," Andrew said.

"Then what is it?" Belle was going to strangle someone if they pulled their usual dragging out routine.

"We...we've decided to..." Kyle stuttered.

"We're going to have a baby!" Andrew burst out.

Belle's mouth dropped open, and she sputtered disconnected words. She slapped her hand over mouth and glanced back and forth between Kyle's and Andrew's expectant faces. "Are you serious?" Kyle nodded and Andrew smiled. Belle looked at Tara in shock. "What?" she said under her breath, and then she shouted it, "What!" Belle flung her chair out from beneath her and circled the table with her arms wide open.

Kyle and Andrew stood up just as Belle threw herself into their arms. She jumped up and down with unfettered excitement. She couldn't believe this was happening. Belle always knew she would be so happy the day her very best friends decided to start a family, but she had no idea it would be like this.

"I'm going to be an auntie! Oh, Tara, can you believe it?" Belle looked at Tara who watched the three of them with a wide smile and sparkling eyes.

"It's amazing, love." Tara stood and congratulated them on their news.

Belle was enamored with the news, but when she heard the word love spoken from Tara's lips, her heart skipped. It was just a word, an endearing phrase, but it hit Belle in her gut. Belle's heart soared in the beautiful moment between her very dearest friends and someone she could feel deep within her soul.

Tara called over the server and ordered the best wine they had available. The day had begun casual enough, but it had turned into one to remember.

Belle took several deep breaths and sat down. "When? How? Give me all the details! How long do I have to wait?"

Kyle, Andrew, and Tara all laughed at her eagerness for details. Belle looked over at Tara who stared at her in a way she had never seen before. She smiled with more than her lips, and Belle's stomach filled with swarming butterflies. Her face flushed and her ears burned as the world around them disappeared. The server set her plate in front of her, and she blinked out of her trance.

Kyle raised an eyebrow at her. "Uhm, right, so we have our first surrogate interview next week. If everything goes right, they're saying we could have a baby by next year."

Belle was full of joy. "Oh, guys, I am just so very happy for you."

They spent the next hour eating and discussing baby names and decorating ideas while Tara never once let go of her hand.

CHAPTER TWENTY-FIVE

When they returned to the house, Kyle and Andrew called it a night, but Belle's mood was dampened just for a moment. She hadn't stopped smiling the entire ride home, and Tara couldn't keep her eyes off her. Belle was a deep and passionate person. She felt life so strongly that it was next to impossible to be in the same room and not be affected. Tara found it so easy to get caught up in the emotional energy that Belle emanated. She felt her fear, joy, and sadness as if they were her very own.

"Would you like to come up?"

There wasn't any other place Tara would've wanted to be. "Absolutely."

Belle flitted around the kitchen for a couple of glasses and a bottle of wine. She was buzzing with happiness, and Tara was enjoying the show. "Can you believe it? I never. Well, I hoped, but I never thought I'd see the day that Kyle and Andrew would become dads! Andrew's been so wrapped up in his career. Isn't it wonderful?"

"It is." It was clear that they were all ecstatic about the decision, and Tara couldn't help but feel the same way.

Belle took the wine into the living room, and Tara followed. She poured two full glasses, flopped down onto the couch, and curled her legs beneath her. "I can't tell you how many afternoons we've spent at the park daydreaming about starting families."

Tara didn't think she had ever done such a thing in her entire life, not even pretended with Cate and Lucy. "Oh." Tara sipped on her wine.

"It's sort of our thing. We get lunch, go down to the park, and ogle all the happy families doing their thing. We always kid each other about who will be the first to be a parent. Him and his workaholic husband or me and well, me." Belle swirled the wine in her glass.

"So, you want a family?" Tara surprised herself that she didn't choke on the question.

"Oh, yes. Very much. This is the closest I've ever come to having a real family."

"You don't have any nieces or nephews?"

"I don't even have brothers or sisters to get them from."

Tara might have never thought about it the way Belle had, but she couldn't imagine her life without Eden and Olivia in it.

"You are so very lucky to have such a wonderful and beautiful family. I'd give up everything I have for a third of it."

"I guess I've never thought about it. About what it would be like not to have them. It's hard to imagine since they've always just been there."

"We all take for granted the things we have an abundance of."

Belle was most definitely right about that. Tara had long lived on that very thing. "So why don't you have a 'real' family?" Tara stuttered out the awkward question. "Sorry, that didn't come out the right way."

Belle chuckled. "It's fine. Umm, I don't know. Nobody wanted me?" Belle laughed, but Tara didn't think it was funny. "I went into the system when I was four. I got bounced around to about eight different houses and four fosters by the time I was fifteen, and by then they've long given up on you. At that point I was just a paycheck and a nuisance."

Tara almost felt sick to her stomach. "So, you don't remember your mom?"

"Nope. I used to think that I had flashbacks of a woman I thought could've been my mom, but I don't know. I heard she was a single mom that couldn't handle a child, and she didn't know who my father was. But stories like those were sort of the 'go-to' explanation for curious foster kids."

"Oh, Belle. I can't even imagine what it was like for you."

"Oh, no worries, Tara. Giles saved me from all that and showed me that there is love in the world. He gave me more love in five years than I'd gotten my entire life, and now I'm hopeful that one day I'll be able to give that love to someone else."

Belle spoke with such passion and confidence that Tara was rendered speechless. She was mesmerized by how intensely Belle expressed so much of herself in everything she did in life, art, and love. Even in the darkest and most frightening moments of her life, Belle exuded a dedication and determination that Tara had never seen in anyone, not even herself. "How do you do it?"

Belle poured them both more wine. "Do what?"

"Give so much of yourself in so many ways, without ever expecting or wanting anything in return?"

"Oh. I wouldn't say I don't want anything in return. Because for as much as I want a family to love, I still hope to be loved equally in return. So my dreams are not without some selfishness."

How could anyone call the desire to be loved a selfish act? Especially Belle who might have been the most deserving of it. Tara scooted closer to Belle and their knees touched. She took Belle's glass and set it with hers onto the table. Tara reached for Belle's hands and held them firmly in her lap. "Belle, I've never met anyone like you. You might very well be the most beautiful woman I've ever known, both inside and out. You deserve everything that you've ever wanted and so much more."

Belle touched her soft hand to Tara's cheek. "Everything I could hope for is sitting right here in front of me."

Tara's heart swelled in her chest. "Belle, I—"

Before Tara could finish her sentence, Belle kissed her. It was a kiss full of all the words left unspoken and all of the charged emotions that swirled around them. Tara wrapped her arms around Belle and pulled her tight against her chest. Tara felt Belle's supple breasts pressed into her own, and a heat rushed through her body.

Belle stood and pulled Tara up with her. She slid her hand down Tara's forearm, weaved their fingers together, and led her toward the bedroom. In that moment, Belle could have taken her anywhere, and she'd have followed.

Up until then, Belle had taken control of their intimate encounters. Tara had no problems with that and had been more than happy to give Belle what she needed. But this time Tara wanted to take her time. She wanted to savor the sights of Belle's body and revel in the sounds of her pleasure, and she had all night to do it.

❖

Belle led Tara into her bedroom. Her heart beat in her chest as desire and want coursed through her veins. The way Tara's eyes had flicked and feasted over her body all night kept Belle's entire body simmering with need. She wanted to touch and taste every last inch of Tara's body until she begged for release. Belle pushed Tara against the edge of her bed and was surprised when Tara resisted the pressure at the back of her knees.

Tara grabbed Belle and spun her around so that their places were reversed. Belle gasped at the unexpected change in direction, and her body burst into flame as Tara took control of the moment. She watched Tara's eyes darken like midnight as they grazed the length of her body. Belle's skin ignited, and a rush of heat burned between her legs. Her thighs trembled as Tara ran a slow, firm finger along the inside seam of her jeans.

Belle bit her lip as Tara's hand brushed over the top of her throbbing center. Belle felt the pulse of her heartbeat against the pressure of her hand. Tara slid her hands beneath the hem of Belle's shirt. When her hands swept across her bare skin, Belle's body shuddered. She raised her arms as Tara slipped the blouse up and over her head. She drew her fingers down along the satin straps of Belle's bra and teased the nipples through the black lace. They rose into tight peaks and strained against the fabric.

Tara dipped her head and licked the firm nipple through the fabric. When Belle hissed with pleasure, Tara pushed away the barrier and took Belle into her warm, wet mouth as she held Belle's side firmly. Belle wrapped her hand around Tara's neck and pushed herself deeper into her mouth as her tongue flicked over the sensitive tip. Tara moved her hand down Belle's belly to the waistband of her jeans. She released the button and slid her hand down over Belle. She imagined just how wet she was, and when Tara slipped a finger down into her panties, she knew. Tara moaned with pleasure as Belle whimpered. Tara's finger flicked quickly over Belle's clit as she pulled her hand out and Belle's body jerked.

Belle needed more. She needed to feel Tara's body pressed against hers. Belle opened each button on Tara's shirt and pushed it down off her shoulders. A white tank did little to disguise her full and braless breasts. As Belle unbuttoned Tara's pants, she was surprised that Tara had chosen to forego both bra and panties. She pushed the offending pants off her hips and Tara kicked out of them and her shoes before she lowered Belle onto the bed.

Tara hovered over Belle as she removed Belle's jeans before she pressed the length of her body down onto her. Her skin burned in every place they connected. Tara covered Belle's mouth with a deep and fevered kiss as she pressed her thigh firmly between Belle's legs. Belle moaned and rocked herself against Tara. As Tara pressed into her, Belle slipped her hand between them. She reached down, cupped Tara in her hand, and slid her fingers through her smooth, wet folds. Tara bucked and gasped from the sudden touch. She pulled herself away and looked down at Belle.

"Please let me touch you, Tara." Tara closed her eyes, and Belle touched her again. This time she didn't pull away.

Belle brushed her fingers against Tara's firm clit, and she gasped. Tara's wetness coated her hand as she stroked her. Tara moaned and moved her hips rhythmically with Belle's hand. When Belle slipped two fingers into Tara, she released a carnal groan and pressed herself down onto Belle's hand, but just once before Tara pulled away again. This time she gripped Belle by the arms and turned her over onto her stomach. Tara held both of Belle's wrists with one hand and slid her hand down over her ass.

Belle's heart raced and she ached for Tara to be inside her. She opened herself and pushed back into Tara. Belle felt Tara's soft breasts brush against her back, and she exhaled. When Tara slipped her hand down between Belle's legs and into her, Belle cried out. "Oh, yes."

Tara thrust her fingers in and out of Belle. She writhed and panted desperately as Tara kissed and nipped at her neck. "Come for me," Tara said.

Belle was close. She could feel herself growing tight around Tara's hand. Belle gripped at the sheets and screamed as Tara pulled the orgasm from her. "Yes. Oh, yes!" Belle's body jerked and quivered with pleasure as she came.

Belle panted as she rode the last waves of ecstasy and Tara wrapped her slick body around Belle. She listened to Tara's own labored breathing in her ear. The puffs of hot breath on her neck did little to cool her libido. When Tara pressed herself wantonly against Belle's leg, she rolled over and pushed Tara to her back. Belle straddled across Tara's hips, placed her hands next to Tara's shoulders, and hovered above her. Tara bucked herself up against Belle. They both moaned as Tara's swollen peak pressed against Belle's. Belle rolled her hips over Tara's wet center. Belle watched the pleasure on Tara's face as she slid firmly over her. She sat up and reached behind her and flicked Tara's clit. She growled and jerked beneath Belle as she twisted Belle's nipples between her fingers. Belle sucked in a quick breath between her teeth. Belle slipped in one, and then two fingers, deep into Tara. "Oh, shit!"

Encouraged by the sounds of her passion, Belle maneuvered herself from atop Tara and slipped down between her legs. Tara's breath caught and she cupped Belle's face. "Belle," she said breathlessly.

"Please?"

Tara's head fell back in approval and Belle pressed her lips to Tara. She slipped her tongue in and out of her. She gripped her hips and sucked Tara deep into her mouth. She writhed beneath Belle and clutched the sheets at her sides. She felt Tara begin to shudder and contract. Belle teased her fingers just inside Tara until she begged for more. "I need you inside me, please."

With two fingers plunging deep inside Tara, Belle licked and sucked her into frenzy. Her body shook and tightened as she screamed Belle's name in pure gratification. Tara fell back in sated bliss, and Belle rested her head on Tara's leg and gently stroked her inner thigh. Belle slid up and let Tara wrap her in a tight embrace. Emotion overflowed in Belle as she listened to Tara's perfect breaths in her ear. As Tara fell fast asleep, Belle stayed perfectly still so that she could feel their heartbeats thrum together in harmony. The cadence of their hearts hypnotized Belle, and before her eyes fluttered closed, she whispered, "I love you."

CHAPTER TWENTY-SIX

Tara lay as still as she could after she heard what Belle had said, but she said nothing in return. So many thoughts and emotions flooded her brain, and she waited for the fear. The strangling, binding, fight or flight response that she had every single time a woman said those words to her. But it did not come. Instead, the feelings of contentment, happiness, and peace settled into her mind.

She had also let Belle touch and please her in ways that she hadn't experienced in so long. Tara had let herself feel the raw pleasure and passion that was Belle and gave it to her without fear. Belle had allowed her into the deepest parts of her heart and soul without want or price. Tara had one thing she could give Belle that even came close to what she deserved, and without asking, she'd given it to her willingly.

With Belle wrapped in her arms, she felt a sense of fulfillment wholly unfamiliar to her that went beyond physical pleasure. It was so deep that even if she had wanted to run from it, she wouldn't have escaped it. Wrapped around her, Tara listened to the soft sound of Belle's breathing as it lulled her into a blissful and beautiful sleep.

Tara gathered the bags from the Jeep. She hooked them onto her wrists one after the other until her forearms were loaded. As she lifted them up and out of the vehicle, Tara thought twice about how much weight she believed her arms could handle. She bumped the door closed with her hip and hurried inside as fast as the extra hundred pounds would allow.

Tara lifted one side onto the counter with the momentum she had going. The other arm wasn't so lucky. With the extra weight pulling her down, she struggled to get her tangled arm free from the bags on the counter. Tara laughed at herself and her predicament.

"Would you like some help, babe?"

Tara peered over her shoulder and smiled. "Yes, please."

Belle crouched and untangled the bags one by one from Tara's dangling arm. "You do this every time. You could just wait for me, and I'd help you."

Once the bags were free, Tara worked on the others. Her forearms were ringed with red and white marks from the plastic handles. "It's okay, my love. I got it. Besides, in the time it takes you to waddle outside, I've already gotten everything in the house."

"Aww. I can't help it," Belle said as she rubbed her swollen belly. "This gets bigger and I get slower. Soon I won't be able to roll myself out of bed."

Tara put her hands on Belle's stomach. "If I have to I'll push my babies around in a wheelchair like old times."

"Oh no, you won't. Not with this and my ridiculously tiny bladder." Belle tapped her fingers on her stomach.

Tara leaned down and kissed her bump. "Don't worry, munchkin. There's always the stroller."

"Oh geez." Belle wrapped her arms around Tara's neck.

"You are so beautiful. My babies."

"Just one baby. I couldn't fit another one in here."

"Two. This one," she said as she rubbed Belle's tummy, "and this one." Tara kissed Belle sweetly on the lips.

They swayed in each other's arms. "I'm afraid your family is going overboard on the baby shower. I think they might be more excited than we are."

"No way, I can't wait until we are a real family. I've never wanted anything more in my entire life. I love y—"

Tara's eyes shot open and she sat straight up in bed. Beside her, Belle slept with her bare shoulder reflecting the early morning sunlight through the window. Tara panted and her heart raced. *It was just a dream.* She knew it was a dream, but she still needed air. Tara slipped out of bed, gathered her clothes off the floor, and padded off to the bathroom. She dressed and then looked at herself in the mirror. Her face was pale and clammy so she splashed cool water on it. Tara sat on the toilet for several minutes as she tried to rationalize fantasy versus reality. The spacious bathroom began to close in around her. She needed to get out.

❖

Belle woke to the sunshine squeezing in through the open blinds. She stretched her legs, and a pleasant soreness reminded her of the evening before. She smiled and rolled over. Belle scolded herself for sleeping so soundly that she hadn't heard Tara get up. She pushed away the covers, climbed out of bed, and pulled her robe from the closet door.

As she tied the belt around her waist, she headed out into the living room. Belle was surprised to see that Tara was nowhere in sight. "Tara?" Belle called out as she returned to the bedroom. Belle noticed that her clothes were still scattered on the floor, and she smiled.

Belle went back to the living room and pulled back the blinds. She looked down into the driveway, and her heart stuttered when she saw that Tara's Jeep was gone. Belle tried to keep a rational head. *Maybe she went out for coffee?* Belle didn't even know how long she'd been gone. Had she left as soon as Belle had fallen asleep? Belle ran her fingers through her hair and took several deep breaths. She was being irrational. "You're overreacting, Belle. She wouldn't leave without saying good-bye," she told herself.

Then she saw it, a slip of yellow paper on the kitchen island. Her heart dropped into her stomach with a thud. Belle walked over to the kitchen and stared down at the handwritten note. She read it quickly before the tears filled her eyes and blinded her.

My dearest Belle,
I am so sorry. I don't think I'm ready for this. I don't want to hurt you, but I need to get a few things straight in my head. I truly wanted to be everything you needed me to be, I'm just not sure I have what you deserve.
Please forgive me.
T

Belle backed down onto a barstool before her legs could give out from beneath her. Tears streamed down her face as she sobbed into her hands. She had opened herself up to Tara, given her heart and body willingly, and she'd taken it with a vengeance. Belle had spilled out her soul filled with dreams of love and family, and Tara gathered the pieces. Only to scatter them to the winds.

Belle pushed herself from the stool and stumbled to the couch. Her heart felt as if it was ripping from her chest. A cold chill settled inside her. She clutched at her robe and curled herself into a ball. The words Tara had spoken hours earlier reverberated in her head. *"You deserve everything that you've ever wanted and so much more."*

Belle desperately wanted one of those things to be Tara. *"Everything I could hope for is sitting right here in front of me."* And then they'd made love.

How could she be so stupid? She knew the kind of woman Tara was, and she'd never denied it. But Belle thought she could lock away her heart and play the game. She took Kyle's advice, against her own judgment, and it got her where she always knew it would—hurt and alone in a crumpled ball on her couch. She ignored every warning sign and alarm just so she could feel what it was like to have Tara, even for a fleeting moment, and in spite of her expectation of disaster, her heart still paid the consequences.

Belle grew angry at herself, at Tara, and at the unfairness of life. How naive could she be to think that she deserved something better than what she already had? Giles had given her the life she never could have dreamed of. He had taken her from squalor and gave her a future. One she never in a million years could have accomplished without his generosity and love. Who was she to think that life owed her something more?

But now, as she wallowed in the misery she had created for herself, she remembered that the life he had given her was gone, too. In her pursuit of Tara, she had taken her eye off the one thing she promised to always protect. From the moment she'd allowed Tara to pull her heart and mind away from the job, all hell broke loose. Her life had officially fallen apart at the seams, and she had no idea how she was going to put any of it back together. She was powerless to correct or control anything. It was all gone—Tara, Giles, and the collection. As if someone had literally stolen the sun, her world was cast in shadow.

Belle stared at the floor as she lay on the couch. Her arm hung down onto the floor and her face was pressed into the cushion. She hadn't the strength or motivation to move, but she needed to get out of the house or she'd go crazy. She pushed herself off the sofa, snatched random clothes from the laundry basket, and put them on. She grabbed her keys and phone off the counter and left. She didn't know where she was going; she just went.

Belle drove around until she found herself in downtown Altamonte near Rosenberg's Gallery. Belle was deafened by the sound of blood as it whooshed in her ears. She clutched the steering wheel with her sweating palms while her heart pounded in her chest. Her head swirled with ideas. She told herself that she wasn't going to do anything stupid or try to be some sort of superhero. She just wanted to see if what her instincts were telling her was correct, and then she would call Agent Campbell.

Belle drove past the storefront twice before she selected the perfect parking spot across the street. She pulled forward into the slip that angled toward the store. She could see the shop ahead, as well as anyone who went in or out. She reclined her seat and slunk down behind the wheel. Two large SUVs flanked her small car so she felt secure that she wouldn't be seen by random passersby. Belle's anxiety was in overdrive, but she also felt an unexpected sense of exhilaration.

She sat in her car and focused all her attention on the activity, or lack of it, around the gallery. When a couple approached, Belle took out her phone and snapped a few photos of them as they entered. She didn't recognize them, and she had no idea what she would do with the pictures. The only thing she knew about surveillance or stakeouts was what she had learned watching *NCIS* reruns. She decided that she might want to stop watching so many crime dramas.

Several people came and went from the store in the first hour, and no one looked suspicious or familiar. Unless she could get inside, there was no way he was going to walk out with the stolen art, and in spite of what she was starting to feel, she wasn't that stupid. A sense of unease began to wash over her. *What am I doing? Belle, you're not Angela fucking Lansbury for Christ's sake! Call the damn police!* She had tried to convince herself that there was no connection, yet here she was pretending to be some sort of private investigator because of a feeling she couldn't shake. She had lost her damn mind.

Belle pulled her phone from her purse and dialed Detective Campbell. "Hi, Detective. This is Belle Winters."

"Belle, what can I do for you?" he asked.

"I think I know who may have been behind the robbery," Belle whispered.

"Uhm, why are you whispering? Where are you?"

She wasn't sure how to answer his question. If she told him the truth, he would blow a gasket, if he believed her. But if she lied to him, he would know it. Caught off guard, without even a relatively believable fib, she told him. "I'm sitting outside the Rosenberg Gallery in Altamonte. I think Otto Rosenberg might be behind the stolen collection. I was doing some research and I think he might be behind the whole thing. He sued Giles for the collection after a falling out, and he lost. Plus, I'm pretty certain that he deals in stolen art."

"Miss Winters, that is not a good idea. I need you to get in your car and get out of there immediately." Detective Campbell's voice was stern and loud.

"But what about—"

"We know all of this already. We made the final connections this morning and the FBI TAC team is preparing to respond to his gallery. Get out of there now!" His voice was shrill to the point Belle thought dogs would start to howl.

"Okay. I'm just sitting in my car. I thought if I could see him with the art that maybe—"

"Belle, you are in serious danger being anywhere near him or his shop. Where is Tara?"

Belle's stomach twisted at first, and then a fire rose in her chest. "Tara? I don't know. I came here on my own. I don't need her."

"Ms. Winters, you are not safe. Leave now."

"Okay. I'm leaving," she said as she turned the key in the ignition. But as the engine turned over a loud click reverberated in her ear.

"Hang up," a deep voice commanded.

"Belle? Who is that? Belle, answer me," Campbell shouted.

Belle lowered the phone, and a man reached in and snatched it from her. Belle could hear Detective Campbell calling her name as the man threw it onto the ground and stomped it into pieces. "Get out."

Terror coursed through her veins as Belle did as she was told. "I was just sitting—"

"Shut up and move." He pressed the gun to her back and forced her across the street toward the gallery she'd been watching for the last few hours.

Belle felt the blood rush from her body as she marched on trembling legs into the building. When he locked the deadbolt behind them, Belle felt the jolt in every nerve ending. He pushed her forward hard and she stumbled. "Please. I—"

"I said shut up." He pushed her again, and she fell through a large tapestry that obscured the opening behind it.

CHAPTER TWENTY-SEVEN

Tara had driven around for a couple of hours as the sun rose from early morning. She drove without destination or purpose, but she kept herself moving. She found herself at Cate's store just as she arrived to open. Tara lingered near the entrance as Cate approached.

"Hey."

"What's wrong?" Cate looked down at her watch and then back to Tara.

"Nothing. Well...maybe...I don't know." Tara ran her hands through her hair and tousled it in frustration. "I left."

"Left what?" Cate reached out and pulled at Tara's hand.

"Not what, who. Belle. This morning. I had a dream. When I woke up, I freaked out and left."

"Please tell me you didn't leave without telling her."

"I told her. Sort of."

"You left a note didn't you?" Cate sighed before Tara even admitted to it.

Tara followed Cate back to her office and slumped down into one of the chairs. "I didn't know what else to do. The dream it was just so real."

Cate sat in her own chair and leaned forward across her desk. "What was it about?"

"It was crazy. We were married and pregnant and I was buying groceries. I...who...I never in a million years, Cate." Tara could barely string a complete sentence together.

"Oh. Wow." Cate sat back in her chair and stared at Tara.

"I know. So I woke up and got my stuff and bolted."

"Okay. But before you woke up, how did it make you feel?"

Tara rolled her eyes at Cate. "What are you, a shrink?"

"Sometimes. So?"

"Ugh. I don't know. It felt..." Tara let herself remember the dream she'd tried all morning to forget. How had she felt? It wasn't until she woke up that the fear and panic set in. Tara could see Belle's intoxicating smile and beautiful swollen belly as if she stood in front of her. Tara smiled. "It felt nice."

"Huh. Okay. So why did you run?"

"I don't know. It was the only thing I could do. I mean, part of me wanted to wake her up and tell her about it. But then what?"

"What do you mean? It was a dream, Tara. It wasn't real."

"But what if a part of me wanted it to be real?"

"Oh." Cate's eyes grew wider than Tara had ever seen.

"I mean it wasn't the dream that freaked me out. It was my reaction to it. I was disappointed, Cate." Tara rubbed her face with her hands. She couldn't believe that she was saying it out loud.

Cate pushed out of her chair and came around to Tara's side. She knelt beside her and rubbed her leg. "Sweetie, this might be the best thing that has ever happened to you. You cannot let your fear keep you from holding on to it."

"I left her a note. I told her that I didn't have what she deserves. And maybe I don't. What have I ever done that makes me worthy of having someone as amazing as she is? She's struggled through her entire life, yet she still has so much hope and love. I can't compete with that. What can I give her that she hasn't already gotten for herself?"

"Love, Tara."

"I heard her say it," Tara admitted quietly.

"Say what?"

"That she loved me. But I didn't say it back. I felt it. I wanted to, but I couldn't get the words out."

Cate smiled and covered her mouth as her eyes sparkled. "You love her?"

"Yes. I think so. I've never felt this way about anyone. But I just know I broke her heart. I took everything she offered and then I walked away. Her pride is as strong as her passion, how do I..." Tara sighed in defeat.

"Go and tell her. Tell her that you're sorry. Tell her that you're a big doofus. Tell her that you love her, Tara."

"You think it's just that easy, huh? Knock on her door and say 'Sorry about the note, but I love you?'"

"What is there to lose? She either forgives you or she doesn't, but how will you know if you just sit here and beat yourself up for your mistakes?"

Tara knew Cate was right. And if she had any chance of making it right, she had to move. It had taken her all her life to find love. She couldn't let it slip from her hands now. "Okay!" Tara stood up. "I have to go."

Tara drove like a bat out of hell back to Belle's apartment. She turned into the driveway and was out of her seat before she even killed the engine. As she rounded the Jeep toward the steps, Kyle bolted out of the house. He screamed at her, "Tara! It's Belle!" Tara's stomach leapt into her throat at the way he screamed her name.

"Kyle, what's wrong? Where's Belle?" Just then, she noticed that her car wasn't parked in front her place.

"Get in the car, now!" he ordered Tara as he dialed Belle's number on his phone. "Andrew!" he shouted back toward the house.

Andrew came out of the house and slammed the door behind him. Tara had no idea what was happening.

Andrew ran past her. "Get in the car!"

Tara jumped into the backseat as Andrew started the car and sped out of the driveway.

"She's not answering. It's going straight to voice mail," Kyle said.

"Will someone please tell me what the hell is going on?" Tara asked as Andrew took the corner so fast that she was flung across the backseat. "Fuck!"

"Agent Gulker called."

Tara's heart stopped short. She listened as he explained that Belle thought Roz was involved in the heist and that she had gone that morning to his store in Altamonte. "What?" Tara couldn't believe what she was hearing. "Why would she do that?"

"We don't know. But Detective Campbell was telling her to leave when the phone cut out."

"What do you mean cut out?"

"He heard a man's voice and then nothing. I think she was right about Rosenberg and now they have her," Kyle said to Tara.

"This cannot be happening," Tara said in shock.

"This might be the dumbest shit she's ever done." Kyle growled as he slammed his fist on the dashboard.

"Relax, babe. She didn't know what she was walking into. And if she was in her car, there was no reason for her to think she was really in danger."

"Spying on a man in connection with a multimillion dollar art heist by a gang of criminals who tried to kill three people doesn't scream fucking danger?"

"I know. I was just—"

"I'm sorry. But they have her, Andrew."

"I know."

Tara's head was spinning. She was consumed with fear and helplessness. Her vision faded in and out, and she had to remind herself to breathe. She blamed herself for the danger that Belle was in. Had Tara not left her that morning, had she made her call the FBI about her suspicions, Belle would still be safe in her arms.

Belle landed on all fours onto a hard concrete surface. Stacked against the walls around the room were rows of art and paintings. He pulled her up off the floor by her hair and sat her at a large table. On the table in the center of the room was a large overturned canvas and gold frame. It was clear that it was in the final steps of being mounted for display, but there were two canvases instead of one.

A corner of the top canvas curled up and exposed a ragged edge. Belle reached over and turned more up. She recognized the colors and brushstrokes of Lempicka's *La Musicienne* and she gasped. She stood to turn the entire piece when she was knocked back down into her seat. "Please. Let me go. I promise I won't—"

"Tie her down!" a voice commanded. "You won't what? Tell anyone that you found Grayson's precious collection? I find that hard to believe considering what you've gone through to get here."

Belle pulled against the rope that locked her wrists behind her. She turned her head toward the voice behind her and recognized the man as Roz. "Please, why are you doing this?"

"Why are you doing this?" He mocked her. "What does it matter to you? You should be dead," he said matter-of-factly as he pulled his gun from his waistband and pointed it at her chest.

Every last breath of air rushed from her lungs. Belle gasped and turned her face away from the muzzle. "No! Roz, don't."

"Give me one good reason. And for the record, none of them will be good enough."

"Giles."

Roz laughed like a maniac. "You're kidding, right? Out of all the reasons you could give to save your life you choose that. I should kill you right now for even mentioning his name." He jerked the weapon at her.

Belle flinched. "Why me? I didn't do anything to you."

"Oh, but see you did. You don't know it, but this"—he motioned to the piles of stolen art around them—"this is your fault."

Belle had no idea what she had done. "I don't understand."

"I built this collection. It was mine. When that old man died, it should've come to me."

Belle had no idea what he was talking about. She had nothing to do with where the collection went after Giles died, as he had long before donated his entire collection to the museum. "His collection belongs to the Grayson. It always has, long before I'd even met him."

"Wrong. And that's why I need you out of the way."

"But I'm not in the way. I promised him that I would protect and care for it the way he had. I owed that to him."

"What in this world is worth that kind of dedication besides money?"

"Money? I don't have any money. Everything he gave me went toward school. There was nothing left."

"You have no idea, do you?"

"About what?" Belle asked as she struggled against her restraints. Her hands were going numb.

"It's yours. Not mine, not the museum's, it's all yours. That son of a bitch left everything I worked for, everything we made together, to some homeless street urchin."

"What?" was all Belle could get out before a knot tied in her throat. *He gave it to me?* Belle struggled to breathe around the invisible weight that pressed down on her. Her breaths were short and quick, and her head spun.

"So, that is why I want you out of the way. You don't deserve any piece of my collection, and that includes the insurance payout."

Belle gasped for air. "I don't want it, I swear. I didn't know. You can have it all, just please let me go." Belle cried. She cried for Giles and his kindness, and she cried for her life. She never wanted the money, and her love of the art went so much deeper than any worldly value. Belle hung her head and sobbed. The room was still and silent except for Belle's sadness.

"That's enough! Pete, gag her," Roz ordered his goon and threw a rag at him.

"No. No! Please?" Belle could barely breathe as it was. If he gagged her, she knew she would suffocate. Belle kicked her feet out at Pete. "He loved you!"

"Stop!" He held up his hand to Pete. "What did you just say?"

CHAPTER TWENTY-EIGHT

As soon as Andrew pulled the car to a stop at the police barricade, Tara jumped out. She ran toward the shop, but was halted by two officers. "I need to get through!" Tara demanded.

"Ma'am, you need to step back."

"My...Belle is in there. She could be...Do you know who I am?" Tara was no one to them, but she couldn't think of any other way to help Belle.

"Excuse me. Kyle King, from the Grayson Gallery. I need to speak to Agent Nicholas Gulker immediately."

Andrew stood next to Tara as Kyle waited for him to arrive. "Mr. King, if you'll come with me." He motioned to the officers and lifted the tape for Kyle.

"Let's go," Kyle said to Tara and Andrew. "Where is Belle?" Kyle asked him as they headed toward the command vehicle.

"We've confirmed one hostage inside with two known suspects. We've called in a hostage negotiator, but I don't think he's what we need."

"Why?" Tara asked.

Agent Gulker turned his attention toward her. "Because if our intel is correct, Otto Rosenberg isn't looking to negotiate."

"Why wouldn't he negotiate? I'll pay anything he wants if he lets her go. I'll buy him a Goddamned helicopter if he wants one!"

"He isn't in this for the money, Ms. Hicks."

"It's about getting back what he thinks is his," Kyle said.

"What? What's his?"

"The Grayson Collection. He was partners with Giles Grayson when he amassed the bulk of his collection. Until Giles met Belle, the value of his works were willed between the Emily J. Grayson Museum and Mr. Otto Rosenberg."

"Okay. So what? He wants more than half? Who cares? Just give it to him!" As far as Tara could see, it was most definitely about money.

"We can't. Neither the museum nor Otto own any portion of the collection."

Tara's head was about to explode with frustration. "Will somebody just talk in fucking plain English?"

"Ms. Winters is the sole beneficiary of the entire Grayson Collection," Gulker said.

"We house the works as a loan from the estate just as when Giles was alive, but the works belong to Belle."

"What? Are you serious? Does she know?" Tara was dumbfounded by the news.

"No. As a caveat of the will, she wasn't supposed to find out until she completed her education and worked a minimum of fifteen years at the Grayson."

"But as sole owner of the collection, she's entitled to the art and any insurance payouts resulting from the theft."

"Correct," Kyle confirmed.

"He doesn't want any of it. He just doesn't want anyone else to have it. So what are we going to do?"

Just then, a heavily armored officer approached, "Sir, we're ready to breach."

"Breach? Breach what?"

"We have our Tactical Response Team prepared to enter the facility."

"What about Belle?"

"That's what we're going in for. We don't have time to waste. If he realizes he's cornered with no way out he isn't going to hesitate to finish, at least part of his plan."

"To kill her." Saying the words out loud made Tara sick to her stomach. She just couldn't grasp the reality of what was happening when just hours earlier she had been wrapped around the woman she loved. Now that love was being torn away from her before she ever had the chance to feel the freedom of it. "Please. You have to save her."

❖

Belle's eyes widened as she watched Roz raise his pistol and point it at her. "What did you say?"

"Please! No! I said he loved you. Giles did. He told me that in his whole life he'd only ever loved one man."

"He loved himself," Roz snapped back.

"No. He said that he'd just one regret and that was never telling you, or anyone else, how much you meant to him."

"Bullshit. He would never admit that to anyone. Why would he tell you?"

"I don't know. But he did. Maybe he hoped one day I would get the chance to tell you. Although I don't think this is quite what he had in mind."

"I never wanted much you know. Sure, in the beginning it was intoxicating. The money, the art, the career, the exotic travels around the world, it was a dream come true. But then I fell in love. I fell in love with a man who loved all those things more than he loved me." Roz lowered his weapon and paced in front of Belle.

Belle never would've thought anyone could have claimed Giles was a selfish aristocratic rogue. He was kind and generous to everyone, especially Belle. "That's not the Giles I knew."

"All I wanted was him. I didn't need anything else as long as we could be together. But no! He couldn't give up his life and reputation for me."

"Did you ask him to?"

"I shouldn't have had to."

"Maybe not. But how was he to know what you wanted if you never told him? Instead you stole from him. You used his love and trust against him and betrayed everything you had together."

"I deserved it. Just like I deserve this. You don't! You are nothing, and he was my everything!" Roz shouted and raised his weapon back up at her.

"He was mine, too!" Belle screamed and closed her eyes tightly.

❖

Tara blamed herself for this turn of events. "I should have called you. I should have taken her theory more seriously and we could have stopped this nonsense." Tara felt a knot tighten in her chest.

"Ms. Hicks, we're doing everything in our power to do just that. She forced our hand by attempting this asinine reconnaissance mission on her own. I can't even imagine what was going through her head."

Tara could. She didn't know if her leaving that morning had sparked Belle's irrational action. "We talked about this a couple times, and each time we just sort of brushed it off." Tara was angry, with Belle and with herself. "She had to know this was a stupid idea, and she came anyway. It's my fault."

"Tara, there's no way she knew he was going to take her hostage. And there's no way you *made* her do this," Agent Gulker said.

"She had the idea in her head that he was the one. She lost him and his collection and then I up and leave her with just a note. What other choice did she have? What more could she lose?"

"That's shit," Andrew said.

The radio squawked and a man announced that it was time to go. "We're ready," Agent Gulker said. "Stay here. I need you back out of the way until we have the suspects in custody and the scene is clear. Understood?"

Kyle and Andrew readily agreed, but Tara didn't. Without any concern for her own safety, she wanted to be in the middle of it all so she could make sure that Belle would be okay.

"Understood?" he repeated.

"I understand."

She watched as the TAC team assembled on either side of the door. They were so far away that Tara had to squint against the sun to see what was happening. She growled in frustration to cover the pounding sound of her heart. *Hold on, my love.* Tara held her breath as the men opened the door and tossed in a flash grenade. The three of them gasped and jumped back as light erupted from the store followed by an ear-blasting bang. Smoke billowed from the open door as the men rushed into the building.

CHAPTER TWENTY-NINE

Belle saw a black cylinder roll just beneath the tapestry. Roz looked back, and it exploded in a blinding flash and deafening bang. Belle was flung back in her chair and fell onto her back in a painful crash. She could see nothing except a glaring white light. Her brain felt like mush as it sloshed between her ears. The floor vibrated like a herd of cattle were stampeding toward her. Belle rolled to her side and struggled with the binding at her wrists. As she twisted and pulled, a sharp pain shot through her arm.

As her vision cleared, it was still speckled with flecks of light, but she saw several men in black rush into the room toward Roz and Pete. She rolled under the table out of the way when she heard a single gun blast, followed by a quick succession in return. Pete fell to the floor next to Belle, and she screamed. She scooted away from the pool of blood that crept its way toward her.

Roz dropped to the floor and had his arms and legs put to his side as two men restrained him. Belle's body shook as she huddled under the table. The room fell into a sudden silence and Belle could hear her own quick, shallow breaths through a distant ringing in her ears. When a hand reached down for her, she screamed and pulled away. "It's all right, Ms. Winters. It's over."

Belle sat up onto her knees and crawled out from beneath the table. He cut her hands loose and they fell to her sides. Her heart still pounded in her chest as she looked around at the room in a daze.

"We need paramedics for possible gunshot wound to the left shoulder."

Belle heard ringing and muffled voices around her as the officer called out for paramedics over the radio. She was pretty sure Pete was dead and past the point of medical attention. The officer righted the chair she'd been sitting in minutes earlier and sat her down.

"Paramedics are on the way, ma'am."

"Why? He's dead."

"Yes, ma'am. But you've been shot."

"What?" Belle wasn't shot. What was he talking about? She looked down at herself. She felt no pain and saw no blood until she moved her arm. Starting at her shoulder, a trail of blood stained her shirt and ran down her forearm. She watched the red stain spread slowly through the fabric and her head whirled. "Oh my..." Before she finished her sentence, the lights cut out and the world went dark.

Tara paced back and forth as the scene unfolded. Kyle and Andrew gasped when the sound of gunshots rang out, and Tara felt the nausea rise into her throat. She could see no movement inside the building, and outside not a single soul flinched as all eyes were trained on the storefront. Tara held her breath as she waited for any sign of Belle. When she heard the call over the radio announcing a clear scene, she exhaled. But the relief was short-lived when she heard the call for paramedics.

Against Gulker's orders, Tara moved closer as several members of the medical team responded with equipment and stretchers. Three people and two stretchers, the odds were nauseating. "What's happening?" Tara asked anyone who was listening. "Somebody tell me what the fuck is happening!"

"Tara!" Kyle called out to her.

Agent Gulker approached her. "Ms. Hicks, I asked you to stay back."

"I did. Now I want to know what is going on. Where's Belle?"

"My team is clearing the scene now. We will—" A call on his radio interrupted him and he excused himself.

"What is it? What did he say?" Kyle asked.

"Did he say anything about Belle?" Andrew added.

Tara ran her fingers through her hair and gripped it. "No. Nothing."

Kyle rubbed his face and squeezed his mouth in frustration. Andrew consoled him by rubbing his back. "I'm sure she's okay.

When Tara saw movement near the store, she stood up onto her toes for a better look. The first of the two stretchers was being wheeled out by the EMTs. Tara's heart dropped into her stomach when she saw the large black bag strapped down to it. But the feeling of dread was overpowered by relief when she saw Belle being pushed out on the second one. Kyle and Andrew whimpered in happiness when they saw her, and Tara sighed with relief. Agent Gulker be damned, Tara needed to touch her and make sure that she was okay. She ripped away the tape and ran to her. Kyle and Andrew followed behind.

❖

Belle was exhausted. Not only from the hours she'd spent held at gunpoint by a sad and crazy man, but from the last several months of her life. She'd been on a physical and emotional rollercoaster ever since she laid eyes on Tara Hicks. She had turned Belle's calm and boring world into a whirlwind of danger and pain. But it was the moments of pleasure and happiness that weighed heaviest on her, for she felt them much deeper than her tired flesh and bone. She laid her head back against the hard cushion of the stretcher and closed her eyes.

As they wheeled her to a stop, Belle heard the clatter of shoes running across the pavement. Without opening her eyes, she knew it was Tara. She was afraid to look at her and forget the words she'd written that morning when she left her alone and hurt. Belle wanted to remember them so that she knew without a doubt they were not meant to be together. Maybe Roz had been right in a way about Giles. She shouldn't have to ask Tara to love her.

Belle heard Tara's voice, and it twisted at her heart. "Oh, Belle, sweetheart. What happened? Is she okay?" Belle felt Tara touch her hand and squeeze it. It was as if Tara had reached into Belle's chest and gripped her heart instead.

"She has a GSW to her left shoulder. She is stable and alert. We'll transport her to ORMC."

"Belle?" Tara said as she leaned down over Belle.

Against her decision not to, she opened her eyes and looked into Tara's. They were red and glossy with emotion, and it tore at her. "Hey."

Tara cupped her face and smiled. "Hey. I was so scared."

"I'm okay. Just another war wound to add to my ever growing list. It's a good thing the drugs kicked in before the adrenaline wore off because this one's a doozy." Belle tried to make light of the situation.

Tara chuckled nervously, but Kyle didn't find it amusing. He pushed his way to her side, "If you ever do something like this again, I…"

"You don't have to worry about that. Ever." Belle reached out and squeezed his hand.

The techs unlocked the wheels and prepared to load Belle into the ambulance. "Wait," Tara said.

"Ma'am, we have to get her to the hospital."

Tara leaned down toward Belle and fidgeted with the sheet over her legs. "But I need to tell you something. Something I should have said last night, but I didn't."

Belle looked at her and shook her head. "Tara, you said what you needed to this morning in the note you left me."

"No. That wasn't it. That's not how I feel."

The tech tightened the straps around Belle. "We need to go. You can either come with or meet us there."

Tara looked at Belle and she couldn't resist the question in her eyes. "She can come."

"Fine." They loaded Belle into the ambulance. Tara climbed in after her and they closed the doors.

Belle had never been in an ambulance before, and she felt a little claustrophobic. Her breaths became short and quick as the vehicle sped away.

As if Tara knew what Belle was feeling, she took her hand. "Look at me. Deep breaths."

"Tara, what are you doing here? We both know this, us, it doesn't make any sense."

"It makes every kind of sense. To me."

"Then why did you leave?"

"I got spooked."

"By what?" The vehicle took a sharp corner and Belle rolled over onto her arm. She winced at the sharp pain that jolted through her. "Ow."

"A dream. But it was more than the dream. It was how content and happy I felt in that dream."

"But then you woke up and I wasn't what you wanted. You got scared of the reality of being with me."

"Belle, that's not why. I have never felt this way about anyone before. Hell, I'm not even sure what this feeling is. But I don't want it to go away."

"You say that now, Tara. What happens when one day it all becomes too much like a cage and you start to regret your decision and blame me for tying you down?" The sharp pain that was in Belle's arm moved to her chest. Her heart was squeezing into oblivion. "Everyone I have ever loved has left me, Tara. I can't go into this knowing that you inevitably will, too. I've spent my whole life trying to keep this from happening and you—" Belle choked on her words. Tears streamed down her face, and she swiped them away.

"Belle, please. Give me a chance to show you how I feel."

The ambulance pulled to a stop and the EMTs went to work. The doors opened and they pulled Belle's stretcher from the vehicle. As they locked the legs in place, Tara jumped out after them. As they began to push her away, Belle closed her eyes and Tara grabbed her hand.

"Wait!"

"Tara, please go."

"Ma'am, please move."

"Belle, don't." Tara's eyes filled with tears, and Belle's heart shattered.

"No more, Tara. It's over. Just go." It took all the strength she had, but Belle turned her head away and pulled her hand back from Tara. A cold chill of sadness flooded through her body, and she wept. She felt Tara staring as they wheeled her into the hospital and out of Tara's life.

❖

Tara stood in the loading bay and watched as they pushed Belle away from her. She wanted to scream and run after her, but Belle had made herself clear. She wanted Tara out of her life. But she couldn't make herself leave. She never had to fight for anything in her life. And if she did she always gave up because it was never worth the effort. This wasn't one of those times. She met Kyle and Andrew in the ER waiting area and told them her plan.

CHAPTER THIRTY

Belle pushed the button on the bed remote and raised herself. Kyle and Andrew carried a large bouquet of flowers and a gigantic stuffed bear. "Guys, it's not that bad. It didn't even go into my arm. It's just a scratch."

"When did you get to be such a badass, Ms. Tough Guy? You got shot!"

"The only thing I got is some stitches and this big ol' fancy Band-Aid here." Belle laughed at herself.

"And really good drugs, apparently."

"Shhh. Don't tell nobody, but I think there might be morphine in this here bag-o-fun. Fun bag." Belle chuckled and poked her finger at the IV bag that hung next to her bed.

"Oh, good Lord," Andrew said as he put down the teddy bear and sat on the edge of Belle's bed.

"The doctor said your surgery went fine. It was just a graze, superficial, so he just wants to monitor you overnight tonight and you should be out by tomorrow afternoon."

"See. I tol' ya. Tol' ya!"

"Maybe we should have him dial it back on the loopy juice?"

"Eh. Let her have it. Hell, I'd need more than that to handle all the shit she's been through the last couple months."

"Yes! I've been almost strangled to death, kidnapped, shot, robbed, and had my still beating heart ripped out of my chest. See?" Belle pulled her gown down and showed them her imaginary scar. "And all because of her. She did this to me. Tara shot me. Right here."

"No. She didn't, sweetheart."

"She could have. I gave her my heart. And she broke it." She made a gesture that resembled breaking a stick in half. "Snap."

"She came back you know. Yesterday, while you were on the phone with me. She came to say she was sorry."

"I love her, you know. I do. But she doesn't love me." Belle was so tired. She leaned her head back against the bed and her eyes fluttered closed. "I love her, Kyle. So much."

"I know you do, sweetheart. I know." He tapped her gently on the leg as she fell sound asleep.

❖

Tara paced in the lobby as she waited for them to arrive. She hadn't seen Belle in almost ten days. And while it was quite a good stretch of time, it had seemed more like months to her.

Tara hadn't been wasting those days pining for the woman she had lost. Instead she spent night and day locked up in the museum with brilliant and dedicated art geniuses as they worked painstakingly to restore the entire Grayson Sunshine Collection. Kyle had found her the world's most renowned experts in restoration and preservation, and Tara spared no expense on their talents or time.

While the pieces had been irreparably damaged, Tara was amazed by what they had been able to accomplish in order to get the art back on the walls. Tara couldn't wait to see Belle's beautiful face when she walked through the door to see what she had done for her. Tara's pulse raced, and nerve endings buzzed. If she had any chance of getting Belle to believe in her and her love, this was it. Her phone buzzed in her pocket, and she jumped. A text from Kyle announced their impending arrival.

"She's here!" Tara's voice reverberated down the hall. Clicks and scuffing of shoes, along with hushed whispers rebounded back.

Tara took several long, deep breaths as she tried to calm herself. She heard the front door open and the beautiful sound of Belle's voice echoed in the foyer.

"Kyle, I don't think I'm ready."

"We will be right beside you the whole time. They said it'll be good for you."

"I know. I just…what if—"

"Hey, sweetie. Look at me," Andrew said. "Breathe."

As if he was talking to her as well, Tara did the same. When the three of them entered the lobby, her eyes met Belle's. They were just as fathomless and alluring as she had remembered. They walked toward each other, and Tara wasn't even sure that her feet ever touched the ground. "Hi."

"Hi. What are you doing here?" Belle tucked a piece of her hair behind her ear.

"I've been here. Waiting for you."

"Me? Why?"

"I need to show you something. Will you come with me?"

Belle looked at Kyle and Andrew for some sort of sign that it was all right. When they nodded and smiled, she said yes.

"Okay. One sec." Tara slipped back behind the docent desk and came back pushing a wheelchair.

Belle laughed. "Are you serious?"

"Yes, ma'am. It's even got your name on it." Tara pointed to the blue embroidery on the seat back.

"Oh good grief," she said as Kyle, Andrew, and Tara all snickered. "Fine, but no speeding." Belle sat in the seat.

"I promise. But you have to close your eyes, please."

Belle looked at her skeptically but did as she was told. "You promised."

Tara pushed her down the hall and into the Grayson Gallery as Kyle and Andrew followed along behind. "Keep 'em closed."

"Tara, I don't know if I'm—"

Tara locked the wheels and came around in front of the chair and knelt in front of Belle. "Just one more second." Tara grabbed Belle's hands and held them on her lap. "You are so full of love and beauty that sometimes I think I might drown in it just being near you. You are fearless, intense, and awkward. You deserve nothing less than to be cherished and adored like the priceless masterpiece that you are. You are my moonlight and my sunshine, and I want to spend the rest of my life with you." Tara wiped away the tears that ran down Belle's cheeks. "You can open them now."

Belle opened her eyes. Tara stood, pulled Belle to her feet, and turned her around. On the wall before her was *Impression Sunrise* flanked on each side by *Auvers sur Oise* and *Vase with Viscaria*. Belle gasped and covered her mouth in surprise. She turned in every direction around the room. All eleven paintings in the Sunshine collection had been restored and remounted in one room.

Belle smiled through tears as she sobbed. "Tara, I..."

"One more thing. Okay!" she shouted into the hallway and more than thirty people flooded into the room.

They stood against the far wall beneath a large blank canvas banner. Kyle and Andrew joined the group of people on either end and grabbed the ropes that hung from each side. When Tara nodded, they pulled down the fabric and revealed a gold sign that read "The Grayson-Winters Sunshine Collection."

Belle turned to Tara with sparkling eyes. "Tara, I don't know what to say. This is more—"

Tara interrupted her before she could continue. "Tell me you love me, again."

"What?"

"I heard you say that you loved me, Belle. My biggest regret is that I didn't say it back when I had the chance. If you still love me, please say it again."

Belle hung her head and Tara's heart stopped. She held her breath as Belle looked up into her eyes. "Tara, I love you."

Tara soul cried out with joy, and she wrapped Belle into her arms. "I love you too, Belle Winters." She dipped her head and pressed her lips against Belle's. She never again wanted to know what it was like to go more than a day without tasting her sweet kisses.

"Do you just love me for my money?" Belle asked with a grin.

"I'm not interested in pretentious muckety-mucks. But I can review my stance."

Belle laughed and Tara kissed her again.

About the Author

Tina Michele is a Florida girl living on the banks of the Indian River Lagoon in the biggest small town on the Space Coast. She enjoys all the benefits of living in the Sunshine State. During the day, she pretends to do what they pay her for, but really spends most of that time daydreaming and plotting some wild adventure. She graduated from the University of Central Florida with her BA in interdisciplinary studies—the most liberal of the liberal arts degrees—majoring in fine art and writing with a minor in women's studies. To say she is motivated by her Right brain is a major understatement. Afflicted with self-diagnosed Sagittarian Attention Deficit Disorder, she spends a lot of time starting projects that she may, possibly, one day, probably finish. When she isn't writing, playing, drawing, painting, or creating something of some sort, she feeds and waters the three dogs that are permanently tethered to her hindquarters.

Tina can be contacted at: tina@tmichele.com
Website: www.tmichele.com
Facebook: www.facebook.com/tmicheleauthor

Books Available from Bold Strokes Books

Dyre: By Moon's Light by Rachel E. Bailey. A young werewolf, Des, guards the aging leader of all the Packs: the Dyre. Stable employment—nice work, if you can get it…at least until silver bullets start to fly. (978-1-62639-6-623)

Fragile Wings by Rebecca S. Buck. In Roaring Twenties London, can Evelyn Hopkins find love with Jos Singleton or will the scars of the Great War crush her dreams? (978-1-62639-5-466)

Live and Love Again by Jan Gayle. Jessica Whitney could be Sarah Jarret's second chance at love, but their differences and Sarah's grief continue to come between their budding relationship. (978-1-62639-5-176)

Starstruck by Lesley Davis. Actress Cassidy Hayes and writer Aiden Darrow find out the hard way not all life-threatening drama is confined to the TV screen or the pages of a manuscript. (978-1-62639-5-237)

Stealing Sunshine by Tina Michele. Under the Central Florida sun, two women struggle between fear and love as a dangerous plot of deception and revenge threatens to steal priceless art and lives. (978-1-62639-4-452)

The Fifth Gospel by Michelle Grubb. Hiding a Vatican secret is dangerous—sharing the secret suicidal—can Felicity survive a perilous book tour, and will her PR specialist, Anna, be there when it's all over? (978-1-62639-4-476)

Cold to the Touch by Cari Hunter. A drug addict's murder is the start of a dangerous investigation for Detective Sanne Jensen and Dr. Meg Fielding, as they try to stop a killer with no conscience. (978-1-62639-526-8)

Forsaken by Laydin Michaels. The hunt for a killer teaches one woman that she must overcome her fear in order to love, and another that success is meaningless without happiness. (978-1-62639-481-0)

Infiltration by Jackie D. When a CIA breach is imminent, a Marine instructor must stop the attack while protecting her heart from being disarmed by a recruit. (978-1-62639-521-3)

Midnight at the Orpheus by Alyssa Linn Palmer. Two women desperate to make their way in the world, a man hell-bent on revenge, and a cop risking his career: all in a day's work in Capone's Chicago. (978-1-62639-607-4)

Spirit of the Dance by Mardi Alexander. Major Sorla Reardon's return to her family farm to heal threatens Riley Johnson's safe life when small-town secrets are revealed, and love may not conquer all. (978-1-62639-583-1)

Sweet Hearts by Melissa Brayden, Rachel Spangler, and Karis Walsh. Do you ever wonder *Whatever happened to...*? Find out when you reconnect with your favorite characters from Melissa Brayden's *Heart Block*, Rachel Spangler's *LoveLife*, and Karis Walsh's *Worth the Risk*. (978-1-62639-475-9)

Totally Worth It by Maggie Cummings. Who knew there's an all-lesbian condo community in the NYC suburbs? Join twentysomething BFFs Meg and Lexi at Bay West as they navigate friendships, love, and everything in between. (978-1-62639-512-1)

Illicit Artifacts by Stevie Mikayne. Her foster mother's death cracked open a secret world Jil never wanted to see...and now she has to pick up the stolen pieces. (978-1-62639-472-8)

Pathfinder by Gun Brooke. Heading for their new homeworld, Exodus's chief engineer Adina Vantressa and nurse Briar Lindemay carry game-changing secrets that may well cause them to lose everything when disaster strikes. (978-1-62639-444-5)

Prescription for Love by Radclyffe. Dr. Flannery Rivers finds herself attracted to the new ER chief, city girl Abigail Remy, and the incendiary mix of city and country, fire and ice, tradition and change is combustible. (978-1-62639-570-1)

Ready or Not by Melissa Brayden. Uptight Mallory Spencer finds relinquishing control to bartender Hope Sanders too tall an order in fast-paced New York City. (978-1-62639-443-8)

Summer Passion by MJ Williamz. Women loving women is forbidden in 1946 Hollywood, yet Jean and Maggie strive to keep their love alive and away from prying eyes. (978-1-62639-540-4)

The Princess and the Prix by Nell Stark. "Ugly duckling" Princess Alix of Monaco was resigned to loneliness until she met racecar driver Thalia d'Angelis. (978-1-62639-474-2)

Winter's Harbor by Aurora Rey. Lia Brooks isn't looking for love in Provincetown, but when she discovers chocolate croissants and pastry chef Alex McKinnon, her winter retreat quickly starts heating up. (978-1-62639-498-8)

The Time Before Now by Missouri Vaun. Vivian flees a disastrous affair, embarking on an epic, transformative journey to escape her past, until destiny introduces her to Ida, who helps her rediscover trust, love, and hope. (978-1-62639-446-9)

Twisted Whispers by Sheri Lewis Wohl. Betrayal, lies, and secrets—whispers of a friend lost to darkness. Can a reluctant psychic set things right or will an evil soul destroy those she loves? (978-1-62639-439-1)

The Courage to Try by C.A. Popovich. Finding love is worth getting past the fear of trying. (978-1-62639-528-2)

Break Point by Yolanda Wallace. In a world readying for war, can love find a way? (978-1-62639-568-8)

Countdown by Julie Cannon. Can two strong-willed, powerful women overcome their differences to save the lives of seven others and begin a life they never imagined together? (978-1-62639-471-1)

Keep Hold by Michelle Grubb. Claire knew some things should be left alone and some rules should never be broken, but the most forbidden, well, they are the most tempting. (978-1-62639-502-2)

Deadly Medicine by Jaime Maddox. Dr. Ward Thrasher's life is in turmoil. Her partner Jess left her, and her job puts her in the path of a murderous physician who has Jess in his sights. (978-1-62639-424-7)

New Beginnings by KC Richardson. Can the connection and attraction between Jordan Roberts and Kirsten Murphy be enough for Jordan to trust Kirsten with her heart? (978-1-62639-450-6)

Officer Down by Erin Dutton. Can two women who've made careers out of being there for others in crisis find the strength to need each other? (978-1-62639-423-0)

Reasonable Doubt by Carsen Taite. Just when Sarah and Ellery think they've left dangerous careers behind, a new case sets them—and their hearts—on a collision course. (978-1-62639-442-1)

Tarnished Gold by Ann Aptaker. Cantor Gold must outsmart the Law, outrun New York's dockside gangsters, outplay a shady art dealer, his lover, and a beautiful curator, and stay out of a killer's gun sights. (978-1-62639-426-1)

White Horse in Winter by Franci McMahon. Love between two women collides with the inner poison of a closeted horse trainer in the green hills of Vermont. (978-1-62639-429-2)

Autumn Spring by Shelley Thrasher. Can Bree and Linda, two women in the autumn of their lives, put their hearts first and find the love they've never dared seize? (978-1-62639-365-3)

The Renegade by Amy Dunne. Post-apocalyptic survivors Alex and Evelyn secretly find love while held captive by a deranged cult, but when their relationship is discovered, they must fight for their freedom—or die trying. (978-1-62639-427-8)

Thrall by Barbara Ann Wright. Four women in a warrior society must work together to lift an insidious curse while caught between their own desires, the will of their peoples, and an ancient evil. (978-1-62639-437-7)

The Chameleon's Tale by Andrea Bramhall. Two old friends must work through a web of lies and deceit to find themselves again, but in the search they discover far more than they ever went looking for. (978-1-62639-363-9)

Side Effects by VK Powell. Detective Jordan Bishop and Dr. Neela Sahjani must decide if it's easier to trust someone with your heart or your life as they face threatening protestors, corrupt politicians, and their increasing attraction. (978-1-62639-364-6)

Warm November by Kathleen Knowles. What do you do if the one woman you want is the only one you can't have? (978-1-62639-366-0)

In Every Cloud by Tina Michele. When Bree finally leaves her shattered life behind, is she strong enough to salvage the remaining pieces of her heart and find the place where it truly fits? (978-1-62639-413-1)